THE SUMMER
OF '39

David Lowther

Sacristy
Press

Sacristy Press
PO Box 612, Durham, DH1 9HT

www.sacristy.co.uk

First published in 2017 by Sacristy Press, Durham

Sacristy Limited, registered in England & Wales, number 7565667

British Library Cataloguing-in-Publication Data
A catalogue record for the book is available from the British Library

ISBN 978-1-910519-70-7

Saboteurs

Berlin, Tuesday 6 December 1938

Black clouds hovered over Berlin, emptying heavy rain over the city. A brisk northerly wind made for a very uncomfortable day for the citizens. The Tiergarten was deserted and there were no signs of sodden Berliners or Nazi bigwigs taking their daily exercise, either on foot or horseback. It was as if the weather gods were taking revenge on Germany's capital for the atrocious treatment of the Jews by the Nazis during the Reichskristallnacht, the night of broken glass, in the previous month.

The rain was making mini fountains splashing on the surface of the Landwehr Canal, which ran alongside Tirpitzufer, on which stood an impressive but forbidding group of buildings stretching northwards almost as far as the Tiergarten. The Bendlerblock, as the complex was called, housed important government departments including the headquarters of both the OKW, the German armed forces, and the Abwehr, the secret intelligence service.

The buildings nearest to the canal had a frontage of numerous windows embedded into stone as grey as the clouds above. Between the canal and the majestic entrance, a number of black Mercedes limousines were parked beneath an avenue of leafless trees, indicating the importance of some of the visitors.

Two tall blue-eyed men, uniformed and helmeted in black, flanked the entrance with rifles held bolt upright in white-gloved hands. Above them a pair of blood-red flags, in the middle of which appeared a black swastika on a white background, fluttered in the breeze.

The exterior of the building was matched by the magnificent reception area. Across a polished grey marble floor, men and women, some in uniform and others not, scurried to and fro carrying files or briefcases, seemingly engaged in tasks of great importance. At one large table, an attractive dark-haired girl was checking the credentials of three male visitors, one in the uniform of a general in the army and the other two in dark business suits. The girl picked up the telephone and spoke briefly into it.

In another office on the first floor, a matronly fair-haired woman of competent appearance instructed the girl below to send the visitors up. This was a fairly large office with more than two dozen filing cabinets and six desks, each occupied by a female clerical assistant. One of these work stations, where the matron was speaking on the phone, was located close to a large set of double doors, each with a golden handle.

Inside these doors was a much bigger room with a high ceiling and a large table set out in conference style with ten chairs. A slight man sat with his back to the windows. He was impeccably dressed as an admiral of the German navy, which was slightly unusual because he normally wore civilian clothes. He was a short man, barely five feet two inches tall, and seemed dwarfed by the size of his antique desk and the high-backed chair on which he sat. Although he was only fifty-one years old, Admiral Wilhelm Canaris, the Head of the Abwehr, looked older. His heavily pomaded hair, parted on the left-hand side, was mostly silver, with some streaks of black. His rather untidy eyebrows, growing a little wildly above his alert brown eyes, were almost completely grey. Canaris was making notes on a large sheet of white paper when his telephone rang.

"Yes Gerda," he said to the matron on the other end of the line.

"General von Lahousen and two other gentlemen are here to see you, Admiral. The General thinks you may wish to see him alone before the others."

"That's fine. Thank you, Gerda. Please send him in and ask the others to wait."

Gerda opened the door and admitted von Lahousen. He was at least four inches taller than Canaris and appeared to be the perfect Aryan specimen with his blonde hair and blue eyes. He looked a lot younger than Canaris too, although he was almost a year older. The Admiral stood up, crossed the room and greeted his guest with an outstretched hand. The traditional German greeting, "Heil Hitler", was noticeable by its absence.

Canaris looked pleased to see his visitor.

"My dear Erwin, thank you for coming. How are you?"

"Very well thank you Admiral. And yourself?" replied von Lahousen with a broad smile. "I see you're dressed formally today. Have you been to the Reich Chancellery?"

"Yes, busy doing our leader's will," Canaris replied with the tiniest hint of sarcasm. "Please take a seat."

Von Lahousen couldn't fail to miss the tone of Canaris' voice and he glanced around the room with a slightly nervous smile on his face.

"Never fear, Erwin. This is one of the few government offices the Gestapo haven't bugged. I have it swept regularly."

"Of course, Admiral. I got your note and I've done some preliminary work. I've brought Clissmann and Hoven with me. They're outside now."

"Excellent. Shall I send for some coffee?"

"Perhaps we should wait until the others join us."

"As you wish."

"Why now, Admiral, and why England?"

Von Lahousen was referring to the note from Canaris instructing him, as Head of Abwehr II in charge of sabotage, to bring him ideas for causing trouble in England.

"You remember, Erwin, when I first took this job, the Führer warned me in no uncertain terms to keep my hands off the English. He saw them as our natural ally. Then, about a year ago, in best Hitler fashion, he changed his mind. He instructed me to begin intelligence gathering in England. So I ordered Piekenbrock, your equivalent in Abwehr I, to begin infiltrating agents into England."

"Has that been successful?"

"Moderately so. We've contacted some sympathisers and placed a number of refugees in sensitive positions. Also, a number of agents in various guises are travelling the length and breadth of that country, sketching airfields, docks, factories and so on."

"But surely most of the refugees are Jewish. They'll not work for us."

"Of course not, but not all of them are Jewish, although they may claim to be."

Von Lahousen nodded and immediately understood the Admiral's game.

"At our most recent meeting, Hitler ordered me to do everything I could to disrupt England's preparations for war."

"I thought that war was off the agenda since Hitler's Munich triumph," Von Lahousen replied, tongue in cheek. "Surely he's not afraid of Chamberlain."

"Quite right, he's not. He thinks him weak and frequently refers to him in the most uncomplimentary terms imaginable. It's Churchill he's afraid of. If he ever becomes Prime Minister, the Führer knows that he won't roll over like his predecessor. So we must prepare for the worst, although, if at all possible, our involvement shouldn't be known. Himmler and Heydrich were at this meeting. They, of course, were keen to have a part in this but Hitler said it was the Abwehr's responsibility. Can you envisage the SS or SD keeping something quiet? There are quite a few Gestapo operatives in England now posing as journalists and so on but they are being uncovered and deported every week. Can you imagine, Erwin, the quiet approach from the Gestapo—the experts at pulling fingernails out and beating testicles with rubber truncheons? No, the Führer wants the subtle touch and that's where we come in."

"I see. And when is all this going to start?"

"Early in the New Year. Hitler plans to seize the rump of Czechoslovakia in March and I've been told to send in agents ahead to undermine and disrupt, just as I did in Austria and the Sudetenland and will soon, presumably, in Danzig. Hitler thinks that England will stand by and watch again but our sources there suggest that they are accelerating their re-armament programme. So, in case they do change their mind and threaten us, we need to upset things as much as we can."

"OK Admiral. I understand. Perhaps it's time to bring in Clissmann and Hoven."

Canaris nodded, picked up the phone, and asked Gerda to send in the two visitors and to organise coffee for four. Von Lahousen and Canaris welcomed the men, both of whom clicked their heels together, and gave a rather half-hearted German greeting and received an equally unenthusiastic one in return. Seated around the conference table, Canaris asked Clissmann what plans he had to upset the English. Helmut Clissmann had thick straight brown hair with matching eyes which hinted at mischief. He was of medium height, certainly taller than the Admiral, and walked with the jaunty step of a man on a mission who was looking forward to serving his country.

"Admiral, I've been in touch with the Irish Republican Army for some time. They are planning to declare war on England within two months."

"Good heavens," an astonished Canaris said, rolling his eyes in disbelief. "What do they plan to do? Row across the Irish Sea?"

Clissmann joined in with the general chuckling and then resumed. "Perhaps I should have said guerrilla war, Admiral. Their intention is to carry out a bombing campaign on the English mainland."

"Refresh my memory, Clissmann. Why would they do that?" the Admiral asked, fixing the Abwehr agent with a penetrating stare.

"They hate the English, Admiral, and would do anything to force them to withdraw from the north of Ireland."

"And how do they feel about Germans?"

"If I may say so, Admiral, that is of no consequence. They would deal with the devil himself if it meant getting rid of the English."

"I understand. My enemy's enemy is my friend. Please continue."

"Thank you. Doctor Hoven and I", Clissmann said, nodding towards a small man with black hair and moustache, "have many contacts with the IRA, both in Ireland and the USA."

"My God! The United States. The Führer won't thank us if we start upsetting them."

"You need not worry, Admiral. We don't operate in America yet and would only do so following your express orders."

"I'm pleased to hear it. Go on."

"As you know, there are many Irish people in the United States, and large numbers of them sympathise with the IRA's objectives. We've established a link with them and meet with them in Mexico."

"OK. What does this guerrilla campaign consist of?"

"Sabotage. We supply the training and the explosives as well as safe houses. They blow up power stations, railway stations, bridges, government buildings, ordnance factories, banks and so on."

"Hmm," Canaris mulled the idea over for a few seconds while glancing at the ceiling, "yes, it does sound feasible. It would most certainly cause a great deal of confusion, and would also keep the English police busy and allow our agents there to continue gathering intelligence without too much interference."

Hoven spoke for the first time. His voice was quiet and nervous. "Perhaps, Admiral, I could identify some IRA people whose skills are rather more in the espionage game than in blowing things up?"

"Thank you, Doctor Hoven. That indeed may have merit, but please keep General von Lahousen completely informed of what actions you plan and carry out."

Hoven lowered his head towards his chin. "I will, Admiral. Thank you."

Von Lahousen summed up. "We three will put together a detailed draft plan", he said, glancing towards Clissmann and Hoven, "and we'll submit it to you for your approval. We'll include details of training, possible targets, escape routes, sources of explosives, places where we can meet IRA leaders from time to time, preferably outside of England, and other sources of intelligence which might be useful to us."

Canaris turned to Clissmann.

"Who is your main contact within the IRA?"

"A man called Donovan, Admiral."

"What's your assessment of him? Is he reliable?"

"He's been fighting the English all his life. He has the respect of fellow members of the IRA and he carries the scars of war. He lost three fingers of his right hand in an earlier explosion."

"He sounds a bit clumsy to me," Canaris sniggered, "but I trust your judgement. I think that's all, gentlemen. Thank you. Please let me have your proposals within a week."

As the three visitors stood up to go, Canaris delivered one final piece of advice, scanning the men's faces to make sure they were paying attention.

"Whatever you do, please don't underestimate the English police force's Special Branch or their MI5. They're almost as cunning as me."

CHAPTER I

Terrorists

London, Wednesday 29 March 1939

A shabby-looking man of medium height was standing on Euston Road opposite the entrance to King's Cross Station. A fine drizzle, made more penetrating by the cold breeze, was gradually soaking his crumpled khaki raincoat. His head was being kept dry by a flat cap pressed down on his forehead. Under his left arm, a copy of the *London Evening Globe* was tucked. This hand was thrust deep into his pocket to make sure the paper didn't blow away. Drawing nervously on his Woodbine with the other hand, he pinched the end so hard that the smoke could only find its way into his lungs with great difficulty.

The man was walking gently on the spot to keep his feet warm. It was eight o'clock in the evening and very dark. Silently, he cursed the English weather, which had been generally cold since the beginning of the month. He dropped his cigarette end onto the pavement and was about to put a fresh one between his lips when a black Austin Six drew up at the edge of the pavement. The front passenger-side window was wound down and, from the dark interior of the car, a quiet but forceful Irish accent enquired:

"Connell?"

The man nodded nervously.

"Get in."

The man did as he was told and slipped in alongside the driver, who was also wearing a flat cap, with a dark blue overcoat, black gloves and glasses. Neither spoke as the car moved cautiously along Euston Road. Being pulled over by the police was the last thing either man wanted. Just after the junction of Euston Road and Upper Woburn Place, another man, slightly taller than Connell and dressed in a darker raincoat, was standing wearing the regulation flat cap, cigarette in mouth and *London Evening Globe* tucked under his left arm. The car pulled up alongside him.

"Wind down the window," instructed the driver, barking out the order.

Connell did as he was told and the man in the overcoat spoke again.

"Brown?"

"Yes."

"Get in the back."

When Brown had settled himself in, the driver passed each of them a black woollen balaclava without any eyeholes. He spoke harshly.

"Put these on."

"Why's that?" asked Brown.

"Don't ask questions, just do it," the man said, a hint of annoyance in his voice.

Neither of the two passengers said a word but followed orders and, by the time they'd reached the top of Tottenham Court Road and were proceeding along Marylebone Road, neither could see a thing.

"What's all this about?" asked Connell, in a thick Northern Irish accent.

The driver remained silent as the car moved smoothly off Marylebone Road on to Abbey Road, then, via Willesden Lane, on to Dartmouth Road before turning left into Walm Lane. Most people had been kept off the damp roads and pavements by the unpleasant weather so nobody was about to spot two hooded men sitting in the Austin Six. Manoeuvring the car into the narrow passage behind Walm Lane, the driver pulled up alongside a dark gate. He parked the car carefully, praying that nobody would appear in another vehicle in the next hour or so. If they did there would be a fuss. He was blocking the lane and the car would have to be moved and a potential witness or two added to the dangers of the evening. The journey from King's Cross had taken about half an hour.

"Get out," the driver ordered.

The men obeyed their orders fearfully and, still hooded, were guided through the gate along a narrow path to the back door. They had one longish set of stairs to climb and, when they reached the top, were ushered into a room which was immediately flooded in light.

"You can take your masks off now and give them to me."

Connell and Brown opened their eyes slowly to grow accustomed to the light.

"What was all that about?" asked Brown, another Irish voice.

"Simple. If things go wrong and you end up in a police cell, I don't want you telling them where you've been or who you've been with."

"OK," said Connell reluctantly, examining the man, who was black-haired and clean-shaven, thinning on top, with almost jet-black eyes. He had the face of a fighter and the manner of a leader. He took off his overcoat. He had on a green roll-necked jumper underneath the coat but, curiously, kept his black gloves on. He motioned them towards the bed, where the men spotted two well-worn suitcases. Both had their lids down and were a sort of faded brown, but they had different dimensions. The boss pulled the catches of one of the cases and lifted the lid.

"Bloody hell," Connell exclaimed, viewing the contents of the case, which comprised old rags and newspapers with, as the centrepiece, six sticks of gelignite bound together and attached to a detonator and an alarm clock.

"Will it go off?" gasped a timid Brown.

"Of course it'll go off, but not until I set the clock."

"Is the clock OK? It does work doesn't it?"

"Course it bloody well works. The bomb will explode when the alarm goes off. These two should cause a very nice explosion and upset the British. The target is Hammersmith Bridge. You'll put one suitcase at either end and then scarper. I'm setting the alarm for one o'clock. There shouldn't be anybody about at that time."

"So we won't kill any British? Pity."

"The idea is to cause maximum disruption. With the bridge lying at the bottom of the Thames, there'll be traffic chaos for years. If the British want to stop these bombs going off, they'll have to clear off out of the north of Ireland bloody quickly."

Connell asked if they would be picked up after leaving the bombs. "No, and I'm not taking you either. It's too risky riding round London in a car with two terrorists as passengers. You can reach the target by Underground."

"Won't that look funny?" asked Connell again. "Two men travelling together each carrying a suitcase?"

"You won't be travelling together. You'll be on separate trains. Besides, it's late at night. There won't be anyone around."

Brown chimed in: "When we've finished there'll be no trains running. Can't we pick up a cab?"

"Don't be stupid. As soon as the bomb goes off, the coppers will be all over the place. They'll be asking every cabbie in town if they've picked up a couple of scruffy Irishmen. They'll have you in no time."

Both clocks were set for one in the morning, lids lowered and the suitcases closed but not locked.

"If the bomb squad find these before they explode, they'll make 'em safe in less than thirty seconds. No point in turning the key in the feeble lock. Time for a cup of tea."

Tea was quickly brewed and the three men sat down to sip from their mugs.

"Brown, I'll drop you at Russell Square tube station. Here's your ticket. I don't want men with Irish accents carrying suitcases talking at the ticket office. Go down in the lift and catch the first westbound train to Hammersmith. Walk towards the bridge. On your left is Queen Caroline Street. There's a bit of rough ground between the street and the river. Whoever gets there first, hide yourself. That'll probably be you, Brown. Conceal yourself and wait for the other. No bloody smoking."

"Why's that?" asked Connell.

The man looked at them impatiently.

"The red glow at the end of your fag can be seen from miles away. Someone'll get suspicious and tell the coppers."

The man repeated the process with Connell, handing him a ticket from Holborn to Hammersmith. Brown was told to hide his case on the north side and then wait for Connell who would have hidden his on the south side.

"Straight back home to Kilburn through Kensall Green and Notting Hill. Don't wait to watch the bombs go off."

Connell asked what would happen if the bombs went off accidentally.

"You'll be killed, but think of it as a sacrifice in the service of our beloved Ireland. But they won't go off before one."

Both men paled.

"But they won't," he emphasised. "Check your watches. Both alarm clocks say eleven o'clock. Put your watches to that."

Half an hour later, after plenty of smoking and with the tea drunk, they were ready to go.

"Right lads, looks like we're off. Hoods on and grab a case each. I'll guide you to the car."

"One thing," said Connell, "won't the people in the upstairs flat be suspicious about all this activity?"

"No, they may be two separate flats, but they're both safe houses, each with a different owner and resident."

"Very clever," said Brown.

Soon the suitcases were carefully and safely stored away in the boot of the car. The rain had stopped and the temperature had gone up a notch or two.

"Can I ask you something?" said Brown.

"Go on."

"Why don't we just drop the suitcases in some busy spot like Piccadilly Circus and kill a load of British bastards?"

The man replied in exasperation.

"I've told you, we're not after killing them. We're looking to disrupt everything until this stinking country realises we mean business. And we'll not stop until the shits get the hell out of the north of Ireland. And our friends who are paying for a lot of this want that as well."

That seemed to satisfy the other two Irishmen. The rest of the journey passed in silence. The car turned right off Euston Road and was driven down Woburn Place. Outside the Hotel Russell on Southampton Row,

Brown got out, collected one suitcase from the boot, and made his way to Russell Square station. A couple of minutes later, Connell got out at Kingsway and went down to the west-bound platform of the Piccadilly Line at Holborn station. The man drove off. He would never see either bomber again, but he thought how nervous both might be and crossed his fingers for them. He drove across London to Western Avenue and pointed the car to Uxbridge where he had a safe house.

◆　　◆　　◆

Brown was one train ahead of his partner and, as he sat with the suitcase behind his legs, his mind began to wander. Back in Derry, where he grew up, he hated the English. He'd been told by his brothers, his father, even his local church's Catholic priest, that the English were occupying their country and that they had been at war with the invaders for centuries. Brought up to believe that violence was the only way to get rid of the occupiers, he'd joined the IRA with his pal Connell in his late teens and, together, they had moved to England ten years ago to find work. Though the IRA had kept in touch with him, this was his first big job and he was determined to make it pay. His family back in Derry were always in his mind and he was often thinking, as he was now, whether he'd be better back there fighting the British on his own patch. But no, that was one battle they could never win. Better by far, he thought, to frighten the life out of them on the mainland.

The train cruised into Hammersmith station and its arrival shook him out of his daydreaming, but his thoughts had helped to overcome his nervousness. With a handful of passengers, none of whom were paying a scrap of attention to a man in a crumpled raincoat carrying a suitcase, he went into the street, found a quiet doorway and had a cigarette. Drawing the smoke deep into his lungs, he felt relaxed, and he began walking towards Queen Caroline Street, which he found without difficulty.

Few were about and the houses in the street were dark. The piece of rough ground was exactly where the man had told them and he settled down, out of sight, behind a garden wall. Fifteen minutes passed and he caught sight of Connell, who had also stopped for a smoke on the way from the station. They sat for quite a while in silence. After some time, Brown tapped his watch and signalled to Connell, who had the longer journey, that it was time to go. Off he went, clutching his suitcase, followed, about five minutes later, by Brown. Both men found excellent places of concealment where the pavement met the bridge fence. There was not a soul nor a vehicle in sight and the dark night looked to be fast asleep. "That won't last for long," thought Connell as he rejoined his fellow terrorist at the rough patch behind Queen Caroline Street. Each gave the other the thumbs up and they walked back along Queen Caroline Street until they found a quiet spot for a smoke.

"Good job we've got them rubber-soled shoes," said Connell. "Nobody would have heard a thing. Let's have a smoke or two, then we'll watch the show and clear off."

"But the man said we shouldn't hang about."

"We won't. We'll just watch the firework display and then bugger off home. Nobody's about to see us. I'm not risking my life and liberty and then not seeing the results of my handiwork. You can suit yourself." It was a decision they'd come to regret.

◆   ◆   ◆

Maurice Childs, a hairdresser from Chiswick, had spent a pleasant evening with friends at a house in Barnes on the south side of the river. So much had he been enjoying himself, he had completely forgot the time, so it was almost one in the morning when he set off home. The rain had stopped but the brisk north-easterly wind was keeping the temperature down. Nevertheless, he reasoned, a good walk would warm him up. If he saw a cab on his way, he'd flag it down. The first part of his journey took him across Hammersmith Bridge.

He confidently strode past the first suitcase without noticing but, walking towards the end of the bridge on the north side, he spotted smoke and sparks coming out of something. Approaching this mysterious object, Childs, who'd had enough to drink to make him reckless, flicked open the lid and was astonished and terrified to find a bomb. Reckless he may have been, but stupid he was not, and the suitcase was quickly lifted up and dispatched into the river. As soon as it struck the surface, there was a huge explosion and a jet of water shot sixty feet into the air. Soaked to the skin, the hairdresser dashed along Hammersmith Bridge Road to a phone box on the corner of Rutland Grove and called the police. As he was speaking, an enormous boom, accompanied by the sound of breaking glass, came from the south side of the bridge.

Connell and Brown watched the proceedings from their observation point. It was too dark to see Childs, so they were amazed when the first bomb went off in the river.

"Something's gone wrong," said a disappointed Brown. "Let's be off."

"Hang on. It's time for the second. I want to see the bridge fall into the river."

Right on cue, the bomb obliged and this time, not muffled by the river as the first had been, the bang was enormous and windows shattered on the south bank.

"That's more like it," said Brown, "now let's get out of here."

"The bloody thing's still standing."

"I can see that, but we won't be unless we get the hell out of here."

Lights were going on in houses on both sides of the river. A motorist crossing the bridge had to swerve quickly to avoid girders that had fallen and lay in his path. This turned out to be the only damage.

"Perhaps it'll fall in later," said an increasingly angry Brown. "We'll split up. I'll see you back in Kilburn."

Brown set off, quickly followed by Connell. By the time they were near the tube station, the night air had been filled with the sounds of bells and whistles. Connell turned left and ran slap bang into a patrolling policeman, who grabbed him by the arm and asked him what he was up to.

"Nothin'," said Connell.

Detecting an Irish accent, the burly copper arrested Connell on suspicion of causing an explosion and marched him towards the police station. Brown, who'd set off in the opposite direction eastbound along Hammersmith Road, had a spot of good fortune when he spied a flat-backed lorry, with its engine idling, outside a terraced house. A man, who was probably the driver, was getting in and closing his front door. Brown quickly and quietly jumped over the tailboard on to the back of the lorry. He'd no idea where the lorry was going and didn't care as long as he could get away from Hammersmith. Then he'd melt into the background of the vast city. Unfortunately for the Irish bomber, an eagle-eyed policeman in the passenger seat of a black Flying Squad Austin saw all this and ordered his driver to get after the lorry. The pursuit didn't last long and Brown was soon being hauled off the back of the lorry and into custody, much to the surprise of the clearly innocent driver.

Brown and Connell were next heard of two weeks later when they were sent for trial at the Old Bailey by Bow Street Magistrates. The damp hero of the hour, Maurice Childs, later received an MBE for his bravery.

CHAPTER 2

Newspaperman

London, Monday 3 and Tuesday 4 April 1939

Crowds swarmed over the concourse of Waterloo station. Although there were repeated rumours that Monday was less busy than the rest of the week due to over-enthusiastic weekend partying, it was still very congested. Roger Martin had squeezed onto the train at New Malden and stood for the entire journey, and had almost been thrown onto the platform at Waterloo due to the rapidly exiting passengers. Still, he wasn't too bothered about this. He'd just had a great weekend, which started on Friday when he witnessed the beginning of the end of the government's appeasement policy. Sitting in the press gallery in the House of Commons, he'd heard Prime Minister Neville Chamberlain guarantee Poland's borders from the threat of Nazi Germany, making war more likely.

With his girlfriend Jane, Roger had been that evening to see *Q Planes*, starring Laurence Olivier, at a West End cinema after a meal at Lyons Corner House in Coventry Street. Jane had collected him at mid-morning on Saturday and they'd set off for the Thames to watch the Oxford and Cambridge Boat Race which, to Roger's great pleasure, was won by his old university, Cambridge, by four lengths, with Oxford evening things up by taking the women's race. On the way there, the two spoke of their plans for the future. Later they sat having tea with Jane's parents, and further chat ended with more smiles and embraces between the four of them.

On the Sunday, the two families gathered at Roger's house to celebrate the couple's engagement. As well as Reg and Mary, Roger's parents, and their younger son John, Jane's parents and the happy couple were present. Questions about the timing of the wedding were brushed aside by Roger and Jane, who said they'd decide when the international situation became clearer. If there was a war, they'd wait until it was over.

These pleasant memories were swimming around inside Roger's head as he moved with the herd towards the station exit. He was tall and good-looking, with curly brown hair, and very fit. The morning walk across Waterloo Bridge was pretty quick, since the temperature was unseasonably cold. Below the walkers, the Thames looked grey and uninviting and the bridge itself was still propped up with a temporary steel structure that had been in place since 1934. The replacement bridge was not expected to be completed until 1942.

Turning up the Strand and then into Fleet Street, Roger began to wonder what assignment he'd be given today. That would soon become clear as he did a right turn into Bouverie Street and stepped inside the offices of the *London Evening Globe*, where he worked as a newspaper reporter. His boss, news editor Ben Rogers, was waiting for him as he walked into the newsroom.

"Morning Prof, had a good weekend?"

"Yes thanks. You?" Roger asked.

"Fine, step inside and take a pew," Ben gestured. "Just a little chat."

Ben, and everyone else in the office, called Roger "Prof" because he was the only university graduate on the staff, having been a student at Trinity College Cambridge just under three years earlier.

"Your stuff from the 'ouse on Friday was good," Ben continued, referring to the young journalist's report on the Prime Minister's guarantee to Poland in the House of Commons the previous week. "Now you've more or less won your battle over that, I've got a new assignment for you."

Roger leaned forward expectantly.

"You know Bill, does general news stories?"

Roger nodded.

"'E's had an 'eart attack. I'm not sure how bad it is or how long 'e'll be off, but it's unlikely 'e'll be back here before the autumn."

"I'm sorry for him and his family."

"Well, 'e's like most journalists, smokes like a chimney, drinks like a fish, eats lousy food. Anyway, 'e's been covering the Irish business, the bombs and so on. I'd like you to pick that up."

Roger nodded with a grin on his face.

"You all right, Prof? You look like a dog with a bone."

"Sorry Ben. I was just thinking back over the weekend. Had a great time."

"Oh? What 'appened?"

"Jane and I got engaged."

"Bloody marvellous. When's the big day?"

"After the war."

"War? What war?"

"The one that's going to be fought between us and Germany. After Friday that's bound to happen."

"I 'ope your wrong. Congratulations and pass on my best to Jane."

"I will. Thanks. Now, the Irish. I haven't been following it all that closely. I've known it's been happening, but that's about all."

"Take the day off and mug it up in the library. I've got a nose for that sort of thing and I'm sure that there's more to this business than just a load of mad paddies going round blowin' things up."

"Right, I'll get on to it. I was at the Boat Race on Saturday afternoon. Hammersmith Bridge looked a big mangled."

"They nabbed 'em, you know. Up before the beak next Wednesday. Check the lists for the Bailey and get yerself there. And keep an eye on what's goin' on at the Police Courts."

"OK." Roger got up to leave. "I'll keep in touch."

◆   ◆   ◆

Roger spent the afternoon getting up to speed on the IRA. It surprised him how little he knew about them. The Easter Rising of 1916, the Irish Civil War, and people like Michael Collins were familiar to him, but the recent bombing campaign was not. It had started with a letter to Lord Halifax, the Foreign Secretary, threatening war if the government didn't pull British troops out of Northern Ireland within four days. The day before the ultimatum expired, the IRA posted notices all over Ireland announcing the forthcoming war and, the following day, five bombs exploded in London.

Atrocities had continued on an almost daily basis right up to the Hammersmith Bridge attack five days ago. At first, Roger guessed that the utilities were the main targets; power stations, electricity pylons and gas holders for example. Then he realised that disruption of communications was clearly an objective, as road and rail bridges, railway stations and bus termini suffered. Then it was department stores, cinemas, banks and even tobacco kiosks. What on earth was going on? Judgement was postponed until Roger felt he knew a lot more about what was happening. A short stroll to the Old Bailey and an examination of the following day's lists was enough to decide Roger on the agenda for Tuesday and he skipped off home about half an hour earlier than usual.

Roger found his quarries the next day in court five. Both men, whose names sounded Irish, were accused of offences under the Explosives Act. He'd never been into a big court before. Plenty of police and magistrates' courts, but never anywhere as important as the Old Bailey. He found the press seats easily enough, nodded to a couple of acquaintances, pulled out his note book and pencil and waited for the day's proceedings to begin. The young journalist was soon to learn that the action in courts was as likely to start on time as a London bus was to run to schedule. He spent time trying to answer some questions that might help him to figure out what was going on with this bombing campaign. Where were they getting their explosives from? Who was training them in the use of explosives and bomb making? How many of them were there? Where did they all live, or even hide? What were they really after? What were their future targets? Would anybody be killed? He was jotting these questions down as an assortment of clerks and wigged barristers began to drift in and take their seats.

Roger had just finished noting down his questions when a man in a black gown appeared and ordered everyone to stand, shouting out some incoherent orders. Then in shuffled what seemed to be an incredibly old man with a wig and red gown. He took his seat and everybody sat down. He nodded at one of the men in wig and gown, addressed him as Mr McGowen, and then settled back to listen to what was being said. McGowen, at times addressing the jury and, at others, the ceiling, summed up the evidence against the defendants and, after about twenty minutes, sat down, after first asking the jury to find the two men guilty. The judge then invited the defence lawyer, another wigged and gowned man called Cooke, to sum up. He took only ten minutes and made a pretty feeble effort. The main thrust of his argument seemed to be that the men were both quarrymen and had accidentally taken home some sticks of gelignite. In a rather embarrassed manner he asked the jury to find the men not guilty. The judge roused himself from his slumber, briefly summed up, and instructed the jury to retire and reach their verdict. The ageing man left slowly and serenely, perhaps for a cigarette and a visit to the toilet. An usher led the jury out of the court.

Some of those in the press seats took advantage of the break to stretch their legs or have a smoke but Roger stayed in his seat and wrote up his notes. He'd privately forecast to himself that the jury wouldn't be long and this proved to be the case, as the members of the jury soon returned, avoiding the eyes of the prisoners in the dock. The clerk reappeared and repeated the earlier process, and the judge, looking as if the quick turnaround had disturbed his morning coffee-drinking, asked the foreman of the jury, a bald-headed man in a grey suit who looked like a banker, to deliver the verdict. It was, to no one's surprise, guilty.

The jury were thanked by the judge and the convicted men were ordered to stand. Two rather nondescript middle-aged men grudgingly got to their feet, each wearing what appeared to be a second-hand sports jacket, a creased shirt and a faded tie. Both had smirks on their faces. The judge sentenced both of them to ten years in prison. "Up the IRA," shouted one before they were rushed out of court by four policemen. Roger finished his notes and was on his way out when he felt a hand grasp the sleeve of his jacket.

"Good morning, Mr Martin."

Roger turned to his left and immediately felt a strange combination of fear and anger.

CHAPTER 3

Unlikely Allies

London, Tuesday 4 April 1939

Roger looked at the man and, in a few fleeting seconds, unpleasant memories of their previous encounters rushed through his mind. He recalled with disgust the verbal threats, the physical assault which had left him in hospital, and, finally, the pathetic attempt to frame him for a nasty crime which he hadn't committed. Had it not been for an anti-fascist journalist, his friends, and a cheerful and brave teenage East End boy called Joe, heaven knows where he might be now.

He glared at the man.

"What do you want?" Roger asked, a note of distaste in his voice.

"Just a quiet chat, Mr Martin."

"I've nothing to say to you," Roger replied and turned to go.

"'Ang on a minute," and he touched the young journalist's sleeve.

"Take your hands off me. What are you planning to do? Drag me outside, bundle me into your van with your mates and drive me off to God knows where?"

A look of resignation passed over the other man's face.

"Look, I know 'ow you feel, and in your shoes I'd feel the same. But there might be summat in this for you."

"What could you possibly have that I'd want?"

"A story."

Despite his intense dislike for this man and the awful memories dredged up by this chance meeting, Roger's journalist's antennae shot up.

"Go on."

"Not 'ere. There's a caff across the street."

Roger shrugged his shoulders and followed his nemesis out of the building. He still wasn't convinced that some kind of reception committee wouldn't be waiting for him outside, but what the hell. He'd done nothing wrong. The two carefully threaded their way through the heavy traffic outside the Central Criminal Court. Roger's unwelcome companion guided him to a smoke-filled cafe which was fairly full with an interesting cross-section of customers, who were either chatting, smoking, drinking mugs of tea, eating bacon sandwiches or, in some cases, doing all four, more or less simultaneously. A few heads turned and gave a quick cursory examination of what, at first sight, appeared to be a bit of an odd couple; one was a tall, brown- and curly-haired handsome young man and the other a short, tubby, dark-haired older man, thinning on top, with ruddy cheeks and a black moustache.

"Tea?" asked the shorter man.

"Thanks."

Roger found a couple of seats at a reasonably clean table while the man with the moustache left for the counter, returning a few minutes later with steaming white mugs of tea.

"Thanks," said Roger. "Perhaps you'd be good enough to tell me who you are and what you do."

"Of course, sorry. Bert Moss. Detective Sergeant Bert Moss. I work with the Special Branch at Scotland Yard."

Roger was relieved to note that Moss was slowly losing his unpleasant aura.

"I guessed as much."

"Guessed what?"

"That you're with the security services."

Moss nodded. "First thing I should tell you is how our paths crossed."

"OK."

"Just under two years ago us and the spooks were told to close down all opposition to Chamberlain's foreign policy—you know, suckin' up to 'Itler, turnin' a blind eye to the German shit's land grabbin', that sort of thing."

"Who ordered you?"

"My guvn'r, of course, but 'e will 'ave got 'is orders, in a roundabout way, from Number 10. Any 'ow, the PM didn't want journalists tellin' their readers what a bunch of sods the krauts are."

"Yeah, well I think I know all this. Where do you reckon this actually came from? Not Chamberlain himself, surely?"

Moss shrugged his shoulders.

"No, probably Ball. Know about 'im?"

Joseph Ball was a thoroughly nasty anti-Semitic former Secret Service man who now worked for the Conservative Party. He frequently described Fleet Street as being "Jew-infested".

"I do," replied Roger, a sour look crossing his face, "and not with any liking."

"As far as I'm concerned, he's a revolting bastard. Being Jewish myself, I've certainly got no love for him. Did you ever read that filthy rag of his, *TRUTH*?"

"Several times. You're right, it's dreadful. But don't you think you went a bit far with me? It's one thing warning me, but quite another using physical violence and trying to frame me."

"Probably, but it was orders. I could've refused but then I'd 'ave been sacked, and then who'd 'ave put food on the table for me wife and kids?"

"OK. Point taken," Roger said as he took a first sip of his tea. All these stories of dirty tricks were confirming just how desperate the Prime Minister must have been to quash opposition and how uncomfortable some members of the security services, especially a Jew like Moss, felt about it.

Inwardly Moss heaved a sigh of relief. He'd hated the task he'd been given in harassing Roger and other newspaper men and women. To cap it all, he'd been indirectly following the obnoxious policy set by the notorious anti-Semite Ball. To make matters worse members of the anti-appeasement press had been loudly voicing their opposition to the Nazis, who were the greatest Jew-baiters of all. He could hardly have felt more unhappy about his mission, but he didn't want to come on too strong, as he wanted Roger to trust him and too many over-the-top anti-Hitler rants might cause the young journalist to smell a rat. Besides he felt he owed Roger some help.

"Anyhow, you won. You're clever, determined and you got some great allies," referring to Claud Cockburn and his team. "And what's more, you're right. Do you think there'll be a war?"

The atmosphere between the two relaxed. Roger was inching towards trusting the policeman.

"Certain of it. As you know, I've seen the Nazis in action first-hand. They like inflicting pain and suffering on innocent people. Sooner or later they'll do something that even Chamberlain can't ignore. Then we'll be in it."

"'Ow about we just draw a line under what's gone before?"

Throughout their conversation, Roger had been weighing up whether or not Moss had been trying to lure him into a trap but, so far, he could sense nothing. But, such was his hatred of Moss, he was finding it difficult to come round. Despite this, Roger's instinct as a Fleet Street journalist told him he had to hear the Special Branch man out.

"OK. Let's hear what you've got to say."

"When I saw you in Whitehall on Friday, I tried to speak to you, but you wasn't 'avin' any of it. I thought a lot about you over the weekend and wondered 'ow I could give you a leg up."

"So, what did you come up with?"

"Nothin'. Then I saw you in court today and got an idea."

"What was that?"

"Well, are you workin' on this Irish business now?"

"Uh huh."

"Good. 'Ow about we share some info?"

"How will that work? I haven't got anything to give you."

"Ha! Knowin' you, you soon will 'ave. I'll give you a tip. You follow it up. If it leads anywhere, you pass on to me any stuff you think might be useful."

"Where does that leave me in protecting my sources?"

"I'm yer main source and any others are likely to be on the enemy side anyway."

"Fair enough, but I'm not going to give you any information that might cause anybody to end up dead."

"Yeah. That's fine. OK, let's start. I've been on this Irish thing since the bombs started goin' off in January. Of course, bein' IRA most of them are thick and they're always gettin' caught. And so far no one's been killed, thank God. But, however useless they are, they seem to be well organised and with plenty of weapons and explosives. Where does all this come from? It can't be the intelligent paddies. They wouldn't touch the IRA with a bargepole. So, who is it?"

"I don't know much about it. My boss only gave me this assignment yesterday morning. I've been doing a bit of reading up and I must say I've asked myself the same question. Who is behind all this?"

Roger was thinking furiously. This Irish story was making him quite excited, so much so that he had forgotten to drink the rest of his tea. He took a quick swig but it had gone cold so he put it down.

"Why are you doing this?" Roger asked.

"Three reasons; because I feel I need to after treatin' you so badly, to 'elp you to 'elp us by 'elping you, and get one over the spooks."

"Do Special Branch need help?"

"There's bombs going off all over England—London, Birmingham and so on—and we're short-staffed. The big boss has asked the Home Secretary for more police officers but, so far, no joy."

"What's your gripe with the spooks?"

"They won't work with us, share information or anythin'. They treat us like the dirt on their shoes. They're all ex-public school types. You're not a public school boy are you, Mr Martin?"

"Grammar school boy."

"That's alright then," he laughed.

Moss pulled out a note book, scribbled something down and tore out a page.

"There's me phone. Keep me up to date."

Roger was about to speak when Moss interrupted him.

"'Ere's yer start. Tomorrer mornin' Richmond Magistrates' Court, first up, a paddy called O'Shaughnessy. Charged with possessin' explosives."

"From what I've read, there's nothing unusual about that, is there?"

"Yer right, but this is different. 'Is wife shopped 'im. The woodentops made their arrest and didn't bother to question 'er very closely. We 'avent got anyone spare with all these bombs going off on Saturday mornin' and more yesterday."

Moss stood up and offered Roger his right hand. The young journalist gripped it.

"Thanks."

"My pleasure, Mr Martin. See what you can get out of 'er."

◆　　◆　　◆

Moss made his way back to the Yard by bus. His boss spotted him as he walked into the Special Branch office.

"Ah Bert. How did it go at the Bailey?"

"Alright sir. The paddies got a ten year 'oliday apiece at the Scrubs."

"Good. Right, got another job for you tomorrow. Nothing on, have you?"

"I'm chasing up on Saturday's bombs."

"The others can deal with that. Get yourself down to Richmond Magistrates' Court. They're kicking off with another Irish madman. This one's called O'Shaughnessy. His wife grassed him up. Found a pile of explosives in their garden shed. Have a word with her, will you? The local plod didn't bother questioning her."

Moss smiled inwardly. This suited him just fine. Tomorrow morning he'd call in sick when it would be too late to send a replacement, leaving the coast clear for Roger. Then he'd volunteer to go to wherever she lived when he was fit again.

"Very good sir. Thank you."

Roger was close enough to the *Globe* offices to walk back from the cafe and it wasn't too long before he was drinking more tea, hot this time, with Ben.

"All go well at the Bailey, Prof?"

"They locked them up for ten years each."

"Good to hear it."

"There was something else though," and Roger proceeded to tell his boss about his encounter with Moss.

"That's very interesting," said Ben. "Do you trust him?"

"I can't see why not. He seems to be on the level."

"Alright, it seems OK. All that can 'appen is he sends you off on a wild goose chase and then sniggers when you come back empty-handed. Right, give the court a bell, ask them to check the lists for tomorrer and, if this bloke is on it, get yourself down there and try to have a word with the wife. Take five quid in ones and ten bob notes and see if you can't grease her palms. Second thought, take a tenner in ones and ten bobs. Start at the bottom and work up. I've got a nose for this. Could be big. She'll be short with her old man inside."

Roger smiled. He couldn't hide his pleasure.

"Thanks Ben. I'm off to write up the stuff from the Bailey."

"You never know Prof. This could be the start of something very interesting."

CHAPTER 4

Housewife

Roger was sitting munching cereals at the breakfast table in the New Malden home he shared with his mother, Mary. She had some toast on the go under the grill and was making a pot of tea.

"You're up early," she said.

"Got to look at a court case at Richmond Magistrates. Ten o'clock start."

"How are you getting there?"

"Dad's giving me a lift to Kingston station on his way to work. It's only twenty minutes from there to Richmond."

Roger had spent the last hour of the previous afternoon at work on the phone, checking the lists at the court and finding out where it was. It turned out that it was only a five minute walk from the station.

"What's the court case about?" his mother asked.

"Some Irishman hoarding explosives in his house."

"Most of the cases I read about in the *Globe* seem to concern the Irish. They always appear to be getting caught. Why's that, do you think?"

Roger gave his mother a wry smile.

"The bombers are a bit dim. Those that planted stuff on Hammersmith Bridge stayed to watch the fireworks and got nabbed by the local police."

Roger's dad Reg walked in, surprisingly jaunty considering the time of the day.

"Morning all. Ready in fifteen minutes, Roger. OK?"

"Sure Dad. Morning."

"Cereals, tea and toast Reg, OK?"

"Lovely. Thanks Mary."

Roger's father was the manager of Bentalls, a large department store in Kingston. He enjoyed his job and was proud to be in what local people regarded as such an important post.

"Roger's been telling me he's reporting on an IRA case at Richmond this morning," Mary said.

"Really," his father said, "seems a bit tame for a journalist who poked his tongue out at the Prime Minister and got away with it."

"Just," Roger replied. "Ben thinks this might lead to something."

"You look after yourself," Mary said, a slight look of concern spreading across her face.

"I will mum."

"Changing the subject," Reg came in, "a colleague at work's got a second-hand Morris Minor for sale. 1934. It hasn't done many miles and he only wants a hundred pounds for it. Do you want me to ask him to fetch it in to the store one day? I'll check it out and, if I think it's OK, you can pop over to his place one evening and see for yourself."

"Sounds good. Where does he live?"

"Worcester Park."

"Right on the doorstep. Thanks Dad."

"I thought you might like your own transport now you've passed your test. Needn't cadge off your old man any more."

Roger laughed, but it immediately crossed his mind that a car might come in useful in his latest assignment.

They said goodbye to Mary, climbed into the family car, a 1938 Ford Prefect, and made their way towards Kingston station. It had been a particularly unpleasant spring and today was no different: cloudy, cold and damp. The train deposited Roger in Richmond twenty minutes later and he was at the court building within a further five minutes. This looked as miserable as the weather and was in need of refurbishment. In the waiting area outside of the court room the usual cross-section of society had assembled. He'd no idea why they were there, but obviously they were answering charges of minor crimes; traffic offences, unpaid bills and so on. Some might have been witnesses, including perhaps Mrs O"Shaughnessy, but the man himself would not have been there; such was the seriousness of his alleged offence, he would have been held in police custody since his arrest.

Roger took his seat on the press benches. The only other person present there was a man of about his own age who was probably a reporter for the local paper, hoping to sell the story to national dailies or London evening papers. Various clerks and other officials arrived in dribs and drabs and one or two others took their places in the public seats. Disappointingly, none could have been Mrs O'Shaughnessy, because there wasn't a woman amongst them. Perhaps, thought Roger, she was being kept in another room as she was a key witness.

As the magistrates made their way to the bench, Roger pulled out his notebook and pencil. He examined the trio and was surprised to see a woman in the middle, indicating that she was the Chair. Women had only been permitted to serve as magistrates since 1919. She also looked quite young, perhaps in her forties, and was thin, with straight brown hair and a severe-looking face. Flanking her were what Roger considered to be the more typical types. On her left was a slight man with greasy black hair, immaculately groomed and wearing a well-pressed charcoal suit with white shirt and dark blue tie. Some kind of local businessman, Roger assumed, possibly even an undiscovered spiv. The third member of the trio was a stout man, with thinning grey hair, possibly in his late fifties, wearing a light grey suit, white shirt and a maroon tie. A bank manager, Roger guessed. All were duly assembled and Michael O'Shaughnessy was brought in by two uniformed policemen and ushered into the dock. Here Roger had his second shock of the day, because the accused bomber bore no resemblance to what the young journalist believed an IRA man would look like. Instead of the angry looking scruffy bomber with lodgings in Kilburn that Roger expected, a smartly-dressed man in his forties, wearing a sports jacket and flannels, shirt and tie, with well-brushed straight brown hair, was seated in the dock looking thoroughly miserable. Still, what did he know? This was only his second IRA story and he hadn't learned much from the first.

The charge was read out by a clerk. O'Shaughnessy was ordered to stand and confirm his name and address, which was in North Sheen. He sat down and the lady magistrate took over.

"This is a very serious offence and we are almost certain to refer this to the Central Criminal Court if the prosecution can persuade us that the evidence merits a full trial."

A uniformed police sergeant was called and gave a brief summary of the evidence against the alleged IRA man. Tipped off by the defendant's wife, officers had searched a property in North Sheen and found a quantity of explosives and other bomb making equipment. That evening, O'Shaughnessy had been arrested. Magistrates had granted a warrant enabling the police to keep him in custody until today, thirty-six hours after his arrest.

The sergeant closed his note book and stood in silence. He was excused and the magistrates went into a huddle.

"We feel that the statement signed by the chief witness is sufficient for us to commit the defendant for trial at the Central Criminal Court. He is remanded in custody until the date of the trial."

O'Shaughnessy remained impassive, with only a slight lowering of the head indicating that he understood the outcome of his brief appearance before the bench.

The prosecution solicitor asked if Mrs O'Shaughnessy's name could be kept from the newspapers for her protection and the Chair agreed, adding that the only details that could be printed in the press were that Michael O'Shaughnessy, aged thirty-nine, of North Sheen, was remanded in custody by Richmond Magistrates on 5 April, to appear at the Central Criminal Court charged with explosives offences.

O'Shaughnessy was led out by the police and the magistrates departed for a cigarette and a cup of tea before their next case. Roger was bitterly disappointed with the non-appearance of Mrs O'Shaughnessy and felt he'd had a wasted trip. It quickly occurred to him, however, that the police couldn't possibly have known that the magistrates would have accepted Mrs O'Shaughnessy's statement without her appearing, so she must be in the building. With a hurried goodbye to the local man, Roger dashed out just in time to catch the police sergeant talking to a rather handsome dark-haired woman.

This had to be the alleged IRA man's wife, so Roger followed her, accompanied by the sergeant, to the street. Sometimes luck is just on your side and this was one of those occasions, as Roger watched the two part and go in opposite directions after a handshake. A lift home in a police car had been rejected in favour of some shopping, perhaps. Swift confirmation of this came when the lady walked towards a busy shopping street. Roger followed, quickly working out what he was going to say. When he was certain that both of them were out of sight from the policeman, the young journalist walked up to her and spoke.

"Excuse me. Mrs O'Shaughnessy?"

"Who wants to know?"

"My name is Roger Martin and I'm a reporter with the *London Evening Globe*. I'm sorry to trouble you but I wonder if I might have a few words with you."

"The magistrates said that my name wasn't to appear in the papers."

"I know that and I won't be using your name. It's your husband and the Irish I'm interested in."

Roger had detected a local accent and hoped that Mrs O'Shaughnessy had no great love for the Irish.

"What do you want to know?"

"Look, would you like me to buy you a cup of tea?"

"And a scone?"

Roger chuckled and Mrs O'Shaughnessy smiled. The young newsman was tall and very good-looking and had been known to turn many a head, although it was doubtful that he was aware of it. Possessed of charm, a sharp mind and a gregarious personality, the Fleet Street man knew how to use these qualities to get people to open up to him.

"Two if you wish, and obviously with jam and butter. Let's go in here."

They were just outside a cosy-looking cafe. Stepping inside, Roger headed for a table away from the window. A waitress appeared and took their order for a pot of tea for two and two scones with strawberry jam and butter.

"Before we begin, I promise you that not one scrap of what you tell me will appear in the papers."

A nod in response.

"You're not Irish, are you?"

"No I come from Norbiton."

"I know it well. My home is in New Malden."

"Oh. You must be alright then," Mrs O'Shaughnessy laughed.

Roger, with some relief, thought to himself that this was going well and felt his hopes rising.

The waitress arrived with tea and scones. Mrs O'Shaughnessy stirred the leaves in the pot and left it to stand and the pair of them buttered their scones and set about eating them.

After the tea was poured, Roger's companion resumed.

"I met my husband at the Regal. I was having tea with two friends before the pictures. He smiled at me. He was very good-looking and ever so nice. It was just before the General Strike. He'd come over from Belfast looking for work. He got a job on the railway. We were married about six months later. Had a lovely honeymoon in Bournemouth. We were both working. I was in the haberdashery department in Bentalls."

Roger kept quiet about his close association with that store.

"After we'd been married for eighteen months, our Anthony was born and, a year later, Richard. We'd moved into a nice little terraced house with a small garden in North Sheen. Everything in the garden was rosy."

"What made you turn him in?"

"I felt happy with him for years, although he was very angry when those in Southern Ireland got some independence and his people in Ulster didn't. He often used to rant and rave against the English. I reminded him that I was English, the English had given him a job, his sons had been born and lived in England. That made him calm down and we were very contented until last January, you know, just gone by."

"What happened then?"

"He started disappearing from the house without explanation. After a while, I started asking him where he'd been and he told me to mind my own business. I thought he was probably seeing another woman. Then, as luck would have it, I bumped into a friend of mine when I was shopping in Richmond who told me she'd seen Michael with a man in the Railway Tavern—you know, on the Quadrant near the station."

"I know it, nice place."

"My friend said she didn't much like the look of this man, so the next time he announced he was going out, I set off after him. It was evening and I could see him through the window in the Railway Tavern talking to two men. One of them looked like a boxer, blackish hair going bald. Black horn-rimmed spectacles. Despite the fact that it must have been warm in there with the fire, this tough-looking man still had his gloves on, black they were and they looked a bit funny."

"How do you mean funny?"

"Well, three fingers of the right hand glove were kind of floppy, like there was nothing inside them."

"Hmm."

"The other one was much younger than Michael and looked like a bit of a tearaway—thick black jumper, corduroy trousers, red face and untidy curly brown hair. He was still there when Michael left."

"What happened next?"

"I kept challenging Michael about where he was disappearing to and he got angrier and angrier. He started slapping my face. I didn't know what to do. I was getting quite scared and was very worried for the children. They knew what was going on and looked frightened. Things came to a head last week when he brought a suitcase home with him."

Mrs O'Shaughnessy paused, took a bite of scone and a sip of tea and continued.

"He took the suitcase straight to the garden shed and closed the door. Then he took the lock off and screwed in a replacement. He threw the old lock and the key in the bin and pocketed the new key and announced it was his shed from now on and nobody else was to go near it."

"What was his mood like?"

"Nearly always bad, although I did notice it was OK when the papers reported a bomb had gone off and bad when someone had got caught. What with meeting mysterious strangers in the Railway Tavern and hiding stuff in the shed I did begin to wonder whether he might be mixed up in this IRA business. He'd kept his feelings under wraps for all those years but this bombing campaign had started it all off again."

"Then, I guess, you decided to take a look in the shed."

"Yes. I unscrewed the new lock, well—you know what I found—and then carefully screwed it back again and went straight to the police station. I didn't want explosives in my garden. I've read where some bombs went off accidentally. I wasn't having that. Any of us could have been blown to bits. He was arrested by two plain-clothes men as soon as he got home from work. I'd already made a statement at the station. I hid in the bedroom with the kids when he arrived. None of us have seen him since."

"I expect you'll be glad not to have had to give evidence today, but you will have to at the Old Bailey you know."

"I'm not looking forward to that."

"I'm not writing this, but you've been very useful. I think it might help me to get to the bottom of this IRA business and pass anything I learn to the police. I expect you'll be a bit short of money now, so please accept this," reaching in to his pocket and pulling out the ten pounds.

"Oh thank you. I was a little bit bothered about money. This'll certainly help for a while. I'd like to get my old job back now the kids are nearly finished school."

"Leave that to me. Please let me have your address."

"How can I get me job back?" she asked.

Roger smiled and tapped his nose. Mrs O'Shaughnessy gave Roger her address and he wrote it down.

They finished their teas, left the cafe, shook hands on the pavement outside and went their separate ways.

CHAPTER 5

Refugee

North London, Wednesday 19 April 1939

"Thank you my dear," said the tall distinguished gentleman to the pretty, young, dark-haired maid as she took his hat and coat and hung them on the brown coat stand inside the opulent entrance of the grand white detached house just to the north of Hampstead Heath. It was still cold for April, and the coat had proved essential to the visitor, who must have been over six feet tall and had beautifully combed silver hair.

"Sir John is expecting you, sir," she told him in good English inflected with a strong German accent. "Please come with me."

The maid led the way to the back of the house and through a pair of sturdy oak double doors into an expensively furnished sitting room. Inside another elderly man sat reading the *Daily Telegraph*. As soon as he saw the two enter the room, he jumped to his feet, belying his sixty-five years, crossed the carpet and walked towards his visitor, extending his arm.

"Ah, my dear Nigel, glad you could make it without freezing to death. I wonder if spring will ever arrive." He turned to the maid.

"Esther, this is Nigel Williams, a colleague of mine at the Foreign Office."

"I'm pleased to meet you sir," Esther responded.

"And you too my dear."

"I'm sure Mr Williams is in need of a good hot cup of coffee, and I think I'll have one too, so you'd better make it a pot."

"Certainly sir," and with another gentle bow, Esther left the room.

Wearing a baggy green jumper and a pair of brown corduroy trousers, Sir John was at least four inches shorter than Nigel, but both shared the same air of confidence that being rich and successful brought. Apart from height, the big difference between the two was the thick curly brown hair which the host sported. Nigel often wondered whether he used hair dye but the occasional sly close examination suggested not.

The pair sat in two all-embracing armchairs with a low table in front of them.

"What a charming young girl," Nigel said. "Where did you get her?"

"I'm sure you've noticed that she's not English. German in fact, and Jewish to boot."

"That makes sense," Nigel replied, knowing that Sir John was a regular worshiper at the nearby synagogue. That he had risen loftily in the Foreign Office hierarchy was testament to his ability, for in 1930s England being Jewish was often an obstacle to attaining high office.

"Why do you think that?"

"We've had a large influx of young German women coming here looking for domestic appointments over the past couple of years, and they've been told on arrival by the local Huns, quite specifically, not to work for Jewish employers—you know this filthy anti-Semitism that the Nazis seem to enjoy practising so much. Obviously that doesn't apply in Esther's case. I doubt they care who she works for."

"You're absolutely correct. In fact she's a refugee."

"Interesting. Is there a story here?"

"Between you and me, but not something I'd welcome being passed on to your journalist friends."

"Of course not."

"I was only joking. Her family are from Berlin. The father was a very capable and successful lawyer, and our paths crossed in embassy business from time to time. I don't suppose he's got many clients now since the Nazis put all professional Jews out of business . . . "

"So you got her out? Impressive."

"Not quite. The credit for that goes to a Nazi-hating German gentile who once worked at the German Embassy here in London."

"Ah yes! Van's Carlton House Terrace spy."

Vansittart had been, until recently, the senior civil servant in the Foreign Office, but had been promoted to a position where he could do less damage to the appeasement lobby. He had been a vociferous opponent of Prime Minister Chamberlain's policy of appeasing the European dictators, especially Hitler.

"Well, our source in the German Embassy has been transferred to The Hague, but an MI5 guy codenamed Harry is still in touch with him, so he was able to make the necessary arrangements."

"How old is she?"

"Seventeen."

"Family?"

"Parents both still alive, living in Berlin, and a much younger brother, twelve I believe, who came over here with the Kindertransport. He's been taken in by a family in Cambridge."

"And you say she's Jewish?"

"Yes."

"Well, at least she won't be pestered by other Germans living here. They won't come near her with a bargepole."

"Let's hope not. I give her a half-day off every week and all of Saturday. I believe she meets other young Jewish women who've fled from the Nazis when she goes into town, or else takes a train to Cambridge to see her brother."

"Is she a good worker?"

"Excellent, and highly intelligent too. She wouldn't be doing this kind of thing in other circumstances. She seems very happy. Apart from one thing."

"What's that?"

"She's worried about her parents stuck in Berlin."

"I'm not surprised."

There was a knock on the door and Esther came in carrying a tray with a large coffee pot, two cups, spoons, a small jug of milk and a bowl of sugar.

"Thank you, Esther. We can pour our own, thanks."

"Very good, sir. Will Mr Williams be staying for lunch?"

"No thank you, Esther," Nigel replied. "I have to get back to the office."

"Very well, sir." Turning to Sir John, she said, "It's my half-day today. After I've served lunch and done the washing up, I'll make my way into London. I'm meeting some friends and we're going to the cinema. Is that alright?"

"Of course, my dear. Any idea what you're going to see?"

"No. One of my friends usually buys a copy of the *Globe* and finds a film that she thinks we might like."

"Have a good evening, Esther."

"Thank you, sir."

Esther left the room with a smile on her face and closed the doors, leaving Sir John and Nigel to talk about whatever Foreign Office staff talk about. She'd fallen on her feet with this job, knew it, and was determined to repay her employer's confidence by performing admirably. She joined Cook in the kitchen and told her that it would just be Sir John for lunch. Lady Blum, Sir John's wife, had died from cancer three years previously. Apart from Esther, Cook and Sir John, the only other occupants of the house were the chauffeur and handyman Maurice, Paul the gardener, and his wife Winnie, who shared the cleaning with Esther. It was too big for Sir John. His son and daughter had long since left home but he loved it here, tucked up against the beauty of Hampstead Heath.

Waiting until she heard Mr Williams leave, Esther collected the coffee tray and washed up the crockery. After laying the table in the dining room, she informed Sir John that lunch was served. An hour later she completed her duties for the day and went to her room to prepare for her outing.

Sitting on the bed with her head in her hands, Esther wondered how her parents were coping with the horrors of Berlin. She'd written to them at least a dozen times since she left Germany six months earlier, but had had only two replies, the most recent at the end of February. Letters, both in and out of the Reich, were being read, sometimes censored, and fairly often, in the case of correspondence between Jews, destroyed. Parental replies to her letters had left her without an inkling of what was happening to them.

On Kristallnacht, during November of the previous year, what she had witnessed at first hand had left Esther without any illusions about what would happen to Germany's Jews, and this had prompted her and her brother's departure soon after. They'd travelled separately but by the same route, across Germany by train and then steamer from Ostend. Another train had taken the refugees to Liverpool Street station in London, where they'd been met by their new families and taken to a new life far from Berlin.

Esther snapped out of her misery. She reckoned that there was little or nothing she could do at the moment. Getting children out of Germany at present was much easier than smuggling her parents out. In fact, she knew that was well-nigh impossible. Even more so if the threatened war came. A letter to her parents would be sent tomorrow and she'd travel to Cambridge at the weekend to see her brother. For the time being, she'd just enjoy her afternoon and try to expel these gloomy thoughts. That might be easier said than done, she realised, but she would certainly try. The kindness shown to her by Sir John had helped to alleviate her unhappiness. She put it all in the back of her mind, took off her uniform and dressed for the cool April day. As she put on her royal blue winter coat, her thoughts took a more optimistic turn as she looked forward to meeting her friends, perhaps eating a nice meal in a Lyons Corner House, and then the pictures. London cinemas were plentiful and there were so many films to choose from, they were bound to find something worth seeing.

Sir John was probably having his afternoon nap and, as she didn't wish to disturb him, she asked Cook to tell him that she'd set off. Stepping out of the front door, Esther was pleasantly surprised to find the sun was shining. A chilly north-easterly wind was keeping the temperature down but still the weather was showing a distinct improvement on the recent cloudy days. So it was with a cheerful step that she made her way on to Hampstead Lane. Trees swaying gently in the breeze greeted her. In her short time in England, she'd regularly taken long walks around the Heath and several times had made her way through the North Wood to visit the small gallery there. At times during these excursions she'd been reminded of family walks around the Tiergarten in Berlin, but these were now very much a thing of the past.

Esther walked along the pavement, thinking of the evening ahead, so she didn't notice the black saloon car parked on the opposite side of the road.

Inside, two men, both wearing fawn raincoats and grey trilby hats, watched her closely. Earlier they'd done a quick reconnaissance of the area and knew that the bus stop was just around the corner, and they reasoned that she was heading for it. Striding purposefully, Esther rounded the corner and walked briskly towards the bus stop about one hundred yards away. The man in the passenger seat of the watching car nodded to his companion, climbed out of the car, crossed the road and set off in pursuit. When he spotted the bus stop, Esther was standing there alone. Thinking that this might be his chance to speak with her, he quickened his stride, but when he was about ten yards away the number 513 trolley bus hissed its way into view. Esther climbed on and sat downstairs towards the front of the lower deck. She bought a ticket to King's Cross, where she was meeting her friends, and settled down to enjoy the journey, totally oblivious of her pursuer, who had positioned himself not far behind where he could keep a close eye on her.

CHAPTER 6

Gestapo

Carlton House Terrace, London,
Friday 21 April 1939

A short distance from Buckingham Palace, busy people were scurrying about in the magnificent reception area of a superb four-storey building. The furniture was the very best, comprising large sofas and matching chairs scattered around a number of small tables on which lay the latest newspapers and magazines in several languages. The carpets were deep enough to cause shoes to be lost from sight. Visitors were kept in comfort while waiting for their appointments.

Someone unfamiliar with the function of the building could have been forgiven for mistaking it for the lobby of a five-star hotel or perhaps a lounge on the deck of a transatlantic liner. But it was neither. Instead here was Hitler's favourite architect Albert Speer's vision of what a Nazi foreign embassy in one of the world's major capital cities should look like. Nine Carlton House Terrace had been the German Embassy in London since 1849, or, more properly, the home of the Prussian Legates until the founding of the German Empire in 1871. In the twentieth century, the neighbouring property of 8 Carlton House Terrace had been acquired, and the two formed a fitting overseas base for Europe's newest great power, the Third Reich.

The present Ambassador, Herbert von Dirksen, seemed harmless enough, but his predecessor, Joachim von Ribbentrop, had behaved in a most irresponsible manner, even clicking his heels and giving the Hitler salute when presenting his credentials to the King. Having upset just about everyone, he was recalled to Germany, not to be locked up in a concentration camp, where most felt he belonged, but to be promoted to the post of Reich Foreign Minister. The former wine salesman— he insisted it was champagne—had bluffed his way almost to the top, helping himself to a *von*, to which he was not entitled, on the way. His one legacy was to have the whole embassy decorated while he was in office. He thought he was being clever when he had hidden microphones installed while the painting was going on, but all the staff knew about it, so they made sure the stupid man heard nothing but lavish praise for himself. All this was a far cry from the previous distinguished occupants of 8 Carlton House Terrace, amongst whom were four prime ministers, including Palmerston and Gladstone.

Not far from the top of the wide and magnificent red-carpeted central spiral staircase, which led from the reception area to the upper floors, four men were sitting, standing and generally slouching around, waiting for a fifth man in another smartly finished room with comfortable upright chairs. Five of these chairs had been set up around a polished oak table. The men were modestly dressed in shirts, ties, sports jackets and trousers. Their raincoats, trench coats and broad-brimmed hats had been taken away by a receptionist on their arrival. All appeared to be in their late twenties or early thirties. All were clean-shaven and had oiled flat straight hair, two brown, one blonde and one black. While they continued to smoke and discuss the latest news of the German football season, the door opened and a remarkably small man in a black uniform, carrying a black peaked cap, entered, followed by a woman carrying a tray of coffee and cups. Hurriedly stubbing out their cigarettes, the other men stood attentively behind the chairs.

"Sit down. You may smoke if you wish," he snapped.

Coffee was poured and the small man placed a pad of writing paper and a pencil beside him, as he took his seat at the head of the table. On his other side he carefully placed his cap, arranging it to so that the death's head badge just below the peak was clearly visible to the rest of those around the table. The man, Sturmbannführer Helmut Wolf, was a senior officer in the most feared and hated police force in Gernany, if not in the world: the SS, an organisation he had joined before Hitler had come to power in 1933. A small black moustache, aping his beloved Führer, completed the picture of a man who enjoyed wielding power and fear, giving him much more satisfaction than his previous job as a bookkeeper.

Wolf cleared his throat, checked to see his tie was straight, and stared straight into the eyes of the four men, one by one.

"I've just returned earlier today from Berlin when I had the honour of attending the Führer's fiftieth birthday celebrations. Everybody had a wonderful time. There were parties held in the streets by the people, a lavish reception for dignitaries, to which I was privileged to be invited, and a parade towards the Siegessäulee which demonstrated the might of our armed forces to the tens of thousands of citizens who lined the streets and the edge of the Tiergarten. I, of course, watched from a specially erected platform of seats which also seated dignitaries from all over Greater Germany and beyond the borders of the Reich. It was a wondrous occasion which showed the world how strong our soldiers, sailors and airmen are and the great love of the German people for our Führer."

Wolf paused for a moment to reflect on the event and his own importance in the rise of the Third Reich. He straightened his tie again before continuing.

"It goes without saying that what I'm about to tell you must not leave this room. You must tell no one, not even your Assistants. Is that understood?"

All four men murmured their assent and nodded their heads vigorously.

"Good. On the day after the birthday celebrations I was summoned to meet Reichführers Goring and Himmler. The Führer was busy elsewhere, but the Reichführers said that what I was about to hear had come from the very top."

Another pause while Wolf considered his own importance in all of this. His staring into space gave the men opportunities to exchange glances and smirk at one another.

"The Führer intends to seize Danzig from the Poles sometime later this summer or perhaps in the early autumn. How this is going to be achieved is not yet clear. He hopes to make the usual noises and threats which delivered Austria, the Sudetenland and the rest of Czechoslovakia to their rightful owners, and expects another round of negotiations like those that took place in Munich last September."

"Excuse me," interrupted Kriminal Inspector Schmidt, "are the English and French expected to back down as they did the last time?"

"Of course. The English Prime Minister Chamberlain is weak and pathetic. We all expect him to back down as before and return to his fishing as quickly as possible. The Führer calls him an arsehole," Wolf chuckled.

"And what about the French?" asked Weber.

"They're useless," replied Wolf dismissing any threat from across the channel with a sweep of his right hand. "Their government is completely unstable. They change leaders as often as I change my underwear."

An image of Wolf walking around in underwear, unwashed for six months, briefly entered Weber's mind, and the others too no doubt, before he quickly dismissed it for fear of breaking into a fit of giggles.

"But what if the English and the French don't back down?" enquired Fischer.

"They will, but nevertheless that's a good question. If they don't back down there will be war, and the generals and admirals have been told to prepare for this. Danzig will be taken and the rest of Poland absorbed in the Reich."

"What about the military capabilities of the French and English?" asked the fourth man, Klein.

"Negligible," shouted Wolf. "It's true the English navy is stronger than ours at present but we're quickly catching up. The world's greatest battleship, the *Bismarck*, has just been launched and, when it's ready for sea, it will blow everything the English fleet has clean out of the water. Our army is superior in strength, weapons and morale, and the Luftwaffe will destroy the enemy air forces. Goring has assured the Führer of this."

"I'm sure this is all true, Sturmbannführer, but we must surely be making some preparations for some kind of armed conflict."

"Naturally, Klein, and this is where you four come in."

A short pause followed while the cups were refilled and the men lit fresh cigarettes.

"The Führer dislikes smoking, but it doesn't bother me. Now, you four will spearhead an intelligence gathering operation and will report to me. Each of you is a trained Gestapo agent and you've already had plenty of experience with this kind of thing in the Reich and indeed here in England. I realise that this is a continuation of work that you are already undertaking, but we must be better organised now that the possibility of war is approaching. Each of you will head a team of three or four assistants, mostly the men you already have working under you. You will report to me weekly and keep me informed of your progress."

"Do we bring any intelligence we acquire to you, Sturmbannführer?"

"No. I will furnish you a list of contacts in our merchant navy. There are several of our ships which deliver our goods to Harwich or collect English stuff on their way to the Reich. When our agents come ashore, you will meet them at a pre-arranged place and hand over what you have. Be very careful. The English customs and secret service agents are both clever and determined. From me you will have a list of the ships, agents amongst the crews, and sailing times, as well as places of contact. These are mostly English public houses. Now tell me your covers."

Fischer chose to speak.

"Everything is well attended to Sturmbannführer. We are a mixture of students, journalists, and office workers in German companies entirely populated by party members. One of my men is a waiter in a German restaurant in Soho. The owner doesn't expect him to serve up many pot roasts."

General laughter followed, but Wolf's face remained impassive.

"He's a party member as well," Fischer continued nervously.

Wolf picked it up.

"Good. Now we already have some other agents in place, mostly Abwehr. They're doing a fine job but, with war possibly approaching, we need to step up the pace."

"What type of intelligence should we gather?" asked Schmidt.

"Everything and anything you can. Our analysts can decide whether or not it's valuable."

Weber then detailed some of the things his assistant had been trying to develop.

"They gather in pubs near to important factories—making aircraft, ships, guns, bullets, larger items of ordnance and so on. They eavesdrop on conversations and see if they can spot anyone likely to be a possible double agent. We recruited a man in the north of England who stole some plans of one of the ordnance factories. Another tried to sell us plans of new aircraft, but it turned out we could have seen these in any aircraft magazine."

"Excellent, but don't forget that, whilst pro-Reich people are an excellent source, mercenaries who do it just for money can be equally useful. However, there's one source that you haven't mentioned. Women."

"Women!" exclaimed Klein. "Do you mean honey traps?"

"Yes, that can certainly be useful, but after Austria joined the Reich, hundreds of their young women came here seeking work. Many were encouraged to do so by the Abwehr. They spend their weekends cycling around London and the countryside, sketching bridges, docks, railway yards, airfields and their locations, factories, army barracks, railway stations and so on. Hundreds of drawings have made their way back to Berlin. We need a complete picture of everything English so that we can plan for attack and perhaps even invasion."

"What about the Irish?" asked Klein.

"That's an Abwehr operation. So far it's not achieved much, a few dozen explosions—nothing much else. There is one of their people, however, a man called Donovan, who seems to be a cut above the rest, who might be of use to us. Klein, get in touch with him and see what he has to say. Most of these Irish terrorists appear to be just anti-English but he's keener that most to see the Reich triumph as well."

"Won't we be treading on the toes of the Abwehr?" asked Weber.

"I'm dealing with that. Heydrich is very close friends with Canaris, so he's going to approach him and get him to agree to share responsibility for Irish operations in England with the Gestapo."

"Just one other thing, Sturmbannführer," said Klein. "We are already tracking a Jewish woman who's working as a servant at the home of an Englishman who is a senior person at the Foreign Office staff. That could be useful. I followed her from her employer's home in Hampstead to King's Cross Station one day last week. There she met some other Jews and they disappeared down the Underground. It was pointless trying to speak to her then. I'll try again next week."

"Is she one of those fake Jews planted by the Abwehr?"

"No, she's the real thing."

"Then why on earth should she help us?"

Klein laughed.

"We have something on her."

CHAPTER 7

Followers

Roger Martin sat in his car on the Quadrant in Richmond with a good view of customers entering and leaving the Railway Tavern. He was well concealed. It was yet another disappointing evening in terms of both the weather and his getting any kind of breakthrough in his search for clues about the IRA's activities in and around London. Although it was almost May, it was still cool for the time of the year, but it was thankfully both windless and dry. The Morris Minor he'd bought from the man in Worcester Park was grey. There were dozens of them on the roads and his was hardly likely to be noticed.

He was nicely set up for his surveillance but, so far, the effort he'd put in had come to nothing. Night after night, he'd sat slumped in the driver's seat of his new car hoping for a glimpse of either a bespectacled bloke that looked like a boxer wearing black gloves or a curly-headed young tearaway. He trusted Mrs O'Shaughnessy and was sure her descriptions of the men were accurate. He'd reported his frustrating evenings to Moss, who sympathised, but was excited to learn that he'd got a lead from Mrs O'Shaughnessy. The policeman told him to be patient. Surveillance work was usually long boring hours with nothing to show for it but, when the pay-off came, it was worth it.

During the day, Roger had been in and out of various courts watching accused Irishmen being either committed for trial at the Old Bailey or sentenced to long stretches inside after being found guilty of various acts of terror. The Hammersmith Bridge bombers had appeared at Bow Street on 13 April. On the previous day two Irishmen, a salesman from Barnes and a barman from Euston, had each been sent away for long spells after being found guilty under the Explosives Act at the Old Bailey. All this he reported dutifully in the *Globe*, to the satisfaction of his boss.

There had been a hint of excitement at the beginning of the week when a bomb had been found outside the home of Leslie Hore-Belisha, the War Minister. It turned out to be a dud. Similarly, the evacuation of an engineering firm near Roger's home at Shannon Corner caused some panic but a bomb was never found. To say it was uneventful was putting it mildly. Roger Martin was bored for the first time in his journalistic career.

Half past nine came and time was called on the surveillance. Roger drove home and telephoned his fiancée Jane and asked her to join him the following evening. They could have beer and sandwiches in the pub, he suggested, and she agreed. As it turned out, the next day, a Thursday, bombs went off all over the West End: two on Tottenham Court Road, and one each on Charing Cross Road, Kingsbury, Holborn and Euston Road, where a woman was blown out of a tobacco kiosk. Nobody was killed or badly hurt and no real damage was done. Roger heard all about this when he went back to the office after seeing another IRA man given ten years by the judge at the Old Bailey. His day ended when he phoned Bow Street to get details of a John Joseph Keane, who'd been remanded for posting a suitcase bomb. By the time he'd written all this up for the next evening's paper it was past six, and it was well after seven when he picked Jane up. It was an evening he was looking forward to; an evening with the girl he loved and a sandwich! He'd had nothing to eat since lunchtime and was famished.

"So what's the plan?" Jane asked, turning towards her fiancé, who was sitting behind the wheel of his Morris Minor, driving towards Richmond.

"A sandwich, or perhaps even two, and a beer. I'm starved."

"Make that a lemonade. You need your wits about you."

"OK."

"Then what?"

"We wait until the bad guy comes in and we follow him."

"In the car?"

"Yes, if he's driving, but if he's on foot I'll follow him. You drive the car home."

Jane had been driving longer than Roger. Her insurance, she knew, covered her to drive his vehicle. She murmured "OK," but secretly hoped that the pursuit would be by car. She fancied a bit of excitement and driving Roger's car back to New Malden alone didn't seem like much fun.

Parking in his usual quiet corner outside the Railway Tavern, Roger began to feel a sense of adventure. He'd felt like this ever since he'd begun his vigil, but he always believed his luck would change. They made their way inside the pub and took up two seats at a table near the fire, which really shouldn't have been alight at this time of the year, but was justified by the chill outside.

"What are you having?" Roger asked.

"Just a lemonade and some crisps please. I've already eaten."

While Roger was walking towards the bar, Jane scanned the room. It was about half full, which meant that there were about twenty customers. She quickly spotted a young man in a black jumper sitting on his own, nursing a half-drunk pint of beer.

Roger returned with two glasses of lemonade and a packet of crisps.

"My sandwiches are on their way," he told her.

Jane sipped her drink and fixed a serious stare on Roger.

"Do *not* turn around," she whispered, "but there's a young man over the far side of the room who might be one of your men. Didn't Mrs O'Shaughnessy say he had curly brown hair and ruddy cheeks?"

"Yes."

"Then that could be him."

Roger's sandwiches arrived, four slices of thick white bread with what looked like half a pig's worth of ham, with mustard on the side. He ploughed into them enthusiastically.

Jane chuckled.

"I expect you'll enjoy those."

With his mouth full, he nodded and then carried on eating. Jane meanwhile chatted on about nothing in particular while all the time keeping a sharp eye on their quarry.

Roger polished off his sandwiches, heaved a sigh of satisfaction, and asked, "Anything?"

"Might be. He's still sipping his ale. He's glancing at his watch a lot and a couple of times he's looked towards the door. I definitely think he's expecting someone. We might be in luck."

Ten minutes of idle chatter passed by pleasantly enough before Jane said quietly: "I think we're in business. A man in a raincoat has just come in. Fawn raincoat, bare-headed with thinning black hair, glasses and black gloves on. His right hand does look a bit funny."

Roger's excitement grew. "What's he doing?"

"He's at the bar ordering himself a drink and now he's carrying his pint towards the lad. There you are, he's sitting across the table from him, shaking hands."

Roger stood up and went to the bar to order more lemonades. On the way back he glanced at the two men, who were hunched over their drinks. Jane continued her observation, reporting to Roger that they appeared to be in deep conversation. Fifteen minutes later the sleuths were presented with a dilemma as the younger one got up and strolled towards the door.

"The boy is leaving. What do we do now?" Roger asked.

"We wait until the other man leaves. I'm sure he's the big fish."

Obligingly, ten minutes later, the black-haired man swiftly downed the remains of his beer and got up. Instead of making for the door, he set off for the Gents.

"Give me the keys," said Jane urgently, "I'm going to the car. If he doesn't emerge from the Gents in two minutes, join me."

The black-haired man didn't seem to suspect anything, and he reappeared a couple of minutes later and left by the main door. Heart hammering in his chest, Roger followed. He opened the driver's side door in his car. Jane was already sitting in the passenger seat.

"He's in that black Austin over there."

Roger started the engine and waited until he saw the Austin ease out of its parking space. Then the young journalist set off in pursuit.

"He could outrun us. His car's more powerful," said Roger.

"If he's up to no good he isn't going to risk being picked up for speeding," replied Jane.

"You're right."

It was getting quite gloomy, so Roger had to tuck in behind the Austin closer than he would have liked, but Jane was right, the Austin wasn't going anywhere in a hurry. He should be able to keep tabs on their quarry quite easily.

Roger sensed they were heading towards Kew. He was familiar with this part of London, but, once they'd crossed Kew Bridge and began motoring along Brentford High Street, both he and Jane were in foreign territory. But everything proceeded smoothly and their guide showed no signs of being aware that he was being followed. Through Southall, they made steady progress, staying two cars behind the Austin. Although they were momentarily held up by a number 607 trolley bus as they approached Hayes when the vehicle stopped to deposit and collect a handful of passengers, the Austin, the two cars behind and Roger were able to comfortably overtake the stationary vehicle.

Jane was making notes of the route and the landmarks on it so that if they ever had to repeat the journey on their own, they wouldn't get lost. They were now on Uxbridge Road, Hayes, and Roger and Jane guessed that Hayes, Hillingdon, or Uxbridge was probably the Austin's destination. They passed the Adam and Eve pub and then the Essoldo Cinema, where Roger remarked that *The Four Feathers*, which he and Jane had enjoyed together in the West End the previous week, was showing.

"Keep your eyes on the road," Jane ordered.

Roger did as he was told. Through Hayes and then Hillingdon, they motored onto Uxbridge High Street. It was fully dark by now and they were grateful for the street lighting. Jane jotted down the Kings Arms Hotel, and the Three Tuns Inn on her left as they passed, and soon, on the opposite side of the road, saw a spanking new Underground station designed in the contemporary art deco mode. Roger knew, because he'd read about it in the *Globe*, that the terminus stations at either end of the Piccadilly Line, Uxbridge and Cockfosters, were designed in this style.

His architectural musings were brought to an abrupt halt when, shortly after passing the George Hotel, the Austin's right-hand yellow indicator flickered and the driver made his way to the middle of the road. Roger slowed down and then crossed the road at a respectful distance, so that he could still see the Austin about one hundred yards ahead. Jane noted they were on Belmont Road, which was straight, so when they saw the Austin pull up alongside a terrace of houses, they had plenty of time to react and park up outside a school. As soon as the Morris Minor pulled up to a halt, Jane jumped out and set off towards the Austin.

"Where are you off?" asked Roger with concern.

"Back in five minutes," Jane replied.

With that she was gone, marching up the right-hand side of the road and just reaching the parked Austin in time to see the driver entering the house. Without breaking step, she continued away from Roger until she came to a Friends meeting house, where she doubled back on herself and soon was back in the passenger seat of the Morris.

"Well?" asked Roger.

"He's in number 10, part of a pair of semis—two upstairs windows and a large bay window on the ground floor. Quite nice—all painted white. Bit of a porch over the front door. I saw him let himself in with a key, so he obviously wasn't a visitor."

"Did he see you?"

"Not unless he's got eyes in the back of his head. When I walked back the light was on behind the bay window and the curtains drawn. That's where he lives. Now we know that and have his car registration number, what next? You obviously can't sit outside his house morning, noon and night."

Roger, who had been playing second fiddle to his fiancée's razor-sharp mind, accepted this and thought furiously for a moment or two, and then, turning to her in the darkness, smiled.

"I think I've got an idea."

CHAPTER 8

Blackmailers

London and Cambridge, Saturday 13 May 1939

Esther was doing the washing up after breakfast. Working quickly but thoroughly, the young Jewish girl was anxious to complete her tasks as soon as possible, because today was Saturday and she was planning to visit her brother Peter in Cambridge. She dressed and called in to have a word with Sir John before she left.

"Ah, Esther my dear. Are you off now?"

"Yes, Sir John. I'll probably be back late."

"Very well. I hope you have a good day."

"Thank you, sir. Goodbye."

The weather had improved since the end of April and Esther set off in a blue cardigan and grey dress. She walked to the trolley stop, her brown leather bag slung over her shoulder. As she strolled along in the late spring sunshine, she thought about how much she was looking forward to her outing, but still, at the back of her mind, anxiety about her parents, stuck in Berlin, loomed large. So deep were her thoughts, she didn't spot the two men watching her from a car near to the trolleybus stop.

"That's her," said Klein. "I think she'll most likely get on the trolleybus. If she does I'll follow her. She's probably going to King's Cross. I'll get off there and see where she goes next. I just hope she doesn't meet another gang of Jews as she did last time. As soon as I'm on the trolleybus, you drive back to base and sit by the telephone. I'll call you the moment I have news and any instructions. Pick up some food on your way back and don't, under any circumstances, leave the house until you hear from me."

Berger, his companion, turned towards his boss and, with a nod, said, "Right, sir." Then, glancing in his mirror, he announced, "here's the trolleybus."

Klein got out of the car and walked towards the stop. Fortunately, half a dozen others were waiting for the bus, so he was able to join the queue unnoticed. Esther sat towards the front downstairs and Klein took a seat towards the rear where he could keep an eye on her. She was staring out of the window while Klein was thinking to himself that this had better work. Wolf had quite liked the idea of recruiting Esther as an unwilling agent and was anxious to see results. As he predicted, the girl got off at King's Cross. This time there was no one to meet her. Klein cursed himself for his bad luck. Had he a colleague and a car, he could have snatched her here. Nobody would have noticed in the hordes milling around the station concourse. He had no choice but to continue following her.

Esther made her way to the ticket office with Klein on her tail. She was far too occupied with her own thoughts to notice him. She joined a short queue, with Klein, looking uninterested, behind her.

"Third class return ticket to Cambridge please."

The man in the ticket office told her the price and Esther rummaged in her bag for money. Having paid and received her ticket, she stepped away from the window and stood for a moment, while returning the change to her bag.

"Third class return to Cambridge," Klein said quietly, making sure that Esther didn't pick up his accent. If the ticket office man found it odd that two consecutive purchases had been by foreigners, he didn't show it. Klein walked a short distance to the platform, presented his ticket at the gate, and got into the carriage behind Esther. He knew where she was going, so didn't need to chance sitting in the same carriage. There was no point in taking unnecessary risks.

Esther, sitting in her compartment, had no idea what was going on. She felt entirely safe. And why not? This was London, not Berlin. She settled down to do some more thinking and the journey passed quickly. It wasn't long before the train pulled into Cambridge. Klein, meanwhile, was plotting what he would do next. He quickly realised that there wasn't much he could do but keep tabs on her until she returned to the station. She only had her shoulder bag with her, so, he reasoned, it was extremely unlikely she would be staying the night.

As the passengers left the station, Klein was dismayed to see a man with two smallish boys, who looked to be in their early teens, walk towards Esther and, with kisses, hugs and handshakes, guide her towards a parked car. All four climbed in and the vehicle drove off. Klein thought quickly. These were her friends, probably more Jews. The adult was maybe taking her for lunch, either at his own home or in a restaurant. Sometime in the afternoon, he guessed, her host would deliver her back to the station and she would return to London. He would arrange to have her picked up at King's Cross.

Klein spotted a telephone box. He called base and gave detailed instructions, again issuing a warning that the phone should be manned at all times. He would call again and leave details of the time of arrival in London of the train that they were on. He ordered that two men, apart from himself, were needed, and that one of them was to meet him at the station and escort him and his guest to the waiting vehicle. He then set off on the mile-long trudge into town. By the time he arrived he was hungry and started looking for somewhere for lunch. He knew he had to take a risk in the hope that it would be several hours before his quarry began her return journey. He'd already made a note of the times of the return trains to London and decided that he would go back to the station for the first of the late afternoon trains.

◆   ◆   ◆

Meanwhile, Esther had reached the home of her young brother's new family. They had a lovely house in a leafy suburb, close to the Botanic Gardens and adjacent playing fields. As the four stepped inside they were greeted by Mrs Richardson, a fine slim middle-aged woman with straight fair hair and stunning blue eyes. Mr Richardson, a teacher of physics at the university, was tall, handsome, and, like his wife, fair-haired. Their son Michael had the same striking features as his parents and had struck up a warm and close friendship with Peter. Both boys attended the local grammar school where their guest Peter, despite initial difficulties with language, was flourishing like his friend.

"How are you, Esther?" asked Mrs Richardson.

"Very well thank you, Mrs Richardson."

"Good. let's have some lunch and then, afterwards, I thought we'd take a stroll around the Botanic Gardens."

"That sounds lovely. Thank you."

"What time do you have to leave?" asked Mr Richardson.

"There's a train at five o'clock. I'd like to be on that if it's possible. Sir John likes me back before nightfall."

"Of course. We'll get you there in good time."

Like Esther, Peter looked happy but a little concerned. He too was worried about his parents. Lunch was served and they settled down to an excellent meal. They talked about how brother and sister were settling down in their new country and Mr Richardson remarked how both would return to their parents, hopefully soon, after their brief but enjoyable stay in England. This caused a small shadow to pass over Mrs Richardson's face. She'd had a miscarriage eighteen months after Michael's birth and the doctor had told her that she would not be able to have any more children. Peter's arrival had given her the second child she'd always wanted and she was desperately keen to keep him. She would never, however, stand in his way if he said he wanted to return to Germany when circumstances permitted.

"There was one thing I wanted to ask you, Esther. Peter hasn't been to the synagogue since he arrived. Is that a problem for you?"

"No," replied Esther. "We weren't brought up as strict Jews. All four of us did attend the synagogue, but not all that regularly. The synagogue near to us in Berlin was burned to the ground on Kristallnacht and Peter's bar mitzvah had to be postponed. I have been to some services with Sir John, who's Jewish as you know, but he is happy that I don't strictly observe the Sabbath."

"That's fine then. I didn't want to upset your family in any way."

Esther smiled in response and then Peter joined the conversation. He asked Esther. "Have you heard from mama and papa?"

"No. I've written several letters but have had only a couple of replies, and both of those had lots of words crossed out."

"You must be terribly worried about them," said Mrs Richardson.

"Yes," replied Peter, "but I don't want to go back to Germany until the Nazis have gone and things have returned to how they were before they came. I love it here," and he turned his dark-haired, brown-eyed face to Mrs Richardson and smiled.

Lunch was over. "Right, let's go for that walk. Michael, fetch the football. You two boys can play on the field while we look at the gardens."

"That's a relief," replied the lively Michael. "I think we'd both prefer that to looking at plants and flowers."

The adults laughed and the boys left the room to collect the football. Soon all five were ready for their outing and, while Mr and Mrs Richardson and Esther set out for the Botanic Gardens, the boys sprinted for the football field. Esther enjoyed the gardens but, after about forty-five minutes, Mr Richardson suggested they return to the field to see how the boys were doing. They found them sweaty, dirty, but still hard at it and obviously enjoying themselves immensely. Mr Richardson suggested they play against one another while he kept goal. Coats and cardigans were put down for the goal and off they went, dribbling, tackling and shooting while Michael's father did his best to keep the shots out.

"Don't you want to join in, Esther?"

"Pah!" said Peter. "She won't be any good. She's a girl. They don't play football."

The three adults laughed. "Not now, perhaps," said Mr Richardson, "but you never know, one day."

"Huh," said Michael. "I agree with Peter," and he patted his friend on the back.

Peter and Esther had a typical big sister-little brother relationship and had often gently quarrelled back in Berlin. But they loved each other dearly and both knew it. Mrs. Richardson called the game to a halt.

"Time for tea. Esther will soon need to leave for her train. Boys, have a quick wash while I make the tea and cut the cake. I'm sure you're ready for more food after that exercise."

Neither needed a second invitation and dashed off, accompanied by Mr Richardson who needed to be at the house before them to unlock the back door.

◆   ◆   ◆

Back in the town, Klein had enjoyed a good lunch and browsed through many of the bookshops. His heart wasn't really in it. He was still worried that he'd left too much to chance, but what the alternative was he'd no idea. By mid-afternoon he'd had enough and began the long walk back to the station. He could have taken the bus, but that would have added one person, the bus conductor, to the list of people who might have remembered him later. He reached the station just before a quarter to four, ample time to make the call to base if the girl turned up for the four o'clock. She didn't and he resigned himself for a long wait. He bought a newspaper from the station shop and sat on a bench outside and read the paper, or rather pretended to. Eyes glued to the front of the station where cars picked up and dropped off railway passengers, he turned each page slowly without reading a word.

His patience was finally rewarded when the same car that had collected the girl in the morning pulled up. Two boys jumped out, followed by the girl and the driver, a tall blonde-haired man who looked attractively Aryan. A further exchange of hugs, kisses and handshakes took place before the three males got back in the car and drove off, the two boys returning the wave of the girl. She turned slowly and slightly sadly away and entered the station. "Five o'clock train," thought Klein, looking at his watch and seeing that he had ten minutes to spare. He quickly went to a phone box and called base. Answering the call promptly, Berger made a mental note of his orders. He put the phone down and repeated them to his companion, who threw on a light jacket and collected the car keys from the mantelpiece.

Klein settled down for the journey, again in a separate carriage from the girl, and watched out of the window as the train pulled out of the station. He reflected on his afternoon in Cambridge. Not a bad town, he decided, a bit like Heidelberg, but he'd spotted far too many Jews for his liking. Also he knew that this university was infested with Communists, another pet hate of his, the Führer's, and, as far as he knew, all Nazis. He was on edge. There were certainly risks in getting hold of the girl. It would still be light when the train pulled into King's Cross and the abduction may not go unnoticed. Hoping that the Saturday evening crowds around the station and on the pavement outside would disguise his actions, he knew that, if he brought this off, he'd shoot up in Wolf's estimation.

In another carriage, Esther was thinking back over her day. The Richardson family were fine people, she thought, and Peter was very lucky to be living with them, as was she at Sir John's house. If only mama and papa could somehow get out of Germany. There were several stops between Cambridge and London, but she daydreamed though all of them and just came back to proper consciousness as the train reached King's Cross. Not noticing the man behind her, Esther handed in her ticket at the barrier and set off for the trolleybus stop on the opposite side of Euston Road. Her follower was now walking side by side with another man and the two crossed the road closely behind her. They spotted their car about fifty yards ahead, the engine idling and the driver standing beside the open rear door. Klein and Berger made their move as Esther passed the open car door and, with great urgency, they pushed her into the car and followed her in. The driver was back in the driver's seat within seconds and was already drawing away as he closed his door. Driving up Euston Road, Berger wrapped his hand around Esther's mouth and climbed over her so that he and Kline were sitting on either side of the petrified girl.

Esther was terrified and continued to struggle, with Berger's hand still securely clamped around her mouth. She tried to think. What did they want? Were they rapists? Then her mind cleared enough to recognise their accents. They were German, and more than that, Berliners. She'd know that rough tone anywhere. This made her even more frightened, and threw her into a fit of hysterics that only ended when Berger gave her a sharp slap across the face.

"Shut up," he said.

"Careful," said Klein. "Don't mark her."

The car was moving north along Hampstead Road, and then it veered to the right and made its way through the densely populated area onto Albert Road. She vaguely knew where she was, somewhere to the north of Regent's Park. She'd been there visiting the zoo, which was now closed for the day. It was still light and the car made its way onto a quiet spot between the road and the canal. Esther had made her mind up that these were Nazis and they planned to kill her. Why else would they have grabbed her off the street? She was sweating profusely and felt her bladder about to give way, although with a great effort of sheer willpower she managed to prevent that from happening. The car drew to a halt, the driver switched off the engine, and Klein turned in his seat and stared deep into her eyes.

"We mean you no physical harm, Miss Abrahams. We need you to perform a task for us."

Sobbing, Esther said in a quiet voice, "what task could I possibly perform for you? I'm just a domestic servant."

"But you work for a very important person."

"I don't understand." Esther was now recovering slightly from the shock of finding herself in the hands of Nazis, but there was no way her terror would go away. She'd seen what they were capable of on Kristallnacht.

"Sir John Blum is a senior man in the English Foreign Office. We want you to provide us with certain information."

"How can I do that? I've just told you I'm only a domestic servant."

"Precisely. No one will suspect you. I would guess you can come and go as you please. He must bring a briefcase home from work. It could contain papers of interest to us. And what about visitors? Some important people must come to his home."

Still horribly distressed, Esther told Klein that she'd never seen his briefcase and, although she admitted that Sir John did have visitors from time to time, she had no idea as to whether they were important or not.

"That's why we're going to give you a month to watch him. See where he puts his briefcase and make a note of his visitors and work out how you can eavesdrop on his conversations with them. I know you're a bright girl, Miss Abrahams, I'm sure you can come up with a way of helping us."

"And what if I don't?" Esther mumbled.

"That's simple. You'll never see your mother and father again."

A pain of shock raced through her body, followed by a second when she realised that they had her at their mercy.

"You won't kill them, will you?" Even on Kristallnacht very few were killed even though there were hundreds of dreadful things done.

"We can do as we please; after all, we're only dealing with Jews. Nobody will miss them."

"You're horrible."

"I'll take that as a compliment," smirked Klein. "No, more likely we'll send them to the camps. The SS guards will have some fun with them there. They've had plenty of practice at Sachsenhausen, and now Reichsführer Himmler has ordered a special women's camp to open at Ravensbrück. If you think we're nasty, just wait until you hear about the behaviour of our women guards. Haha! Yes, your mother would be very comfortable there."

Esther remained silent.

"Right, you'll meet me exactly four weeks today near to the gallery in the woods at the north end of Hampstead Heath. You know it?"

Esther nodded.

"Seven o'clock exactly. Understand? Do not be late."

Esther nodded again.

"We'll take you back to King's Cross. You can catch the trolleybus back to your home."

The car started first time and Esther remained totally silent throughout the return journey.

"Goodbye Esther. Pull yourself together. I'm sure you wouldn't like Sir John to find you in this state. He might even suspect something. See you in a month," Klein said with menace in his voice.

A still petrified Esther stepped on to the pavement. Her legs were like rubber. Staggering towards the ladies' toilets, she rummaged in her handbag, mercifully found a penny, dropped it into the lock and just managed to get her head over the toilet bowl in time before she was violently sick. She left the WC and splashed cold water on to her face. That look of terror just wouldn't leave her eyes.

Back outside the station, the fresh air made her feel slightly better, and she took stock of her situation. The German was right. If Sir John saw her like she was now, he'd know something was wrong. Esther would blurt out what had happened and that would be that. The Germans wouldn't have access to any secrets and her parents would be sent to concentration camps, probably to die. She went back into the toilets, used her make-up to make herself look more presentable and left to catch the trolleybus back to Hampstead. Esther knew she'd be terrified when she had to look Sir John in the eye.

CHAPTER 9

Irregulars

London, Tuesday 16 and Wednesday 17 May 1939

"Two quid, two quid, the paper isn't made of money, yer know."

Roger Martin stared at his boss, Ben Rogers, a determined look on the younger man's face.

"Two quid would keep me in fags for a month." As if to emphasise the fact, the *Globe*'s news editor pulled a packet of cigarettes and a box of matches from his jacket pocket and lit up. Roger quickly calculated his own savings by not being a smoker.

"There's a big story here, Ben, I know. I can feel it."

"I will say you've always delivered in the past, Prof. Anyway, it wouldn't be as much as your jaunts to Paris, Berlin and Scotland over the past couple of years. And, to be fair to you, you delivered the goods then. OK, I'll go and check with the powers that be. You sit 'ere and file your nails. I'll be back in a jiffy."

Roger was quite excited. After identifying a man whom he guessed could be one of the IRA's top dogs in England, someone who might be behind the spate of bombings in London and elsewhere, he was very anxious to find out more about his suspect, and see if there was more to this than just a bunch of angry Irishmen trying to cause havoc. At the back of his mind there was just a touch of uncertainty. He could be wrong. An IRA exercise in causing disruption might just be all that it was. Still, he had to know, and he wanted to know more. To achieve this, he needed help and he knew just where to get it.

Ben returned less than five minutes later. "Right, Prof, you're on. They seem to think you're some sort of golden boy. In fact, if you'd asked for more, you'd have probably got it. Remember, receipts, no cash back without receipts."

Roger was relieved but not surprised. The *Globe* had been an excellent employer during his two and a half years or so with the paper. Despite having been involved with high level political stories until recently, he accepted that the IRA run-of-the-mill stuff he'd been covering lately was important. He was just itching to get his teeth into something bigger again. He thanked Ben and went to his desk, where he phoned Moss, his Special Branch contact. The policeman thanked him for keeping in touch and said that the details Roger had given him would help the Yard identify the IRA man. To Roger's relief, Moss said that they wouldn't be arresting the man yet, since the only evidence they had against him was the word of a journalist who'd reported some slightly suspicious behaviour. That same journalist said thanks, and promised that he would give Moss regular updates.

◆　　◆　　◆

That done, Roger pulled on his jacket and stepped out of the office into the warm May sunshine. He made his way down the Strand, across Trafalgar Square, through to the edge of Leicester Square and on to Coventry Street. By the time he reached Piccadilly Circus, the shoppers were out in force and the crowds were pouring into Swan and Edgar. A minute or so later he entered the hallowed confines of the Café Royal, where, as he'd hoped, he found his quarry enjoying a cup of coffee and a cigarette.

"Roger, my friend, how good to see you. Will you join me?" said Claud Cockburn, who was a vociferous opponent of the government's appeasement policy. He was thinning on top, and that, together with his black horn-rimmed spectacles, made him look older than his thirty-odd years. Cockburn had once been a journalist on *The Times*, but had given that up and taken a part-time job on the Communist newspaper, the *Daily Worker*. Later he'd launched his own news sheet, *The Week*. That journal had been a thorn in the side of Neville Chamberlain when he pursued his policy of appeasing Hitler, as Cockburn published facts and stories that other papers had either been too frightened to print or had failed to get past the government's censorship axe.

Roger thanked Cockburn for the offer of a drink and said he would have one and ordered a coffee. He shook the hand of the man who had not only been his ally in his own battle with the government, but had been responsible for keeping the *Globe*'s man out of the clutches of the police.

"I see you're on the IRA stuff now, and with your own byline! Anything to report?"

"Only what you've read in the *Globe*," replied Roger.

"All rather dull after your previous adventures, isn't it?"

"I suppose so, but Ben seems to think there might be something more to it and I tend to agree with him."

"I do as well but, as of yet, nothing to support that theory."

"I have made some progress," said Roger and he told Claud about Mrs O'Shaughnessy and his vigil at the Railway Tavern and the subsequent visit to Uxbridge.

"I see. Presumably you don't want me to print this. It might upset your plans. Anyway, anything I say would be pure speculation at the moment."

"Of course. I've got a tenuous working relationship with a Special Branch man." Roger outlined his agreement with Moss.

"Well, that's a turn-up for the books. Do you trust him?"

"I think I do, especially as he seems keen to get one over the MI5 boys."

"OK, but watch it. The Branch has been pretty nasty to both you and me in recent times. Circumstances have changed, however. Appeasement, if not actually dead, looks like it's on its knees. Nonetheless, I expect Chamberlain to continue to press for peace. It won't be too long before Hitler's at it again and then it'll be war unless we can get Russia on our side. I see we're having what the government calls 'conversations' on that front. Let's hope they succeed."

"I guess that's left you a bit short of material," said Roger.

"True, but I expect the government will make a mess over any agreement with the Soviets. There's always that. Right, let's get down to business."

"Thanks. Any idea if anybody else apart from the Irish is behind these bombings?"

"I've heard rumours that the Nazis might be involved, but nothing more than rumours. I believe they make contact in the United States. I doubt your editor will let you cross the Atlantic to sort that one out."

Roger laughed. "Not likely. I think my best bet is to follow the mystery man from Uxbridge and see where that leads."

"And you need some help?" Claud knew exactly what was coming next.

"Yeah. Both he and I have got cars, so that side of it's covered. But what if he's on foot? I can't really dump my car in Uxbridge and chase after him. Then again, he might meet someone, and then the two will go their separate ways. Which do I follow?"

"I assume you're not expecting me to carry out these extra duties. You need the help of one of my boys."

It was a statement rather than a question, and Roger could see that Cockburn was thinking along similar lines to him. At the height of the government's battle with *The Week*, Claud had boys posted outside his office in Victoria, keeping an eye on Special Branch personnel disguised as road workers, delivery men, newspaper vendors and so on. The police were keen to find out about *The Week*'s sources. The boys were mostly from the East End, where Cockburn had many sources amongst Communist Party members. They were a 1930s version of Sherlock Holmes' Baker Street Irregulars.

"Are any of them available?"

"Yes. As I said, things are quiet at the moment and I don't need them to watch my back as much as I did. I suppose you're thinking about using Joe?"

Joe was the youth whom Claud had instructed to keep an eye on Roger while Special Branch had been after him.

"If he's free that would be great."

"I'll get word to him and you can ask him yourself. How about two o'clock tomorrow afternoon at my office in Victoria?"

"Your office will be open, even on a Saturday?"

"Naturally. People like Hitler don't take the weekend off."

"Of course not. That's great. Thank you. I've been wondering . . . "

Claud cut Roger off, "How do I pay them? I haven't got a vast amount of money, but I just make sure they're covered for their fares, food and cigarettes."

"That's good. I've got the go-ahead for extra expenses, so food and fares can come out of that. The money for cigarettes can come out of my own pocket. I've got an idea for something extra when this is all over."

"Good. You've got it all worked out. You'll need to tell him exactly what you want and be absolutely straight with him. None of them are stupid. In fact, in a country with a decent education system, they'd still be at school. And if you think anything in this caper could be dangerous, tell him. He's as brave as a lion but he should know what he's getting in to. He's bound to say yes. He loves it."

"Thanks Claud. I'd better be getting back. I'll see you tomorrow afternoon."

"Thank you for coming, Roger. I'm quite excited about this myself."

◆   ◆   ◆

Roger walked back to the office and then spent the afternoon at the Old Bailey. That evening he gave Jane an update. She could see the excitement in his face as he told her of his meeting with Claud and it was clear she wanted some involvement in it all. Not just yet, Roger told her. The next morning he was at Bow Street to see more IRA suspects come up in front of the bench. They all appeared quite young, with ages ranging from nineteen to twenty-five. All five of them were remanded in custody for causing explosions in Holborn, Euston Road and Charing Cross earlier in the month. Roger thought that all of the people he'd seen in the dock seemed pretty useless. He'd seen in the morning papers that the Irish had taken to leaving firebombs at bed and breakfast establishments in seaside towns like Eastbourne, Blackpool and Margate. Desperation? he wondered, then reminded himself that it would only take one effective IRA cell to cause chaos.

Roger was on time at Claud's office but, when he arrived, Joe was already sitting there chatting with the owner of *The Week*. His eyes lit up as soon as Roger walked in.

"'Ow are you guv?" he asked, walking towards Roger with an outstretched arm.

"Very well thanks, Joe," Roger said, grasping Joe's firm and dry handshake. "How about you?"

"OK. Bit bored. 'Ad to get some work on the markets since the coppers stopped pesterin' Mr Cockburn. The chief over there," he began, nodding towards Claud, "says you might 'ave summat for me."

"Do you want me to leave you two alone?" asked Cockburn.

"Not at all," said Roger, "I've no secrets from you."

Joe sat down. Roger, who had only met him once, looked at the freckled brown face and curly brown hair. It was an honest but mischievous face. He had on a pair of dark blue corduroy trousers, black working boots and a grey jumper over a white open-necked shirt. Roger summed him up as a kind of latter-day Artful Dodger from *Oliver Twist*, only older, cleaner and more honest. This isn't going to work, thought Roger, unless I trust him, and that's what he decided to do.

"I need you to keep watch on a man and follow him when he's on foot," Roger began.

"Is 'e a nasty bugger?"

"Not sure, but probably."

"Irish?"

"I think so."

"Good," said Joe with enthusiasm. "Ol' girl down our way got blown out of 'er kiosk on Euston Road the other day. She was lucky not to be killed. I don't like the Irish."

Roger laughed. "They're not all bad, but plenty in England are."

"Right. Fill me in on all the stuff, please guv."

"The man I'm interested in lives in Uxbridge."

"Where's that?"

"West London. Further out than Wembley."

"I know where Wembley is. Never bin. Me dad went the year I was born. West Ham lost two-nil to Bolton in the Cup Final."

"So you know it's a fair way out?"

"'Ow will I get there?"

"Either I'll take you in my car or you'll go on the tube and I'll meet you there."

"What line?"

"Piccadilly."

"I get on at Plaistow. It's on the District. I'll 'ave to work out where I change to get on the Piccadilly."

"Here's how I see it," said Roger. "You and I will watch his house from my car. If he drives off, we'll follow him. If he parks the car and carries on on foot, you get on his tail. If he parks up and goes into a nearby place, we'll sit in the car waiting for him and keep with him until he gets home. We'll just have to play it by ear. See what happens. While you're following him, I'll stay with the car. If you're not back in an hour, I'll set off either home or back to the office. Ring me there and tell me what's happened. OK?"

"OK guv."

"Could be a bit boring."

"Naw. Not wiv you. I've followed you plenty. You always seem to be gettin' into trouble."

Roger laughed. "You're right there Joe. Now I'll give you a quid a week. That'll cover your fares and food. Just one thing. You'll have to keep receipts for these things. Keep any bus and tube tickets and get whoever you buy food off to sign a scrap of paper saying how much you've spent. Give me all the tickets and paper at the end of each week."

"Sounds good to me."

"Right, here's the first pound. We'll start next Monday. I'll pick you up outside Uxbridge tube station at ten o'clock. Leave plenty of time for the journey. It's a long trip. Here's another ten bob. That'll pay for your cigarettes for the week. You don't need receipts for them. If you decide to give up smoking in the meantime, spend the money on something else. When the job's all over, I'll give you something special."

"Great. Thanks guv."

"Here's two phone numbers: my office and my home. If you can't get me, leave a message. Anything else you need to know?"

"What happens if I follow this geezer and 'e meets another bloke and then they split up? 'Oo do I follow then?"

"Er . . . "

"Told you he's a good lad," said Claud, with a chuckle.

"What do you think, Joe?"

"I think this job needs two of us."

"Of course. Anybody in mind?"

"Me mate George."

"He's a good lad too," said Claud.

"And 'e can 'andle 'imself in a ruck and 'e's fast just like me," added Joe.

Roger thought quickly. He'd get nowhere with half-measures. Joe knew his stuff and he'd got enough money to cover the two of them.

"Right. Bring him along on Monday. Ten o'clock at Uxbridge."

"OK. We'll tell our mums and dads we're working for Mr Cockburn. They're Party members. They know him well."

"One last thing Joe. you can't afford to get spotted."

"No trouble guv."

"Well, I spotted you."

"I meant you to. So you'd feel safe."

CHAPTER 10

Watchers

London, Thursday 25 to Wednesday 31 May 1939

"So, what you're telling me, Mr Martin, is that you're going to follow some mad Irish bombers using a couple of street urchins."

"Well they're not exactly urchins. Clean, well-dressed, properly brought up lads with brains, guts and determination."

"What happens if they get spotted? The mad micks will kill 'em," Moss asked, with concern in his voice.

"I'm pretty certain they won't be seen."

"What makes you so certain?"

"You didn't take them out when they kept an eye on me."

Joe had rescued Roger from the clutches of Special Branch on more than one occasion over the last eighteen months or so, while keeping watch on the young journalist.

"How many of them will there be?"

"Two, but so far I've only met one, Joe, the boy who snookered your lot when you tried to have me framed."

"Can you trust the other one?"

"I have to. In any case, as far as I'm concerned, if Joe says he's all right, then that's it for me."

Roger was enjoying himself. He knew he'd got Moss on the back foot and got a bit of a hold on him. The Special Branch detective was keen to make it up to Roger for his persecution in the past, as well as to get a feather in his cap by tracking down and arresting an IRA bigwig.

"But," continued Moss, "we've no idea yet who this bloke is. The house is rented and the car belongs to another feller in Kilburn called Davidson. We daren't question either the landlord or the car owner or else word might get back to the terrorist and he'll just vanish. And we can't arrest him because we've got no evidence."

"I don't want to you to arrest him. We'll never be able to find out where he's getting orders from or the sources of his guns and explosives if you take him in."

Moss stared at Roger with an air of resignation. "OK, Mr Martin, but don't forget you're dealing with dangerous and determined criminals here. There seem to be dozens of them. As soon as we grab one, another one takes his place. They've even got some women on board. I expect you've been following their latest stupidities. One of the idiots tried to leave a bomb in a cinema in Victoria, another let off a tear gas bomb, and some of 'em have started to send letter bombs. None dead so far, but you never know. They've even spread as far north as Scotland—a couple of them were jailed in Stirling last week. You're right though. Bugger all is what we've got. We've even found one or two pistols."

"I know. I was at Bow Street yesterday when the cinema bomber was committed."

Roger was still a bit mystified. Why on earth were the Irish risking their freedom by causing minimal damage? Most of them seemed to be getting caught and locked up. There must be more to it. He was certain of that and absolutely determined to find out what it was.

"Right, Mr Martin, keep in touch." Moss stood up and shook the journalist's hand. Both men left the Lyons Corner House at the bottom of the Strand and went their separate ways.

◆　◆　◆

Back in the newsroom, Roger rang his friend and co-conspirator in the battle against appeasement, Richard Walker, who lived close to him in

New Malden. He arranged to call round and see his ally later that same evening at Richard's house, after a visit with Jane to the Railway Tavern just in case the Irishman put in an appearance. No such luck, so he dropped Jane at home and made his way to the Walkers.

A couple were sitting chatting with Richard when Roger was shown into the lounge by Richard's wife Inge.

"Roger these are two friends who've just escaped from Germany on the MS *St Louis*. You must have read about it."

"Of course I did. It must have been dreadful for you. I'm pleased you got here safely. I'm Roger Martin."

"Ruth and Benjamin Gerber. So happy to meet you," they said in unison in passable English, with big smiles on their faces.

"Their boy Jonathan is staying at your place. He's a tough lad and very pleasant. You'll like him."

"I've heard we're having visitors. I'll try to meet him in the morning before I go to work."

"Roger's a journalist with the *London Evening Globe*," continued Inge. Roger quickly smelt a story.

"I bet you've got some tale to tell. Perhaps you'd be good enough to allow me to interview you some time?"

Ruth and Benjamin looked at each other and some kind of understanding passed between them.

"Certainly. We'd be delighted. Will you be able to write about everything we've been through in the past few years?"

"Definitely. There's no press censorship, not officially anyway, in England," Roger said with a wry grin on his face, "and I've already written a similar piece about Richard, Inge and their family."

"Not like Germany," added Ruth. "When would you like to see us, and perhaps Jonathan as well? He's very grown-up."

"In the next few weeks, if that's OK. I'm chasing another big story just now but, as soon as that's dealt with, I'll get in touch."

"Roger and I have something to talk about. If it's OK we'll take a beer into the garden. It's a lovely warm evening."

Richard fetched a couple of beers and put them on the garden table and the two settled down on seats facing each other.

"How's things?" Richard asked.

"So-so," Roger replied. "Mind you, that was a bit of luck meeting your guests. Definitely a good story there."

"There is, and wait until you hear it. They've been through a lot of misery and worry. Still, all seems well now. They're planning to rent near the Jewish community in North London until things are settled. They've got all this alien registration stuff to get through. I see you're still working on the Irish stuff."

"Yes, I am," and Roger recounted everything he'd been up to after the past couple of months. "I think there could be more to it. Maybe some foreign involvement. That's what I'm trying to find out."

"You could be right. I've been following our Nazi friends and their activities. I reckon they've got a whole load of people over here who are up to no good, and they're well-organised—community groups and so on. Any German who turns up here seems to be put under immediate pressure to join the Nazi party, if they're not already members. I spoke to Harry the other day."

"How is he?"

"OK. I'll tell you a bit more in a minute. He reckons half of our visitors from the Third Reich are agents of one sort or another. Most pose as journalists, although some, especially the women, have got themselves jobs in sensitive positions."

"Who's driving it?"

"Not sure. Harry thinks the Abwehr have been at it for more than a year, but now more sinister characters are appearing, probably Gestapo."

"Bloody hell. The Gerbers had better avoid them."

"I don't think that's a problem. They won't be troubled. The Nazis are glad to be rid of Jews."

"That's something, I suppose."

"So, you're on to your IRA chief and you've enlisted Claud's boys so that between you, you can see if something crops up that might link him with foreigners who might be German."

"That's about it, but so far no evidence."

"Persistence, Roger. You seem to have got a nose for this sort of thing."

"I hope you're right. What have you got so far?"

"Well there's a whole lot going on. For a start, there are hundreds of refugees. Ninety-nine per cent are Jews and totally above board, but I wouldn't put it past the Nazis to slip the odd agent in masquerading as a Jew. Then they get themselves a job in the home or office of a top Jewish politician, civil servant or businessman and, Bob's your uncle, an Aladdin's cave of secrets could be ready for them to get their hands on."

"What else?"

"The Abwehr have been recruiting British fascists to spy for them. Mostly it's things like information about docks, airfields, other communications such as railways and so on. Lots of the Germans have been picked up and deported, including a few from the Gestapo. You may have seen some snatches in the press about people in court stealing plans of ordnance factories and so on, one in Lancashire, another in Sheffield and a third in South Wales. They've all been arrested. Interestingly, two German vice-consuls in the north of England seem to have played a part in this spying. The Manchester man's been expelled and the Liverpool guy is under investigation."

"If I could link the IRA with the Abwehr or the Gestapo, would Harry be willing to lend a hand?"

"I'm not sure. I'm only guessing, but I think he's employed by MI5—not as a full-time agent but on a sort of part-time basis. He's always short of money, you know. He needs to pay his bills and entertain his women."

The pair of them chuckled and Richard continued. "You remember that he had a source in the German Embassy?"

"Yeah."

"I told you he was posted to a similar post in The Hague, but he's still very active in intelligence gathering. Harry has to troop over there from time to time and collect the stuff. Where he is at the moment I couldn't say, but the next time he's in England I'll go and have a word with him. See what he says."

"Thanks Richard," said Roger. They drained the last of their beers and Roger went home.

Just before he left the office on Friday afternoon, Roger got a call from Richard.

"Good news. Harry's on board. He thinks, but doesn't know, that there might be collaboration between the IRA and the Nazis. He'll put his man in The Hague on the alert so he can react quickly."

"Great. Thanks Richard."

"He's sniffed out that something's going on with fake German agents wandering all over England. Although he's never met you, he likes what he knows about you and was very impressed by the way you put pressure on Chamberlain and his cronies. He says if you do get anything valuable on your Irish bloke, tell the police and get them to carry out the arrest. Conclusive evidence on the Nazis, you tell him and he'll get the Branch to do the necessary. That way both Harry and your copper will get the credit and you get a big story or two."

"That sounds fair enough," said Roger.

"Just one other thing. Harry wants you to communicate via me. He's got my number at home and at the store."

Richard worked for Roger's father at the department store in Kingston. Mr Martin senior was happily resigned to Richard's cloak-and-dagger life and recognised what he'd done for Roger.

"Perfect," said Roger. "I'll get on with it straight away. Thanks a lot , Richard."

◆   ◆   ◆

Roger spent much of the weekend either keeping watch on the house in Uxbridge or hanging around the Railway Tavern. He had no luck at either location. He kept telling himself that, if he stuck at it long enough, his patience would be rewarded. He went to bed on Sunday night after a day at home with his parents and Jane, enjoying the traditional Sunday programme of lunch and tea with a walk in between. So it was with a renewed sense of optimism that he set off on Monday morning to meet his confederates.

The two boys were spot on time at Uxbridge tube station. It was a fine and warm Monday morning and, as they left the Underground, Roger looked at two smiling lads, Joe, whom he already knew, and his slightly taller companion George, his black hair flattened with some kind of grease and given a major sharp parting. Both were smiling as he beckoned them to the car. As they came nearer, Roger noticed how smartly dressed they were, in pressed grey flannels and open-necked long-sleeved shirts over which each wore a slipover, green for Joe and dark blue for George. Closer inspection revealed that George was obviously Jewish, with his white face and dark eyes. So much the better, thought the journalist. He'll certainly hate the Nazis and this'll spur him on to do a good job if he comes across any.

"Morning guv," said Joe, stretching out his hand for Roger. "This is George."

"Hello George, good to see you," and the two exchanged warm and firm handshakes.

"Morning guv."

A note of slight worry crept into Roger's mind as he wondered if he was doing the right thing exposing these two young men to what might be extreme danger. No, he reflected. They knew what they were doing, and he'd already seen enough of Joe in action to know he could look after himself. George, he noticed, while looking like a nice lad, was strongly built and, as Joe had reported, looked as if he knew how to look after himself and was quick on his feet. If we have some luck, Roger thought, this could work out well.

"Right lads, jump in." Joe sat in the front seat, letting George into the back first, and they drove towards their destination. Roger parked out of direct sight but with a view of anyone coming and going in and out of number 10 and switched off the engine.

"This could be boring, lads, you know."

"We know, we've done plenty of this sort of stuff for Mr Cockburn."

"OK. We've got to think on our feet and react to whatever he does."

"Mind if I jump out for a fag guv?" Joe asked. "Don't want to fug up your car."

"Course. Make sure you can't be seen."

Joe rejoined them five minutes later and they sat chatting, keeping a watch on the house. As lunchtime approached, Roger caught sight of their quarry as he left the house carrying a shopping bag and alerted the boys. Keeping their distance, Joe and George followed the Irishman towards the shops, watching him in and out of the ironmonger's, the butcher's and the baker's. As he set off home, George slipped into the baker's and bought three sandwiches, remembering to ask for a receipt. Both boys saw their prey safely inside the house and returned to the car and divided the sandwiches between the three of them. Roger had fetched three bottles of lemonade and they took it in turns to guzzle thirstily from the first bottle, thankful for this relief on the warm afternoon.

Just when the day looked like a lost cause, the Irishman's Austin backed out of the narrow drive and set off with Roger following. Fifteen minutes later, Roger realised they were heading for Richmond and it was no surprise to him that he found himself on the road near to the Railway Tavern. Roger left the lads drinking lemonade while he went into the bar and bought himself a half of bitter. He picked up a copy of the *Globe* and settled down to keep an eye on the Irishman who was parked behind a pint, repeatedly looking at his watch and becoming increasingly irritable.

Eventually he gave up, drained his glass and set off for the exit. When Roger emerged, the Austin was disappearing through the car park gate.

"'Urry up guv. 'E's gettin' away."

"Don't worry. He's not going anywhere tonight. We'll pick him up again tomorrow."

Joe and George got out at Richmond station, where he gave them their expense money as well as covering the cost of their tube fares.

"Don't forget lads, receipts for everything. Thanks. See you tomorrow. Make it nine. Same place."

The Central Line train would take them straight home with only one change. Roger drove home, dog-tired, having achieved precisely nothing apart from strengthening the bonds between the three watchers.

◆   ◆   ◆

The next day was no better, but on the Wednesday things began to happen.

Luck was almost certainly on their side. As Roger pulled up to collect George and Joe at the tube station, he saw the Irishman approaching the Underground from the opposite side of the road, about a hundred yards away. He was carrying a small suitcase. The lads saw him and approached the car.

"We're in luck," Roger began. "There he is now. Follow him."

"We'll get tickets at the same price as him from the ticket office," Joe suggested, "and we'll sit one of us at each end of the carriage he's in to keep an eye on him," finished George.

"Brilliant. I'm going straight back to my office. Phone me as soon as you have any news."

"Right-o guv. We've both got your numbers."

It was barely nine o'clock when the boys vanished into the station and the tail-end of the rush hour meant it was still quite busy. Roger immediately pointed the car towards central London. Knowing that he could be held up by the ever-increasing London traffic, he decided to drop the car at Gloucester Road and complete the journey to the *Globe* office via the Piccadilly Line to Aldwych station and then on foot.

Joe and George, meanwhile, were also on the Piccadilly Line into London, having placed themselves at opposite ends of the carriage in which their quarry, handily placed in the middle, was sitting. Neither of them stared at him suspiciously, yet at the same time, neither took their eyes off him for a single second. Much of the early part of the line was above ground, and gazing out of the window or reading a newspaper seemed to be the main preoccupation of a majority of the passengers. The Irishman was reading the *Daily Mirror* and had no reason to take any interest in two boys looking bored at each end of the carriage.

Bored they might have been, but they were fully alert when the Irishman got up and moved towards the exit doors as the train approached South Kensington. As he climbed the steps to the District Line, the boys weren't far behind. All three jumped on the train, but hardly had they settled down before they were off again at the next stop—Victoria. Stepping smartly across the concourse of London Victoria, one of the capital's busiest railway stations, Joe followed their quarry while George located the nearest telephone kiosk, gesturing to his pal where he was going.

The Irishman was standing beside the Continental Departures ticket office and Joe paused long enough as he passed to light a cigarette and hear the booking clerk announce, "Right sir, second class return to Brussels, departing at eleven o'clock and returning on the eleven o'clock from Brussels tomorrow morning." He collected his tickets and travel documents and walked towards the refreshment room. Joe picked up George from near to the phone box.

"Go in the refreshment place, George, and order two teas and sit where you can see 'im. I'll join you as soon as I've phoned Roger."

Joe dialled the *Globe*'s number. A woman answered the phone and Joe asked for Mr Martin.

"You're in luck," the woman replied. "He's just walked in through the door. He's a bit short of breath. Who's calling please?"

"Joe."

"Joe for you, Mr Martin."

"Thanks. Joe?"

"Guv. 'E's at Victoria in the refreshment room. George is keepin' an eye on 'im. 'E's booked on the eleven o'clock to Brussels and the same time back tomorrow. Shall we follow 'im?"

Roger laughed. "No. You can't leave the country without a passport. Go back to the refreshment room and make sure he gets on that train. Then you're finished for the day. I'll check the arrival time of his train from Brussels tomorrow. Call me and I'll tell you the time. See where he goes when he gets back. We'll pick it up at nine on Saturday at Uxbridge station. No need to ring me unless he doesn't get on the Brussels train. Thanks. You're both brilliant."

Roger went up to the newsroom, sat behind his desk, glanced at his watch and saw it was after eleven. He picked up the phone and dialled.

Planners

London and Brussels, Thursday 1
and Friday 2 June 1939

"God Roger, this is short notice. I'm not sure anything can be done to pick this fellow up when he arrives. I'll call Harry now and see what he thinks. Any idea what time the train gets into Brussels?"

"Twenty past five at Midi station. We know he's going there, because the boy overheard him buying a ticket."

"OK. I'll pass that on. I'll get back to you as soon as I can."

"Thanks Richard."

Roger put the phone down and looked at his watch. It was five to eleven. He leaned back and waited. Just after eleven his phone rang again.

"Joe again for you, Mr Martin."

"Thanks Margaret. Put him through please."

"Guv?"

"Hi Joe. What's the latest?"

"He's on the train to Brussels. Just pulled out of Victoria."

"Great. Thanks Joe. You and George get off to where you're going. See you both on Saturday at Uxbridge station at nine."

"OK. You'll tell us what this is all about, won't you?"

"Of course I will. As soon as it's all over, I'll give you the full story, before it appears in the paper."

"Thanks guv. Bye."

Roger put the phone down and waited anxiously for Richard to call back. He made some notes, filed a story from the previous day's proceedings at Bow Street. He'd just finished when the phone rang.

"Mr Walker for you."

"Richard."

"This anti-Nazi pal of Harry's must certainly hate the jackboot brigade. Says he'll do all he can to help. All Harry's told him, presumably in some sort of pre-arranged code, is Brussels as soon as possible. It's impossible to give details over the phone—after all, it is the German Embassy in The Hague and, from what Harry understands, the place is full of Abwehr, Gestapo and God knows what else."

"So, what next?"

"Sit and wait for Harry to call back. Meanwhile, give me a full description of the target."

Roger relayed all he knew, including the information about the Irishman's clothes and baggage that he had got from Joe and George as well as his own observations at Uxbridge earlier in the day.

"Right, Roger. Patience."

Roger could hardly sit still. The Irishman might be going to Brussels to meet a friend or just to have a look around Belgium's capital. He'd look a real fool if just one of those possibilities turned out to be true. Still, as Joe had said, Roger had a nose for trouble and he had more than just an inkling that he was on to something here. He suddenly realised he was hungry and asked one of the messenger boys to nip out and get him a sandwich and, when he returned, make him a cup of tea. He apologised to the boy, explaining that he'd usually do those things himself but that he dared not leave his phone.

Ten minutes later he was munching on a cheese sandwich when the call came.

Nervously he asked for Richard to be put through.

"Harry's rung. I'd already given him your description of the Irish guy. It seems that Harry's man from The Hague has got an aide, manservant or whatever. Name's Willi Schneider. Evidently he's in on his bosses spying activities and does all he can to help. Anyway, he's on his way to Brussels."

"How's he getting there?"

"Motorbike."

"Motorbike! Will he get there on time?"

"Of course he will. It's only about a hundred and thirty miles from The Hague to Brussels. He'll stay with your man until he leaves Brussels, presumably for London. The train back sets off at eleven o'clock tomorrow. As soon as it leaves, Willi will phone Harry with an update. So the rest of the day's yours."

"Brilliant, Richard. Thanks ever so much. And thank Harry and Willi for me as well."

◆   ◆   ◆

While all this was going on the Irishman was settling down, like Roger back in London, to a cup of tea and a sandwich in the cafeteria on board the cross-channel steamer currently moored in the harbour at Dover. It was, he noted, a pleasant day with very little wind. The crossing should be smooth, which was a relief. He'd twice before made this journey, on both occasions en route to Berlin, and each time the sea had been rough, causing him considerable discomfort. As the ship made its sedate way across the channel, he began to try to work out why he had been summoned to this meeting in Brussels. Were his German masters dissatisfied with the bombing campaign? What more did they want? It was true, he thought, that not a great deal had been achieved. England had hardly been brought to its knees by the terrorist explosions. He himself was happy enough. The British people were learning that the Irish republicans were very unhappy with the partition of their country and probably wouldn't stop until all of Ireland was one country. He suspected, however, that the Germans wanted more.

He boarded the train in Calais and, after a stop in Lille, crossed the Belgian border. Three stops later, the train reached Brussels, where the Irishman enjoyed a trouble-free passage through Belgian customs, unlike his visits to Germany where the process was long, exhaustive and full of suspicion. It was just after twenty-five past five, Belgian time.

As the Irishman was making his way over the sea and then through the countryside of northern France, Willi was speeding across the flat roads of the Low Countries. With helmet on his head and googles protecting his eyes from the wind, he was hunched over the handlebars. He stopped at Steen Bergen, just inside the Dutch border with Belgium, and telephoned London for his final instructions. Crossing the Dutch/Belgian border was straightforward enough; the rather laid-back customs officials readily accepted his story of doing a few tourist spots in Brussels, like the Grand Place. He then completed his incident-free journey, arriving in Brussels forty minutes before the London train was due. He pulled off his motorcycling gear and stored it in a bag he'd brought with him. He was a rather striking fair-haired young man of medium height. His hair was straight and his eyes blue. Hitler would have been proud of his Aryan features. But those looks were deceptive. He loathed the Nazis, like his boss did, and was happy to carry out any work which might damage Hitler's government. Willi had allowed sufficient time to take a good look around the station, seeking out familiar faces, of which there were none, and finding a convenient spot from which he could watch the passengers climb off the train. He also needed to be somewhere where he could see visitors entering the concourse without being seen himself.

Midi was a fairly scruffy-looking station with lots of passages, each setting off in a different direction—hardly a railway cathedral like those in Germany, or indeed Antwerp, which he had once visited. Brussels didn't have the type of station which befitted the capital city of Belgium. The labyrinthine layout meant that following his prey might be tricky. He shrugged his shoulders and made his way to the newspaper kiosk where he bought a copy of *Her Laatste Nieuws*, a Belgian paper printed in Dutch. Not that he cared what language it was in, for he had no intention of studying the newspaper closely. As he glanced vacantly at the paper, he had a slight worry at the back of his mind. If he recognised the man the Irishman was meeting, there was a chance that he himself might be recognised. He'd have to be at the top of his game.

The Irishman walked along the platform edge, through passport control, and onto the concourse. He stood for a few seconds and then saw a youngish man with brown hair striding purposefully towards him.

"Clissmann," he said, offering his hand. "You must be Donovan."

"That's right."

"I haven't a great deal of time. I have to be on a train to Cologne in less than two hours. We'll talk in the buffet and then I'll show you to your hotel room. Your train back to England leaves at eleven tomorrow morning, I believe," he said in heavily accented but otherwise impeccable English.

"Yes."

"Right. Let's get something to eat."

Neither man spotted Willi, who was undergoing moments of frustration. He'd recognised the Irishman from the description he'd been given of him over the phone and was pretty certain he'd seen the other man before, but couldn't remember where. He wasn't going to follow them into the buffet and eavesdrop on their conversation, the risk was too great, and so he sat and wracked his brains while waiting for them to emerge.

"You must be wondering why you've travelled a long way for a short meeting?"

"I am," replied Donovan. "Are our efforts seen as unsatisfactory?"

"Not at all. The Admiral is delighted to see the English so unsettled by all these bombs."

"Why, then?"

"Before I tell you that, a little bit of background. I'll try to make it not too complicated. You've been helped by the Abwehr. Admiral Canaris is Head of the Abwehr. He is very close friends with Heydrich and his family. Heydrich is very senior man in the SS and very anxious to carry out a major atrocity in England that will kill lots of people and upset war preparations."

"We haven't killed anybody so far."

"Surely you're not averse to killing English people? You must have done so before?"

"I have, but they were soldiers and we're at war with Britain. Civilians are another matter."

"Yes, I understand that, but you forget the second part of what I said—to upset war preparations. If there is a war between Germany and England, which seems possible, I assume you'd wish us to win?"

"I would, but only if it would leave the British unable to continue occupying the north of Ireland. My main ambition is to see a united Ireland."

"And you feel that a German victory would help to achieve that?"

"Definitely, yes."

"So, would you be prepared to do something that might make this more certain?"

"Of course I would."

"Excellent. When you return to England tomorrow, I would like you to give some thought to a likely target. Your contact will now be with the Gestapo, who have many agents in England. One of them will get in touch with you in the next week or so. By then I hope you have a plan. They will supply you with weapons, explosives and anything else you need."

"Who will my contact be?"

"Don't know yet. He will approach you and ask if you know me. Then you'll know that he's your man. You've got seven days to plan something that will help both our countries."

"I think I can do that, OK."

"Good. Thank you for making the journey. I'll show you to your hotel, and then I must dash off to Cologne."

Willi had barely started reading his newspaper when the two men walked out of the buffet. He'd spent the last hour staring at the entrance and trying desperately to think where he'd seen the Irishman's companion before. Try as he did, he just couldn't remember. Picking up a small bag which contained some overnight things just in case, he followed the pair at a safe distance out into the busy Brussels streets. It was a short trip, as the German pointed his Irish companion to the Hotel Atlanta, a large and smart-looking establishment. The two shook hands and the Irishman walked through the hotel entrance. The other man turned on his heel and headed back towards the station. Willi briefly felt himself on the horns of a dilemma. If he followed the other man he might find out who he was. On the other hand, he'd been told to follow the Irishman. So that's exactly what he did. It was possible that he'd meet another contact, so he settled down with a coffee and pastry at a pavement cafe opposite the hotel.

Donovan presented himself at reception and found he was expected. He signed in and was shown to a small first-floor room, which he found clean and bright, with a wash-basin and freshly laundered sheets. He took his shoes, jacket and raincoat off, lay on the bed and thought about his meeting with Clissmann. He didn't have any problems about killing British people, and he quickly thought that he knew of a location where a big enough bomb would do just that, as well as meeting the German's second objective of disrupting his enemy's preparations for war. After a tiring day, he began to doze off. Realising that he hadn't eaten properly since breakfast, he swung his legs off the bed, put on his jacket and shoes and walked downstairs to the dining room.

The dining room was beautiful. Painted in a dazzling white and extensively decorated with flowers, it had two large bay windows overlooking the street, and it was to a table next to one of these that he was shown. Willi, across the street, watched as the Irishman took his seat, read the menu and placed his order. "That's it," Willi decided. "He's settled in for the night. By the time he's eaten his meal it'll be time for bed." He left the cafe and walked back to the station, where he checked the times of the return train to London. Armed with the knowledge that the Irishman would probably be leaving Brussels at eleven in the morning, he booked into a modest hotel near to the station before going out for a meal. He'd had a tiring day and, soon after his meal, he was back in his room. Unsuccessfully, he tried again to work out where he had seen the other man. The long motorcycle journey and the hours of surveillance had left him dog-tired, so he climbed into bed and was soon fast asleep.

The early morning sun was already inching through the gap in the curtains when Willi awoke with a start. "Of course," he realised. It was at the embassy in The Hague about six months ago when he'd seen the other man. According to his boss, the stranger was a member of the Abwehr named Clissmann. Feeling wholly satisfied, he washed, dressed and checked out of the hotel. He took up post in the same cafe across from the Atlanta that he'd used last night, ate some rolls, drank some coffee and waited.

Stepping out of the Atlanta a little after ten, Donovan walked back to the station with his shadow a discreet distance behind. Safely seeing him on the London-bound train, Willi retrieved his motorcycle and began the journey back to The Hague, stopping only to make a phone call to London.

Roger was like a cat on hot bricks all of Friday morning. What would Richard and Harry think of him if he was wrong and the Irishman's continental trip was just a spell of innocent sightseeing? Not only would he have been highly embarrassed, he would probably have been demoted to reporting on unimportant council meetings dealing with matters like new public toilets in Walthamstow. His heart was racing when his telephone rang in mid-afternoon.

"Roger, you were right. The Irishman met a member of the German Secret Service in Brussels, name of Clissmann. They had a relatively short meeting in the station buffet and then the German vanished and your man went to a hotel for the night. He's on his way back to London. Should be back by late afternoon."

"What a relief. Thank you, Richard, and please thank Harry and ask him to thank Willi when he can. I'll pick it up in the morning."

CHAPTER 12

Connections

Esther was assisting with the Monday morning washing. It was, as always, a pretty boring task, and, however much effort she put into it, it couldn't erase from her mind that she was due to meet the unpleasant German on the north end of the Heath in five days' time. She was, naturally, terrified, not for herself but for her mother and father in Berlin. If she didn't come up with something soon, her parents would be arrested and sent, without trial as always, to a concentration camp. Their chances of emerging from there unscathed, if at all, were nil.

As the dreaded day approached she was becoming more and more agitated. Sir John had noticed it and put it down to Esther's concern about her parents. War was creeping nearer day by day and Hitler had now taken to trumpeting Nazi claims to Danzig, an important Polish port on the Baltic governed by the League of Nations. Britain, of course, had guaranteed Poland's borders. If the Nazis invaded Poland, Britain seemed duty-bound to go to war in support of the Poles. The government was dragging its feet in seeking an alliance with the Soviet Union, which would probably stop Hitler, and his land grabbing, in his tracks.

All this was of great concern to Sir John, and he regularly received visitors at home. Some things couldn't be spoken of openly in the Foreign Office in case one of the appeasers got word back to Chamberlain. Esther had made a mental note of the names of the visitors and found that she could interrupt meetings without arousing suspicion, and pick up the odd word or phrase as she was serving coffee or replenishing cups and pots.

Sir John regularly brought home his briefcase, which looked to be bulging with papers. Getting into the case would be easy, but what would she do once she was inside? Steal the papers? Definitely not. They'd soon be missed and suspicion would immediately fall on her as one of the few, perhaps only, people who had access to them. What then? Copy them out? Not enough time. Memorise the content? No chance. Her English, while good, wasn't good enough to commit what might be complex political documents to memory.

Esther had decided to do what the German demanded. She knew she would be betraying Sir John and committing treason against the country that had given shelter and love to her and her brother. But what other choice had she? It was either that or send her parents to an almost certain death. And that she wasn't prepared to do.

"You do seem a bit unhappy of late, Esther," Sir John said, later on that same Monday morning.

"It's my parents, sir. I can't think of any way that they can escape from Berlin. They'll be taken to a camp soon, I know."

"I fully understand you Esther, and with war perhaps just around the corner the chances of them getting out seem to be diminishing day by day. There is nothing I can suggest to you, Esther, but that you and I pray to God for a miracle."

"Thank you, sir."

◆   ◆   ◆

While Esther was talking to Sir John, George and Joe were spending a fruitless and largely dull day in Uxbridge. Roger had met them at nine. There was no sign of the Irishman as they took up their concealed position near his house, so Roger took advantage of the lull in proceedings by updating the boys on the situation that had developed in Brussels.

"So 'e met a Nazi?" enquired George.

"Seems so," Roger replied, "and a member of the German Secret Service at that."

"Blimey," said Joe. "I said to you when we met at Mr Cockburn's place, you're never far from trouble, guv."

Roger laughed. He was happy keeping the boys fully informed. They were, after all, doing an often tedious, but important and possibly dangerous job, and he'd be lost without them. Acknowledging to himself that the surveillance was very much a hit or miss game—they couldn't keep a watch on the Irishman for twenty-four hours every day—Roger thought he'd give them a treat tomorrow.

Then, suddenly, their quarry was on the move, but it turned out to be a false alarm. A trip to Richmond for some shopping was followed by a brisk walk around Richmond Park in the afternoon sunshine. Roger thought that perhaps contact might be made, and so the three of them followed at a distance, kicking a football that the journalist had brought with him.

Tuesday was no better, at least from the cloak and dagger point of view. The day started with the Irishman paying a visit to the local Catholic church and then he went home. Jane was with them, and the two of them took a calculated risk and left their prey to his own devices after he had returned home and took the boys for a slap-up lunch in Hillingdon.

Jane took to the boys straight away, soon recognising the honest loyalty in the two of them. All four got on like a house on fire and a strong bond was quickly formed. Jane asked about life in the East End, and when they replied calling her miss, she corrected them, telling them her name was Jane and that was what they should call her.

"Thanks miss, er, Jane, I was wonderin' what we should call you," said Joe.

"I thought maybe Mrs, guv," George added.

"We're not married yet," Roger said, amidst the boisterous laughter.

During the happy meal, nobody mentioned the Irishman, but, when it was over, they drove back to Uxbridge to check that the car was still in place. Which it was. They called it a day and the boys were despatched on the tube to head for home while Roger drove Jane back to her office in Kingston.

◆   ◆   ◆

Joe and George were left to their own devices the next day, and it was another barren day. On the following day, however, things really picked up. Just after lunch, the Irishman appeared from his house and set off towards the Underground station. The boys were immediately on his tail, pausing only while he stopped at the station kiosk to buy a *Daily Express*. As usual, they kept their distance. He got a tube to Leicester Square and walked down Charing Cross Road on to Trafalgar Square. Stopping at the base of Nelson's Column, he began to anxiously glance around him. Joe lit a cigarette and took up position at the bottom of the steps leading up to the National Gallery. He smoked in silence, and both he and George, who was at the top of the same steps, swept the square with their eyes, looking for anyone who might be meeting the Irishman. After about ten minutes a tall, hatless blond-haired man, with a newspaper under his arm, approached the Irishman and, after apparently exchanging a few brief words, they set off towards Charing Cross station. The boys followed.

The Irishman and his companion made their way to the station refreshment room. The boys watched from a safe distance. Seated at a table behind two cups of coffee, the two men spoke to each other in low voices.

"I understand that you've met my colleague Clissmann?"

Donovan nodded.

"Were you followed, Donovan?" asked Klein.

"Definitely not. What's your name?"

"You don't need to know that."

"But you're Gestapo?"

"Correct. Clissmann told you what we want?"

"Yes. Why don't you do it yourselves?"

"Because we're not at war with England, yet. You are."

Klein was shrewd enough to recognise that he had to flatter Donovan or else he'd get no help from him. He continued.

"So far your Irish Republican Army has done a fine job. The English have no idea where the next bomb will go off. The police are completely tied up with chasing your bombers, leaving our agents to collect information which will be of great value in a war with England, should it come."

"Will there be a war?"

"No idea, but if there is one, we need to be fully prepared. Surely you'd want the Germans to defeat the English?"

"Naturally."

"You may be interested to know that when we win any war with the English, the Führer has made it clear that a united Ireland, totally independent of the rest of England, will be established and recognised as a sovereign state."

Donovan was a hardened IRA fighter and took this with pinch of salt, but he understood that there would be huge advantages for Ireland if Germany defeated Britain.

"OK," he said. "I'll think about this as a matter of urgency. I presume you'll provide the materials for this incident?"

"We will. You let us know what you want and what your plan is and I'll see you get what you need."

"Right. How do I contact you?"

"You don't. I'll be in touch with you. When should we meet again?"

"Give me three weeks to set it up."

"You'll hear from me at that time. I'll need two weeks or so to get the materials you need to you. Then you can do your worst about the middle of August."

Donovan nodded and Klein continued.

"You leave now and I'll follow in five minutes. Good luck. See you in three weeks."

Donovan got up and made his way out of the refreshment room. He didn't notice two working class boys loitering around the station concourse.

"He's on his own," said Joe. "I'll follow 'im. You pick up the bloke that looks like a Nazi. Now you know why I told Roger this was a job for two. Ring 'im when you've finished. I'll do the same. See you back home."

Joe set off after Donovan, who was crossing Trafalgar Square and appeared to be heading back towards Leicester Square tube station. He boarded the westbound Piccadilly Line train and stayed with him to the end of the line. The Irishman immediately set off home when he reached Uxbridge and, when Joe had seen him safely enter his house, he found a nearby telephone kiosk and called Roger in the *Globe* office.

Roger was relieved to hear from Joe and excited about his news, but felt a shudder of concern when he heard that each boy was on their own. What all three had thought of as a game was now turning into something altogether more sinister. He thanked Joe and went back to writing up a story about the bombing of Madame Tussauds the previous Saturday. There had been quite a bit of damage, but the only casualties had been a few waxwork models of well-known people.

◆　　◆　　◆

Five minutes after Donovan had set off with Joe on his tail, Klein emerged from the refreshment room. George was waiting for him as he walked towards Admiralty Arch. The next part was decidedly dodgy for George as Klein made his way into a labyrinth of streets. George could easily lose him here but, fortunately, Klein hadn't a clue he was being followed and he strode purposefully and arrogantly onto Carlton House Terrace. Joe dropped back and was about one hundred yards behind his man, who turned left into one of the magnificent buildings in the street. George was nonplussed. He'd never seen a street like it, with wide roads and pavements and what seemed to be a small park opposite the building into which Klein had walked. Nor had he ever seen so many statues in such a small place, with a kind of mini Nelson's Column dominating the road.

George thought quickly. He couldn't hang around the building. He'd soon be spotted and that would be the end for him. What possible reason could he give for being there? Then it dawned on him. He was there to look at the statues. He pretended to closely examine the tall column, which he noted was of Frederick, Duke of York, whoever he might be, all the while keeping a watch on the building. Another, he noted, was of King Edward VII sitting on a horse. He glanced at the building, numbers 8 and 9, which was guarded by men in black uniforms, and then walked towards the park before turning left, where a statue of someone called Franklin nestled against the park fence. He spotted a gate but it was locked and so, quick as a flash, he stood on the base of the statue, reached one foot onto the fence in between the spikes and, risking impalement, dropped onto the grass beyond the fence. He made straight for some thick bushes, wriggled his way inside and found he had a direct view of the building. He'd noted people on the lawn inside the park sitting behind tables, chatting and drinking out of cups and glasses. He wondered whether or not they'd seen him but they were so engrossed in their conversations that seemed highly unlikely. He settled down and waited.

Inside the building, Klein was reporting to his boss, Wolf, who seemed pleased with what he heard.

"Excellent, Klein. When do you expect the girl to become operational?"

"I'm seeing her on Saturday, so any time from next week on."

"And the Irish business?"

"Scheduled for mid-August."

"Very good Klein. Well done. Please join me in a cup of English tea and then I can tell you about my attendance at the Führer's birthday celebrations, or have I told you before?"

Naturally Klein had heard it before, but he was too wise to tell Wolf, so he settled down to a boring half-hour. By the time Wolf had finished it was late afternoon and Klein was ready to nod off.

Across the road, George had not moved and never taken his eyes off the entrance to numbers 8 and 9. He was on his feet as soon as Klein emerged. He moved stealthily towards the statue and saw a handy tree close to the fence. He quickly climbed a few feet off the ground and, showing great agility, swung one foot onto the fence and then the other onto the base of the statue, before dropping, unharmed, onto the ground. He'd not given any thought to the hazardous nature of this exercise. His mind was entirely on keeping tabs on Klein.

As if joined by an invisible thread, the two headed north towards Piccadilly where the German turned right. Following him was easy, even in the rush hour crowds, but, as they approached Piccadilly, George realised that he could easily lose his man if he went down the steps into the Underground station. So he quickly closed the gap, risking being seen, but the crowds were so thick in the concourse that that was unlikely. George watched Klein buy a ticket, bought one himself, and descended below ground via the escalator to the Bakerloo Line northbound. Klein got off at Paddington and George tracked him to Sussex Gardens. After Klein had disappeared into one of the houses, George walked past, made a mental note of the house number, and continued to the end, turning into Praed Street. He was famished, so bought himself some sandwiches and ate them on his way down Edgware Road. Spotting a phone box, George reported in. The telephone was answered at the other end by an unfamiliar voice.

"Hello."

"Is Mr Roger Martin there, please?"

"He is. Who shall I say's calling?"

"It's George."

"Hold on please."

Roger snatched up the phone excitedly.

"George, great to hear from you. How are things going?"

"Great," and George told him about his adventures.

"Brilliant. That was the German Embassy, you know."

"I thought it might be something like that. I should have hurled a brick through the window."

Roger laughed. "I'm glad you didn't. The game would've been up."

"I know that, guv. I'm at Marble Arch. I'll get the Central Line home, then I'll look up Joe. I thought tomorrow he'd stay with the mick and I'll pick up the Nazi. Is that OK?"

"Definitely. Good night George, and thanks."

Roger put the phone down and thought to himself how fortunate he was to be part of such a great team, although his worries about them being involved with two such dangerous men wouldn't go away. He silently thanked the lads and Claud, their mentor.

CHAPTER 13

Espionage

Roger and Jane were sitting in the comfortable front room of Richard Walker's semi-detached home in New Malden. It was a fine evening, although still a little cold. Richard wanted an update on Roger's pursuit of both the IRA and the Nazis. The young journalist had no secrets from Jane, or indeed Inge, Richard's wife, who was settling down with them having fetched a tray of drinks while her husband brought in the sandwiches.

Jane had spent the day in her office sorting out the financial affairs of several small businesses in Kingston and was happy to sit back and listen, a welcome relief from poring over columns of figures. Richard, too, was relaxed after his duties at Roger's father's department store, also in Kingston. Inge had been looking after the house, keeping it in good shape while the Walker boys were at school. Roger had been at the Old Bailey watching yet another IRA bomber trial which seemed to be heading towards a predictable outcome.

"I hear you've got visitors?" enquired Jane.

"Yes," Inge replied. "Another Jewish refugee family from Berlin. Benjamin and Ruth, and their boy Jonathan, who's sixteen or thereabouts, I believe. We know them from our days in Berlin. Initially it was a business connection, but as time went by we became friends."

"You'll both like them," Richard added. "The family isn't orthodox, rather like us, but very brave. They've just come through that Cuba business with the *St Louis*. They'll be down soon and you'll meet them, Jane. Their boy Jonathan is staying with Roger."

"So I hear. What's he like?"

"A terrific lad. Big, strong and intelligent, by all accounts. And a sportsman to boot."

"I've met him briefly," said Roger. "He seems a very decent boy. I expect he'll make a good rugby player and cricketer."

Jane let out an exasperated sigh. "They don't play rugby and cricket in Germany, Roger. More like football and athletics."

"Well, I'm sure he'll soon pick them up."

Jane rolled her eyes at the Walkers, and then asked, "How long will they be here in New Malden?"

"As long as they want," replied Inge, "but I expect they'll soon want to buy a place of their own."

"They've got to convert their assets into hard cash first. The Nazis won't let you bring much out of Germany. They had to smuggle their valuable stamp collection out," said Richard.

"Or rather Richard did," added Inge.

"Not exactly," he replied. "I just helped to make it possible. Anyway, what's the latest, Roger?"

"Thanks to you and Harry we've now established a link between the IRA man and the German Secret Service. My police contact tells me the IRA man is called Donovan and that he's quite a big shot. Now we know he's in touch with the Nazis, we can see what this brings about. He had a clandestine meeting with another man in Trafalgar Square last week and one of my spies followed the other man back to the German Embassy."

"By your spies, I assume you're talking about these two lads you've told me about?" asked Richard.

"Yes. Joe and George."

"They're really nice boys," said Jane. "Rough diamonds."

"Isn't it a bit dangerous for them?" asked Inge.

"I've worried about that myself," said Roger, "but Claud Cockburn thinks they'll be OK, and so far they've been brilliant."

"You ought to rope in Jonathan Gerber to help. His parents say he's a real hard case. He flattened a couple of Nazis who were pestering him during the voyage of the *St Louis*."

"I think we should let him settle in first, but he definitely sounds like a rugby player," smiled Roger. "Back to George and Joe: Joe's still tailing Donovan and George is on to the Nazi. We're just waiting for results."

"Harry's very keen on this business, Roger. Let me know when you need him again. He's still got anti-Hitler contacts in the German Embassy, through our friend in The Hague of course. Right, I'll go and ask the the Gerbers to join us. Roger's already met them and he's tapping them up for a story, like any good journalist," Richard laughed.

Benjamin and Ruth made their way into the living room and were introduced to Jane. Roger had made quite an impression on them at their only previous meeting and now they found that his fiancée was equally charming. They chatted easily for the rest of the evening. The international situation was briefly discussed, and Roger said he was not impressed with the pedestrian way in which the government were trying to set up an alliance with the Soviet Union.

◆   ◆   ◆

At the opposite side of London, in the East End, George and Joe were playing football, or rather head football, as each tried to nod the ball past each other in the narrow lane that ran behind their street. Sweating, they stopped for a rest and Joe lit a Woodbine.

"Where's our dads tonight?" asked Joe.

"Party meeting, I think, then a pint afterwards at the George and Dragon. 'Ow yer gettin' on with the Irishman?"

"I'm not. He's hardly been out since we spotted him in Trafalgar Square. A bit of shoppin' and a couple of trips in the car. Otherwise nothin'. He just stops in."

"What d'you reckon?"

"'E's either plannin' summat or waitin' for a call from that Nazi. What about you?"

"Same. I've been 'angin' around Sussex Gardens. 'E's in an' out quite a bit but it's always back to Carlton 'Ouse Terrace or some place in Fleet Street which I found out is the German Press Agency."

"Have you told Roger?"

"I 'ave. 'E just said thanks and stick with it."

"Same wiv me. What d'you think o' the guv?"

"Good bloke, bit of a toff, but a good bloke."

"Yeah bit like Mr Cockburn. I trust him though."

"I do too. Are you ever frightened about all this?"

"No. I can 'andle this. What about you?"

"Don't worry me. This is our town. I know it like the back of me 'and. If things turn nasty, I'll find a way out of it."

"Bit borin' at the the minute though innit?" said Joe.

"Roger said it might be like this. Something'll 'appen soon. I can feel it in me bones."

"Definitely. Knowin' the guv, it'll be somethin' excitin' too. You got a girlfriend, George?"

"Nah. No time."

"S'right. Mind you, when all this is over I think I'll look for one. I used to like all that messin' around at school."

"I did an' all. 'Ow about some more 'eaders.? First to ten then we'll go 'ome for some supper."

"Good idea."

◆　　◆　　◆

As her appointment with the Nazi approached, Esther was becoming increasingly unsettled. He'd told her to be at the gallery on the Heath the following Saturday. She was due to visit Cambridge on that day and was frantically thinking of her reason for leaving early. She racked her brains and came up with a plausible reason.

"Esther. Are you going to Cambridge tomorrow?" asked Sir John.

"Yes, sir."

"What time do you expect to be back?"

Esther was suddenly filled with dread. Why was he asking this? Saturday was when she due to meet the German. Surely he didn't suspect anything.

"About the usual time, sir."

"Good. I'm having some people round at about eight. I'd like you to serve the drinks and help Cook with the supper."

Inwardly Esther breathed a huge sigh of relief. Not only did he not suspect anything, but he'd given her a ready-made excuse to leave Cambridge early.

"That'll be fine, sir."

"Excellent. Thank you. You still seem to be on edge, Esther. Is it your concern for your parents?"

"Yes sir. All that talk from Hitler about Danzig is making me nervous. What if he invades Poland and Britain declares war on Germany? They'll be stuck in Berlin. They could be in even greater danger than now."

"You're right. We must continue to pray for them. Something may turn up."

Esther thought to herself, what does this kind old man know? What could possibly happen to help them to escape?

"Thank you, sir. I'd like to take a short walk before dinner if I may?"

"Of course, my dear."

Esther went up to her room and slipped on a light cardigan. She left the house and set off towards the Heath. She stopped out of sight of her house and used the public telephone box to call the Richardsons. Mrs Richardson answered, and Esther explained to her that she would have to leave early to be back in time for Sir John's gathering. It was a lie, of course. Her normal return time would have got her back in time for Sir John's visitors. She rang off after enquiring about her brother and telling Mrs Richardson how much she was looking forward to Saturday.

◆   ◆   ◆

Klein was sitting in his house in Sussex Gardens. He was looking forward to meeting Esther that evening. Not only did he enjoy frightening people, but he thought that he was launching an operation which would impress his boss, Wolf. He depised his superior, but recognised that if he pulled this off he might gain a promotion, perhaps even a posting back in Berlin. This might become even more certain if Donovan pulled off the atrocity which the Gestapo man had asked for. The two had been in touch, but Donovan had refused to be drawn on what he had in mind, only to say that it would require some highly powerful explosives. Berger had been sent by car to Harwich earlier in the day to contact a Gestapo agent who was posing as a seaman and would take details of Donovan's requirements back to Germany by a steamer which was due to sail later that afternoon.

This left Klein needing to use public transport, but it didn't bother him at all. He had already been to Hampstead Heath and knew the route. It was slightly annoying not to have use of the car, since he had no means of making a quick getaway should things go wrong. But they wouldn't, he was sure. What kind of a girl would sentence her parents to certain death? Even Jews had feelings for their families. He put on a check sports jacket and slipped a small package into his right-hand pocket. Then he set off.

George was loitering at the junction of Sussex Gardens and Edgware Road. He was wearing his usual clothes, plus a flat cap which, for no apparent reason, he'd pulled down on his forehead. Seeing Klein emerge from his house, he quickly folded up the copy of the evening's *Globe* which he'd been pretending to read, put it under his arm and set off in pursuit. Klein, up ahead, was totally unaware that he had a sixteen-year-old East End boy following him. He prided himself that he had a sixth sense with which he could feel a tail., But he wasn't sensitive to the likes of George; rather, he only noticed MI5 agents whom he guessed were "interested" in him. So he was completely at ease when he walked into Paddington station from the Praed Street entrance.

George had made this trip once earlier in the week and wasn't particularly excited about this outing. It usually ended at the German Embassy. Nonetheless, he was totally alert as he followed Klein to the platforms. It came as a bit of a surprise when Klein joined an eastbound District Line train rather than the usual Bakerloo Line towards Piccadilly Circus. He carried on looking at the *Globe*, but was on his feet and after Klein as both alighted at King's Cross. A short trip across the Euston Road and George watched as Klein joined a trolleybus queue. When the bus arrived, he attached himself to the back of the queue and sat downstairs at the rear, with Klein handily located towards the front. So intent was he on keeping an eye on the German, he failed to notice a young woman chasing after the departing bus and then stopping when she realised she had missed it.

The bus made its way towards Hampstead Heath. Ten minutes behind, Esther was on the same route, frustrated that she'd missed the one before. She was now concerned that she would miss her appointment with Klein and worried about all that that might mean. She'd been on edge all day, something that both the Richardsons and her brother had commented on, but they had accepted her explanation that she was very worried about her parents.

Up ahead, Klein made his way onto the Heath and towards the gallery. George, meanwhile, was on a parallel path fifty yards away and well concealed by the trees. Klein stopped at the gallery and waited. A moment later he started pacing about and glancing at his watch. George had edged silently forward, and was now just twenty yards away and concealed behind a bush. Klein was becoming increasingly frustrated, and his obvious concern only subsided when a young woman came rushing up to him. Immediately George heard the man speak loudly in a language he didn't understand, but guessed was German. The girl was sobbing and, in gasps, responding in the same language.

Eventually, both calmed down. Klein appeared to be asking the woman questions and she nodded in reply. Then the German took a small package out of his pocket and gave it her. He left after what appeared to be a few threatening words and marched back in the direction of the bus stop. George had witnessed all this without understanding a word of what had been said. But he instantly knew that the man was making the woman's life a misery. He decided that she was on the side of the angels. He also felt sure that, as far as the German was concerned, the action was over for the day, and so he let him return to central London unaccompanied. He followed the woman. His first instinct was to walk up to her and put his arm around her and ask what the problem was. He might hear something he could report to Roger. He quickly dismissed the idea, and followed her until he watched her enter the poshest house he'd ever seen.

There was no point in hanging about any further, so he jotted down the address and set off home, pausing only at the same telephone box that Esther had used earlier in the week to call the Richardsons. He tried to call Roger at home, but he was unlucky. He was out—probably with that nice fiancée, thought George. When George reached the East End he tried again, and this time spoke to Roger, filling him in on all of the details. Roger jotted these down and thanked George.

"This is getting really interesting," Roger said. "Take tomorrow off and pick him up on Monday. You're doing a great job, George."

CHAPTER 14

Under Surveillance

The June day was hot. The sun blazed. Berlin's traffic thundered along its wide streets: single decker buses, double decker buses, trams, small cars, saloon cars, lorries, small trucks and motorcycles. Along the edge of Unter den Linden, a troop of about twenty Hitler Youth boys marched cheerfully in unison as if on their way to some treat. Outside Goering's Air Ministry on Wilhelmstrasse, black-uniformed and helmeted guards wearing white gloves and belts goose-stepped their way through the changing of the guard.

The fine weather meant that the outside areas of Berlin's cafes were doing a roaring trade. Women gossiped over their tea, husbands and wives danced in the sunshine (or perhaps they weren't married couples, merely betrothed or even lovers). Several miles away, the bathing area at Wannsee was packed. Some sat and sunbathed, while others swam, but a large number of adults merely stood in the shallow water and splashed each other like children. Many would stay until dusk before making their way home by car, bus, tram, U-Bahn, or S-Bahn. All appeared to be entirely contented. Their country was at peace. Adolf Hitler, their Führer, had delivered to them all that he had promised, or nearly all. Almost everyone had a job. The army, navy and air force were strong. Exiled Germans from Austria and Czechoslovakia were now part of the Reich and troops were stationed in the Rhineland, facing the French border, despite being forbidden to do so after the 1914–18 world war by the Treaty of Versailles. Blood-red, black and white flags and streets filled with men and women in uniforms added to the comfort with the regime felt by most, if not all, Germans, except of course the Jews.

The only Germans now stuck outside the Reich were those living in the Free City of Danzig, which was actually in Poland but was governed by the League of Nations. Hitler wanted it back. Most of the people living there were German. Entirely relaxed about it, the citizens of the Reich were confident that Hitler would deliver Danzig, probably with a masterstroke of diplomatic genius, similar to that with which he had grabbed the Sudetenland of Czechoslovakia for the Reich the previous October, when he had outfoxed the rather feeble-looking British Prime Minister Neville Chamberlain. Yes—the Führer would sort it all out. Meanwhile, let us enjoy the fine weather.

◆   ◆   ◆

Two of the many people who were not enthusiastic about the Nazi regime were Simon and Deborah Abrahams. The weather made not a scrap of difference to them. Living in a constant state of terror, they awoke each morning wondering whether they would survive the day. While hundreds of Berliners were splashing about in the water at Wannsee, the Abrahams were pottering about in the markets near Alexanderplatz buying their next couple of meals. After this they would return to their drab apartment in a tenement building nearby, where they lived in a single poorly furnished room with a toilet and bathroom two floors below.

It hadn't always been like this. Until the previous December they had lived in a spacious flat in Charlottenburg with their children Esther and Peter. Simon was a lawyer, and a successful one at that, and, until the Nazis came to power in 1933, had a long list of clients. Gradually his career petered out as Nazi laws forbade non-Jews from employing Jews in any capacity. Eventually the only people left of his client base were, like him, Jewish. Still, until Kristallnacht, in the previous November, he remained both busy and prosperous, although an ever-increasing list of anti-Semitic pieces of legislation made life increasingly uncomfortable. Then everything changed. Although they avoided physical punishment and arrest, the Abrahams were thrown out of their home and told to live with the "other" Jews in East Berlin. Refugees from anti-Jewish pogroms in Eastern Europe in the late nineteenth century made up the vast majority of the population of the area in which they now lived. Many had originated in Poland.

Simon had found a place to live partly because of his past links with the KPD, the German Communist Party. Fighting bravely on the Western Front in the Great War, Simon had won an Iron Cross, Second Class, and had struck up a close friendship with another soldier, Ernst Thälmann. Both were members of the Social Democratic Party. Thälmann had deserted towards the end of the war and made his way back to his home town of Hamburg, where his politics veered ever leftwards. He was in Berlin for the disturbances of 1919 and became leader of the KPD.

Simon maintained his links with the Social Democrats and, as a successful lawyer in Weimar Germany, his and Thälmann's paths inevitably crossed. The strong bond between them lasted through the post-war years even though the political gulf between the two was wide. Thälmann often called on Simon's legal expertise and, in return, established contacts for him with the Jewish Communists of East Berlin. Simon had been saddened when his old comrade was arrested shortly after Hitler came to power, but when needing help in the aftermath of Kristallnacht he found it amongst the working-class Jews. Ernst Thälmann hadn't been seen for six years.

The Abrahams were a handsome couple. Neither looked particularly Jewish. Simon was of medium height, about five foot ten inches, with dark rather than black hair. His brown eyes often had a sparkle in them, but less so in recent weeks. Clean-shaven, with a perfectly formed round chin, his face gave the impression of being completely in control of things. He'd always been sparsely built, but recent events had left him thinner than he would have liked to have been. The same was true of his wife Deborah. She too was slim and of medium height, with long black hair. Her face was just beginning to show the ravages of time and circumstance, but nothing could conceal her beauty, emphasised by her full mouth and hazel brown eyes. Neither looked ill, but both had clearly seen better times.

Deborah had put a brave face on their predicament and had worked tirelessly with her husband to get their children safely to England. Great as the relief was at this, it didn't prevent either of them from trying themselves to escape from Germany. They had made several applications to the British Embassy to be given permission to join their children but had always been refused. However, on this sunny July day their hopes had been lifted by the news that they would be welcome in England. Now all they needed was an exit visa from the Nazi authorities. Hitler and his gang were keen to rid Germany of the Jews, so, since they had the money to pay both for the rail and cross-channel steamer trips, there shouldn't be any problems—should there?

Just a couple of miles away from the Alexanderplatz and at the heart of the government district stood an impressive but forbidding grey stone building in Prinz-Albrecht-Strasse. The entrance was topped by an arch. Five stories the building rose from the pavement, but much of the business was conducted in the basement, where thousands of German citizens were interrogated, tortured and sometimes killed. This was the headquarters of the German Secret Police, the Gestapo.

Far above the screams of those arrested and tortured with electrical apparatus on sensitive parts of their bodies and the crack of the whips on naked flesh, two men sat facing each other. Uncomfortable in his black uniform after a rushed flight from London, Wolf was looking across a desk at the Gestapo Chief of Operations Heinrich Müller. Wolf didn't like Müller, who was younger than him but seriously outranked him. Wolf knew that the man on the opposite side of the desk had only recently joined the party, and he suspected that this was a gesture of convenience to keep the upward path of his career on track, that Müller was not an ardent National Socialist. Not only that, he was frequently seen, as today, in civilian clothes. Was he ashamed of the SS uniform? Wolf wondered. Müller was only just forty years of age. His thin brown hair was short, and swept back and held in place with the aid of hair oil. His brown eyes stared at Wolf and his thin lips were fixed without a hint of a smile. It was impossible to know what Müller was thinking. Wolf was afraid of him, but nevertheless risked a mildly critical opening gambit.

"I had hoped to see one of the Reichsführers, given the importance of my mission."

"They're too busy."

"Or perhaps the Gruppenführer," referring to Heydrich.

"He's busy as well. Besides, he's moving on to more senior responsibilities. I shall soon be Head of the Gestapo."

"I see."

Wolf's discomfort grew.

"Now kindly explain to me what it is that has caused you to fly all the way from London and take up my time in what is a very full day for me?" Müller said, referring to an assignation that he had with his American mistress later in the day.

"I hope my message got through about the Jewish couple, Abrahams?"

"It did. I've had my men keeping an eye on them day and night. Why, apart from being Jewish, are you so interested in these people? They don't appear to be particularly threatening."

"They're not. It's their daughter I'm interested in."

"Ah! An affair of the heart, Wolf. Very dangerous, that. You know what the Führer thinks about sexual relations with Jews. There are even laws against that sort of thing. You could end up in Sachsenhausen or Dachau."

Wolf was clearly getting flustered.

"Nothing of the sort," Wolf replied with a semblance of anger. "Their daughter is in London working in the house of a very senior person in the English Foreign Office. She has agreed to provide us, or rather my man Klein, with secret intelligence, in return for which we have agreed to keep her parents safe and well and out of the camps."

"Right, I follow that. She needs to know her parents are OK, so we'll let their letters to their daughter get though with only mild censorship?"

"Exactly. But we need to watch them in case they try to escape. We need to be continually re-assuring the girl of her parents' safety and continued presence as free citizens in Berlin."

"OK. It seems a good plan. With my men on their tails, there's no chance they'll escape."

"What about if they get attacked by the Brownshirts?"

"My men will prevent that. Those beasts won't get near your protected Jews."

"Thank you. I return to London most reassured."

Wolf got up and saluted Müller, who returned it with a half-hearted gesture. He watched as the tin-pot Nazi left the room. How he hated these people, with their arrogant strutting postures. Still, he would do as Wolf asked. It sounded like a good idea. He picked up the phone and spoke to an immigration official and told him, in no uncertain terms, that the Abrahams should not be given documents which permitted them to leave Germany under any circumstances. Then he sat back in his chair and thought of the evening ahead with his lover.

Simon and Deborah walked around the markets and flea markets of the Alexanderplatz in a very good mood. There was a chance that they would soon be soon be joining Esther and Peter in England. Tomorrow they would apply for permission to leave and show the Nazi authorities their permission to settle in England.

They saw that their happiness contrasted starkly with the majority of Jews in this part of Berlin. They would never reach England, America, or Palestine, even with permission to leave, because they had so little money. Some had left, but that was because they'd been expelled to their Polish homeland where the Germans were expected soon. Many were orthodox Jews and still dressed in long heavy coats and traditional Jewish headgear, the men adorned with elaborate beards. The fine weather made no difference as to how they dressed. They sweated inside their clothing. By contrast the young boys and girls wore what children wore all over Berlin, although their clothing was largely threadbare. Those boys and men not dressed in the almost bear-like traditional hats sported flat caps or kippahs.

This was the maelstrom in which the Abrahams found themselves as they walked confidently to the government district the next day to apply for their permission to leave. Dressed for work in a lightweight grey suit and a homburg hat, Simon held Deborah's hand as they climbed the steps into the immigration office. She was wearing a yellow cool summer dress and her demeanour matched her husband's optimism. Joining a short queue, they edged slowly forward until their turn came.

"Name?" barked an owlish looking man behind a desk.

"Simon and Deborah Abrahams."

"What do you want?"

"Permission to leave Germany and live in England."

"Why?"

"To join our children who are already there."

"Have you a visa to enter England?"

"Yes."

"Wait here."

The official disappeared into a back office. More than ten minutes elapsed and the Abrahams became increasingly concerned.

"What's the hold up?" Deborah asked.

"No idea," her husband nervously replied.

The official strode back into the room holding a piece of paper. He sat down, unfolded the sheet of paper, adjusted his glasses, stared into Simon's eyes and said in a harsh voice: "Permission refused."

Devastated, his voice shaking, Simon asked, "Why?"

"We don't have to give a reason. You and your wife are refused permission to leave the Reich. Good day."

Shocked and shaken, Simon and Deborah tottered out of the building. Deborah began to cry. Simon produced a handkerchief and comforted her. Neither had reached fifty years of age but both seemed old as they made their way home.

"We must write to the children," Deborah said, "and tell them we're safe and well, won't be joining them for a while but hope to at some point in the future."

"Do you believe that?" asked Simon.

"We've no choice. We have to," his wife replied.

"I suppose you're right, but sometimes I wonder if we'll ever get out of Germany."

"You must never think like that."

"You're absolutely correct," said Simon, lifting his shoulders and pushing his chest forward. He smiled and stared deep into his wife's eyes. "We will get out and soon." Then he leant forward and kissed her. Neither noticed the Gestapo agent following them. He kept up with them until he reached their room and then took up watch nearby.

The next day Simon went to help a number of poor clients. Most couldn't afford to pay him very much, if anything at all, but repaid him with drink and often delicious food from the many bakers in the area. Tired at the end of the day, he was approaching his tenement block when he noticed a dozen or so brownshirts heading in the same direction, shouting at the tops of their voices: "Open up Jews, and have your papers ready. We've been ordered to search your apartments." What they were searching for wasn't made clear, but they barged into each room, shoving people out of the way, sweeping plates and glasses onto the floor where they smashed, pulling out and emptying drawers, cursorily examining papers, and delivering the odd well-directed kick into the groins or stomachs of some of the men.

Simon rushed upstairs to warn Deborah, glancing at the scenes of carnage as he did so. He dashed into the apartment and found Deborah cowering against the wall. Closing the door, he walked over and took her in his arms. Then they waited for the inevitable. Ten minutes passed and the noisy chaos all around them continued. After twenty minutes—silence.

"Where are they?" Deborah asked.

"No idea. I'll go out and see."

"Be careful."

Simon looked down the stairwell. The silence had been replaced by sounds of crying, moaning and cursing. Almost every room in the block had been broken into and serious damage done. Simon went back through his own door.

"Have they gone?" asked an anxious Deborah.

"Yes. They seem to have broken into every room except ours."

"Why?"

'No idea, but we are the last room on the top floor. Perhaps they got fed up before they reached us." Simon shrugged his shoulders. "Let's have something to eat."

The next day he set off on his errands. Again he failed to notice his tail.

CHAPTER 15

Woolwich Cell

London, Thursday 29 June 1939

"Hang on. This sounds a bit dodgy. You've got your lad to follow a German to Hampstead Heath, he meets a young girl, has an animated conversation with her and you're suspicious. Come on, Roger."

Roger turned to his friend and held both hands up in an attempt to be convincing.

"Look Richard, we know he's a German, and I suppose he could be just another member of the embassy staff, or perhaps a German citizen living and working in London for a while, but he's been seen having a clandestine meeting with a man called Donovan, whom we now know is a big fish in the IRA. She was visibly upset and he behaved aggressively."

"Your source is a sixteen-year-old boy with a possibly vivid imagination."

"I trust his judgement. If he says they looked as if they were up to no good, I believe him."

Roger and Richard were having a cup of tea in Richard's office in Kingston. The young journalist needed help—desperately—and he could think of no better person to provide it than Richard.

"Let's suppose the woman is the German's girlfriend and he's said something to upset her. Say, for example, he's told her he's found somebody else, or he's going back to Germany. That might bring tears."

"Yes, of course. There could be any number of explanations. But we've established a link between the IRA and the German secret service. This man could be an Abwehr agent or, perish the thought, even from the Gestapo. I don't think we can afford to take the risk. Besides, George . . ."

"Who's George?"

"The lad who was following her. He says the German was threatening her. He couldn't risk getting too close or else he might have been spotted, so he didn't hear what was being said—mind you, he said they were speaking a foreign language—but he definitely said that he was bullying her. It doesn't sound like a lover's tiff to me. Besides, we just can't afford to risk it. At least I don't think we can. Oh, yes, I nearly forgot, the German gave the girl a small package. OK, it could be a box of chocolates."

Richard shrugged his shoulders.

"OK. Let's suppose you're right. What do you want me to do about it?"

"I've not finished telling you about it yet. I know who lives in that house where the girl went. I got my friendly copper to find out that for me. His name is Sir John Blum and he works for the government, although Moss, that's the policeman, hasn't been able to find out in what capacity just yet."

"I presume he's Jewish with a name like that?"

"Probably. She might be as well, the girl I mean."

"That's guesswork, and who's to say she isn't just a relative or a friend of the family?" resumed Richard. "Let's stick to what we know. I suppose you want Harry to try to find out who this John Blum is, and then we'll get a better idea of whether there's a dangerous situation developing."

"Could you?"

"Sure. I could ask him. But what's to stop him running off to his masters and telling them of your suspicions? That would spoil your story, wouldn't it? If this German is up to no good, the Foreign Office would just send him back to Germany. They're doing it all the time. Fake German journalists who are really spies getting their marching orders. Even the German Consul in Liverpool was expelled a couple of weeks ago."

"Yes, I know. It's a bit risky, but something big's brewing. I know it. I told Moss the same and he's agreed that Special Branch are going to keep Donovan under observation, but not arrest him. Not just yet anyway.

Besides, they haven't got any evidence, and they can't just lock him up because they don't like the look of him."

"That's true, although I've heard that Parliament are going to get a bill through that gives the police powers of arrest if they have even the slightest suspicion that someone's involved in terrorism. Just to be seen drinking a bottle of Guinness would be enough to get them clapped in irons."

Roger laughed. "I've heard that as well. We need to move quickly."

"OK, I'll get in touch with Harry as soon as I can. But Roger, you know if you're wrong, you could be in a lot of bother."

"I know. Thanks Richard."

◆   ◆   ◆

Joe had had a frustrating day. He'd parked himself near to Donovan's house in Uxbridge early on and his only reward was to see Donovan leave his house on foot for a couple of shopping trips. He was about to give up for the day around teatime when his quarry appeared for the third time, wearing a light rain coat. Although it wasn't raining, the skies were heavy, and Joe guessed that a longer trip was planned. Just before the tube station, Donovan paused and used a public telephone kiosk for three or four minutes and then headed for the Underground.

Joe again found himself on the Piccadilly Line heading eastwards. Donovan settled down to read the *Evening Standard*, a paper George's parents didn't approve of for some reason, and he kept watch over the top of his copy of the *Globe*. Donovan got off at Holborn in the middle of the evening rush hour and Joe had difficulty in keeping tabs on him in the crowds, but spotted him as he walked briskly across the concourse of the busy station towards the escalator descending to the Central Line platforms. He was slightly surprised to find himself on an eastbound train, but the end of the line was at Liverpool Street. Another mad dash saw the pair catch another eastbound train, this time on the District Line. Joe was getting a little worried by now. Did all this changing of trains mean that the Irishman was trying to shake off a tail? He'd no idea, but carried on until Donovan left the train at East Ham. Joe was almost on home turf, but this did nothing to ease his fears that he had been spotted, and when the Irishman climbed on to the 104 bus he somehow knew that the Woolwich Ferry was their destination. He was some way behind Donovan in the pedestrian queue waiting to board the ferry, but now he relaxed. Once on board there was no need to keep a watch on his target. Donavan was unlikely to jump off the boat halfway across the Thames, and he could easily pick up the trail when the passengers disembarked on the south side of the river. So he concealed himself behind one of the tall funnels on the paddle steamer, which kept him warm on what was becoming a chilly evening, and settled down to smoke a cigarette.

Joe kept Donovan in sight when they left the ferry and followed him to a pub called the Anglesea Arms and settled down to wait. He risked a peek through one of the windows and spotted the Irishman in deep conversation with two young working men, seated at a table in a corner away from the other drinkers. Twenty minutes later Donovan emerged and set off back towards the ferry. Now Joe had a dilemma: continue to follow the Irishman or track the other two? He decided on the latter. There was no point in making the long journey back to Uxbridge. Besides, it was getting late and the light was beginning to fade, and his parents might be getting worried. He waited for the other two and was rewarded twenty minutes later when the pair emerged from the pub and walked towards the back streets of Woolwich. They disappeared inside a grimy-looking terraced house in Wellington Street. That was it for the night, Joe decided, and he made a note of the number of the house into which the men had disappeared and walked back to the ferry.

Arriving at the ferry, he was disappointed to find that there was no vessel in sight, so he had to use the foot tunnel, about five hundred yards long. He reckoned that he could outrun anyone who attacked him, so he set off with a brisk stride and reached his street unharmed about an hour later. He stopped on the way to report in to Roger and was told to have a lie-in the next morning and meet him in the refreshment room at Charing Cross station just before lunch. George was still up so he briefly told of his adventures. Joe was famished and so, after reassuring his parents that he had been in no danger, he settled down to a bangers and mash meal and a cup of chocolate before he collapsed into bed.

◆   ◆   ◆

After lunch on the following day, Roger met with Moss at the Wellington, at the top of The Strand. Joe had given him a full account of his trip to Woolwich, and had had a tasty meal and some more cash as his reward. The young lad had been told to go home. He said he'd be back on patrol in Uxbridge the next day. Roger quickly recognised that things had now taken a sinister turn. He immediately rang Moss and the two agreed to meet urgently at the pub.

"This could be really serious, Mr Martin."

"I realise that, Sergeant. The Woolwich Arsenal."

"We always thought that might be a target. The commies set up a spy ring there a few years back. Our lads reckoned they were trying to pinch secrets and pass 'em to the Russians. We'd 'ad our eyes on the leader, bloke called Percy Glading, for a while. 'E was a member of the British Communist Party. Turned out 'e'd been trained to be a spy by the Russians in Moscow—bastard. They might 'ave got away with it, but MI5 planted one of their secretaries, woman called Olga Gray, in the British Communist Party and she blew the whistle."

"I remember hearing about the spies. What happened to them?"

"Few of 'em got six years. I'd 'ave 'anged the lot of 'em. Bastards."

"What about that accident last month—was that sabotage?"

"Not as far as we know. It really was an accident. Five dead."

"That's awful. It must be a dangerous place to work."

"Yer right there. They make guns, bullets, shells and explosives. if somebody succeeded in blowin' it up, there'd be one 'ell of a bang. 'Undreds would die, not to mention buggerin' up our war preparations. It can't 'appen."

"Why not arrest them?"

"No evidence."

"So what are you going to do?"

"'Ow good are these lads of yours?"

"Brilliant."

"Right. As soon as we get a sniff that they're plannin' somethin' we'll pull the micks in. I'm guessin' they're Irish. Meanwhile, I'll see if some of our people can get into the 'ouse in Woolwich without bein' spotted and 'ave a look round. If there's explosives there, we'll nab 'em."

"And if not?"

"Nuthin'. We can't pick 'em up on suspicion. The 'Ome Secretary's trying to get a law through Parliament that'll let us arrest these paddies on suspicion of 'avin' explosives, but until that 'appens, we're snookered."

"Where do they get their explosives from?"

"They nick quite a lot from quarries an' that, but there's so much about they must 'ave other sources."

"Communists? Germans?"

"Probably the Nazis. We've got the commies bottled up."

"Do you think that's why Donovan's been meeting this German?"

"Seems like it."

"Right, I'll tell the lads to keep on these two, and as soon as we get even a whiff of a rat, I'll let you know."

"That's good, Mr Martin. When we decide to act, I'll let you know when and where and you can be on the spot, preferably with a photographer. Nice result for both of us."

"Won't you get into trouble for tipping me off?"

"Nobody'll know it's me, and besides, journalists are always gettin' good information from their sources, and nobody ever finds out who those sources are. It's the result that matters. And for gawd's sake, tell them lads to watch 'emselves."

◆   ◆   ◆

While Roger and Moss were in the Wellington, George was indeed watching his target, while munching a piece of bread. Klein was in Sussex Gardens. He'd done nothing but to and fro to the German Embassy for a couple of days, but George stubbornly stuck to his task. He'd seen Joe late last night and was excited to hear of the chase across London to the other side of the Thames. He hoped for something as interesting for himself today. Little did he know just how interesting that his day would turn out to be.

It started just after lunchtime. Klein appeared in his raincoat and trilby and set off for Paddington station. He ducked down the steps into the tube station in Praed Street. Walking with a great deal of urgency, the German bought himself a ticket. George did the same. The journey didn't take long. Heading south on the Bakerloo Line, the train stopped at Bayswater, after which Klein stood up. Staying seated as long as he dared, George leapt to his feet just as the doors began to close and was on to the platform at Notting Hill Gate just in time to see his quarry disappear down a passage signposted to the Central London Line. Safely on board and with a good view of his target, George wondered where he would end up today. The train was heading east. Perhaps he'd end up in Woolwich like Joe. The Central London Line ended at Liverpool Street, George knew, so it was either by bus, train or on foot for the onward journey unless—of course—there was some secret meeting at the big station.

Train it was. Klein seemed to be in a hurry, and George didn't have time to buy a ticket. He couldn't risk getting close to Klein so he was in quite a rush as the German went past the ticket collector on to his platform. Ticketless, George skipped past the collector.

"Me dad's forgotten 'is keys," he explained, and raced up the platform without waiting for a reply. A whistle blew and the train prepared to leave the station. He'd seen Klein jump into the fourth carriage from the rear, so he leapt into the rear carriage. He hadn't a clue where he was going and there seemed to be very few stops. Each time the train drew to a halt he leaned out of the window to see if the German got off. He didn't. He stayed on to the terminus, which turned out to be Harwich, from where ships sailed to the continent.

"Maybe he's on his way back to Germany," thought George, but when Klein turned away from the busy quayside, he realised that was unlikely, since the German wasn't carrying any luggage. George had to have his wits about him. There were cars, lorries, trolleys, sailors, civilians and policemen everywhere. In the near distance he could see two steamers ready for departure. Klein was walking away from them, which pleased George, because he didn't much fancy a sea crossing. A short distance from the quay, the German marched into a pub—the Royal Forrester's Arms, noted George. Like Joe the night before, he peered through the window and saw Klein join a sailor at a table. The sailor didn't look much like he was in a British uniform. He was wearing a funny white hat, white top and navy blue trousers. The two men weren't in the pub for long and they stood up and shook hands. George slipped back into a small alcove outside the pub. Klein came out, followed by the sailor. Neither appeared to recognise one another. Klein turned towards the station and the sailor towards the quayside. A British sailor was walking towards the pub entrance.

"Excuse me sir," George said to the British sailor, "'oo's navy is that?" pointing towards the retreating figure of Klein's companion.

"Jerry."

"Thanks," replied George, and he trotted after Klein. One thing had changed. The German was carrying a small, light brown suitcase. George settled down for the return journey. As on the way there, he checked each station to see if Klein got off, but he didn't, and he was easy prey all the way back to Sussex Gardens.

Back in the East End a little later, it was teatime. George and Joe were sitting in George's mum's kitchen munching bread and jam and drinking tea. George had already told his friend about his day. George's mum was busy preparing her husband's supper, but had one ear on the boys' conversation.

"'Ere, you be careful you two. Them Germans are 'orrible. Look what they did to them poor Jews before Christmas."

"We are bein' careful, mum," her son replied, "but we 'ave to take some risks to keep the blokes we're followin' in sight. Besides, there's usually only one of 'em, so if 'e turned on me I'd just use me boots and fists."

"Or yer legs," added Joe.

"Or me legs. I can run like the wind."

"Good thing," replied his mum. "Perhaps one day you'll be in them Olympics."

"I 'ope so. The next ones are in Japan but I'll be a bit young. They're next year."

"Maybe the ones after then," George's mum added.

"Alright if we leave the table mum? I gotta phone the guv."

"Alright. Don't be too late."

"We won't. We'll play football for a while."

The house, which was immaculate inside, was part of a brown and rather depressing looking terrace of twenty. Various adults and children were sitting on their doorsteps, some smoking and all of them chatting. They said hello to the boys as they walked past, and Joe and George smiled a response. When they reached the end of the street and turned towards the phone box outside the Duke of York, Joe said, "I reckon we oughta swap. You follow the Irish guy and I'll follow the German."

"Because if we follow the same one for too long 'e might begin to think we're a familiar face and smell a rat."

"Got it in one. Check with Roger when you ring 'im."

Roger's mother answered the phone.

"Is Mr Martin there please?"

"Yes, he is. Who shall I say's calling?"

"George."

"Hang on."

"Thank you."

Roger's voice came on the line.

"How are you, George?"

"Fine thanks guv."

"Anything to report?"

George told him about the trip to Harwich and back and the collection of the small suitcase. He heard a sharp intake of breath at the other end of the line.

"Right George. Things might be getting dangerous. You'll need to be on your guard more than ever. And don't let either of them out of your sight."

"OK guv. Me and Joe think we oughta swap the people we're tailin' in case they get use to seein' us. Is that OK?"

"That's a brilliant idea. I should have thought of that. Start tomorrow."

"Will do. Thanks guv."

"Thank you, George, and Joe as well."

George looked at his friend.

"Right, we're on. Startin' tommorer. We'd better spend some time cluein' each other up about our new targets."

CHAPTER 16

Exchange

London, Thursday 12 July 1939

Roger was getting seriously worried about the welfare of the two boys. It was one thing following a couple of shady characters around London, but quite another when the two marks were possibly, even probably, terrorists. He shared his concerns with Claud Cockburn on the telephone.

"They're absolutely great, Claud. They haven't put a foot wrong and don't seem likely to."

"So?"

"It's possible that there's some serious plan afoot to blow up the Woolwich Arsenal. The stakes are getting higher and higher and the risks to the lads are increasing each day."

"Yes, I can see what you're getting at. I would suggest that the Irishman is more dangerous than the German."

"Why's that?"

"If they fell into his hands, he'd probably dispose of them immediately. He's desperate and he's got nothing to lose. Nor is he an official representative of any government. On the other hand, the German, Gestapo, Abwehr or whatever, is here officially, albeit pretending to be something he isn't—a journalist for example—and any incident involving him, below actual murder, would lead to his immediate expulsion. That's just the kind of diplomatic incident the Nazi government would wish to avoid."

"Presumably because they wish themselves to be seen as a peace-loving nation pursuing what they believe to be justly theirs—Danzig."

"Exactly."

"That doesn't decrease the threat to the lads."

"Roger, I put Joe to shadow you because I was sure your well-being, liberty and maybe even life were under threat. I trusted him to do a good job protecting you, and he did. We might not be having this conversation now but for Joe."

"I know that, Claud, and you know my feelings of gratitude."

"George and Joe are intelligent, courageous and intensely loyal boys. They come from good Communist stock. They believe that the good things in life should be shared equally between everyone, irrespective of race, colour, creed, and religious and political affiliations. That gives them the motivation to do the right thing. But there's one other thing."

"What's that?"

"They're both as hard as nails. From the outside, they seem to be normal pleasant boys, the best of friends and kind to most people. Scratch deeper and you'll come across two fiendish physical scrappers who would stop at nothing to protect both each other and their mates—and that includes you and me. A few of Moseley's Blackshirts can testify to that, having had their noses bloodied by George and Joe, even when they were just nippers."

"I'm gratified to hear that, Claud, but that won't help them when the bullets are flying."

"You're right, which is why you must brief them never to find themselves completely alone with either man. Always make sure there are witnesses about. I doubt if even Donovan would start blasting away in the crowd."

"Thanks Claud. I'll tell them. I feel much better now."

"Now, the story?"

"As soon as I'm ready to write it, I'll get it to you. My scoop will probably be hacked to pieces by the subs, but I'll let you have the lot and you can do what you like with it."

"Thank you, my boy."

"There's just one thing, Claud. There are actually two linked stories, so there may be some stuff I'll have to keep back from the Irish piece in order not to frighten away certain bad guys who are behind the second plot."

"I'm intrigued. Goodbye, Roger."

◆　　◆　　◆

Roger and Jane were having a night out with Richard and Inge. They were in the Rosebery Hall restaurant at the back of Nuthalls store in Kingston. They'd chosen a quiet corner spot so that they could talk freely, without fear of eavesdropping. It was one of the most stylish eating houses in the town and the four had enjoyed an excellent meal. As soon as the coffees arrived, Roger told the others about his long conversation with Claud.

"The old rascal is probably right," Richard said. "I'm sure they'll be alright."

"I'm glad to hear it," said Jane, "and he's not that old you know. Probably not much older than you."

"Huh, he looks older, don't you think so, darling?" turning to Inge.

"I've only ever seen photographs of him, but maybe he does look perhaps a year or two older than you."

The others broke into laughter which Richard finally joined, after sitting momentarily with a face like thunder.

"Now that's out of the way," Richard continued with a smile, "I expect you want to hear what I've found about your mystery girl, Roger."

"Roger's got a mystery girl, has he?" asked Inge, turning towards Jane with eyebrows raised.

"Well, perhaps I could have put that better. Let's say the young lady that one of Roger's miniature detectives spotted with a man from the German Embassy, who may or may not be an Abwehr or Gestapo agent."

Inge shivered. "God help them if he's Gestapo. They're just about the lowest form of human life. They gave the Gerbers a terrible time."

"We don't know much about him, but Roger's lads need to prepare for the worst. Back to the girl. She's seventeen and Jewish, and came to England from Berlin six months ago. Her parents are still in Berlin, but her twelve-year-old brother came on the Kindertransport at about the same time. He lives with a family in Cambridge and is, I'm told, settled and happy."

"What about her parents?" asked Inge.

"Not allowed to leave Berlin, as far as we know."

"Why?" asked Jane.

"No idea. I think we all understand that the Nazis are totally unpredictable. They've no fixed rules about who comes and goes."

"What about Sir John Blum?" asked Roger.

"He's a senior civil servant in the Foreign Office," replied Richard. "He is certainly privy to secrets. He knows all about the current negotiations with Russia, for example."

"So," continued Roger, "he has access to stuff that the Germans would like to see."

"Definitely. He's involved in the talks with Poland as well. Everything he's concerned with is highly sensitive. We certainly don't want any of this stuff to leak out."

"Is he an appeaser?" asked Jane.

"No. He's a Vansittart man. He doesn't trust the Germans, doesn't believe a word that Hitler says, and thinks the PM is weak."

"So," Roger said, "to sum up, we've got a senior member of the Foreign Office with access to sensitive material living in the same house as a German refugee who's been seen having clandestine meetings with another German who may or may not be some kind of agent."

"She may be a plant, her papers forged, her biography created by the Abwehr, the persecuted parents a figment of the Nazis' imagination, the brother in Cambridge fictitious. Although I doubt that, it's too easily checked," suggested Richard.

"Or she could be genuinely in love with this German, or maybe part of a honey trap," added Inge.

"Or she's being coerced—something's being held against her, blackmail perhaps," continued Jane.

"There's only one way to find out—you're going to have to talk to her, Roger. When we've heard what she has to say we'll decide whether or not to involve the police or security services," Richard concluded.

◆   ◆   ◆

George and Joe set off from their East London homes at the crack of dawn.
This was the first time that they were to tail different people. Joe was on his
way to Edgware Road to keep an eye on the German in his Sussex Gardens
base, while George had the long trek to Uxbridge to shadow Donovan.
They sat chatting on a westbound Central Line train.

"D'yer get the feelin' that fings are pickin' up?" asked Joe.

"Yeah, it's as though summat big's gonna 'appen soon," replied George.

"Excitin' innit?"

"It's bin a bit dull up to now, but the guv did warn us about that. Still,
fings are definitely pickin' up."

"I'm beginnin' to know the tube like the back of me 'and," Joe said.

"Me too, but yer must've known it pretty well when you was followin'
the guv last year?"

"Yeah, but nuthin' like this."

"Anyway, what d'yer reckon the jerry and the paddy are up to?"

"Plannin' to blow summat up, I shouldn't wonder."

"It'll be down to us to stop that 'appenin', and that's what worries me."

"'Ow d'yer mean?"

"I get the feelin' that these ain't ordinary bad guys. Their bombs ain't
gonna blow up phone boxes and such. Much bigger targets. People could
be killed."

"Right, we'd better be on our best form. Them bombs ain't gonna explode."

Joe left the train at Charing Cross and joined a Bakerloo Line train for
Praed Street, and George carried on until Earl's Court, where he stepped
on to the Uxbridge-bound Piccadilly Line. It was a bright sunny day when
he reached the terminus and he made his way quickly to Donovan's house.
He felt relief as he spotted the Irishman's car outside the house, and settled
down for the long wait.

As it turned out, it was only about half an hour before Donovan emerged,
jumped into the car, started it up and drove off towards the main road.

"Now what do I do?" George wondered. "Ring the guv or stay put?"
He decided on the latter. Donovan might just have popped out on a local

errand. So he stayed put. Two hours passed and there was still no sign of the Irishman and George began to worry. It was his first day following Donovan and he'd lost him. Should he go home or call the guv?

While George was chewing over his options in Uxbridge, Joe was on the corner of Edgware Road looking out for his mark to emerge from the Sussex Gardens house. He didn't have long to wait. At about eleven o'clock, not one but two Germans emerged, Klein and an associate, and they climbed into a car. The man that he hadn't seen before was carrying a small suitcase. The boy jotted down the number of the car, which he recognised as a grey Daimler. Then, to his immense frustration, the car turned right down Edgware Road and disappeared. Like his pal up there in Uxbridge, he knew he had an important decision to make. He decided to sit tight and wait for the Germans to return.

Large numbers of people were taking advantage of the fine weather, walking dogs, pushing prams, or strolling about in Richmond Park. Older infants were kicking footballs, chasing birds, indulging in friendly fights with one another, or just skipping along, all under the close supervision of their mothers or nannies. Everybody was far too busy to notice a man with a raincoat folded across his knees reading a newspaper and smoking on one of the many park benches. Nor did they notice when he was joined by two others just after noon. The newcomers, confident that they hadn't been followed, didn't acknowledge the man in the raincoat. One of the new arrivals put a small suitcase on the ground between his feet. Chatting and smoking in the sunshine, they didn't appear to have a care in the world. Fifteen minutes later they stood up and walked away, leaving the suitcase behind. The third man, anxious not to attract attention, quietly slid across the bench and put his feet on either side of the suitcase. He lit another cigarette and continued reading his paper. A quarter of an hour later he folded his newspaper, got to his feet, casually picked up the suitcase and slowly wandered off in the direction of his parked car.

◆   ◆   ◆

Roger Martin and one of his photographer colleagues were near St Paul's when the suitcase was being exchanged in Richmond and the boys were kicking their heels in Uxbridge and Paddington. There'd been an explosion near the cathedral and Ben had sent them to see what was going on. A story and some decent pictures were urgently needed on what was turning out to be a slow news day. It wasn't clear, when they got there, whether the explosion was an accident or the result of yet another IRA bomb. One thing was certain, and that was that a gas main had gone up and there'd been quite a lot of damage, although, thankfully, no casualties. Roger spoke to both a fireman and a policeman, but neither would confirm whether the blast was planned or just a mishap. The photographer snapped some shots and the two of them walked back to the office.

Klein and his confederate returned to Sussex Gardens. The watching and worrying Joe noticed that neither was carrying the suitcase. Of course, it might have been in the boot of the car. Who knew? All Joe could do was to report the facts as he saw them. The two men went into the house without opening the boot of the car. Joe guessed they no longer had the suitcase. He went to the nearest phone box and called Bouvier Street.

"Guv? It's Joe. Couldn't follow the German today because 'e set off in the car wiv another bloke wiv the suitcase. They came back a couple of hours later and 'adn't got the suitcase wiv 'em as far as I could see. Course it could've bin in the boot of the car."

Roger fought hard to conceal his frustration. Joe could have done nothing more, and at least he knew that it was likely that the suitcase was probably no longer in German hands.

"Thanks Joe. Meet me in the morning at ten in the refreshment rooms at Charing Cross."

"OK guv."

Roger went back to writing up his report on the explosion at St Paul's, but his mind wasn't on it. He was now seriously worried. A suitcase, possibly containing explosives, was on the loose somewhere in London. He prayed that George might know the answer.

George was still in Uxbridge. He'd decided to hang on and wait for Donovan to return. It was a momentous decision, because a little after three the Austin drove up the road and parked outside Donovan's house, and the Irishman climbed out. He reached into the back seat, lifted out the suitcase and went into the house. George heaved a sigh of relief and went to call Roger.

In Bouvier Street Roger snatched up his phone when it rang.

"It's George, guv."

"Thank God."

George told of his frustrating day. Roger breathed a huge sigh of relief when he heard that the suitcase was in Uxbridge.

"You both did the right thing, waiting for the two of them to return to their bases. Joe was also left kicking his heels when the German vanished by car. He waited until he could confirm that the suitcase had gone missing and now you've confirmed it's in Uxbridge. Brilliant. Thanks. I've got a few things to do. I'll be in Uxbridge in a couple of hours. Can you hang on till I get there and I'll drive you home? OK?"

"Thanks guv. 'Oo's gonna keep an eye on the case when we're not there?"

"I think it's time we got the police involved. I'll see you as soon as I can."

CHAPTER 17

Special Branch

London, Wednesday 23 July 1939

Roger got up early on the following morning and was sitting behind his desk at the *Globe* well before nine o'clock. He rang Scotland Yard and spoke to Moss. He outlined to the detective the events of the previous few days and confirmed that the suitcase, with its unknown but suspicious contents, was now at Donovan's house in Uxbridge.

"Thank you very much indeed, Mr Martin. I think it's time we took over now."

"Of course, I totally agree, which is why I'm calling you at the first opportunity I've had since the boys tracked the suitcase to Uxbridge. I've told them that, as far as Donovan is concerned, their duties are complete."

"Good. No doubt you've congratulated 'em on the great job they've done. Per'aps they'll make fine police officers one day."

"I'm not sure about that. They're a bit anti-establishment. They might not fancy working for the rozzers."

Moss laughed.

"We'll see. Plenty of time to decide what they're goin' to do with their lives. The way things are goin', it looks like their first job will be in the forces."

Moss was referring to the rapidly deteriorating international situation. The Nazis were increasing the pressure on the Poles to give up Danzig and the Poles weren't having any of it. UK ministers and civil servants were talking to the Russians about a defensive alliance, but were making no progress. War was definitely on the horizon.

"Look, Mr Martin, I need to ring off and set the ball rollin' with our surveillance teams. I'll call you back shortly."

The phone went dead and a slightly frustrated Roger leant back in his chair and waited. He was desperate to continue his conversation with Moss, but understood why the Special Branch man needed to set in motion the climax to this operation as a matter of urgency. He settled down to write up his views on the Prevention of Violence Bill, which had become law on the previous Friday. He'd hardly typed more than fifty words when Moss was on the line.

"Right. Got things goin'. They'll be under surveillance, Donovan and the two men in Woolwich that is, twenty-four hours a day. We've been given more officers at last. This Irish thing has dragged on for more than six months and we need 'em. You know that under the new Act of Parliament we could pick Donovan up straight away, but my guv'nor thinks it'll be better to pick 'em all up in one swoop. Bit of a risk, I know, but we've nothin' at all against the two men and they'd be on the loose if we moved too soon."

"OK."

"Now, about your story. As soon as we're ready to make an arrest near the Arsenal, we'll let you know. I can't guess the timetable, but probably Donovan will deliver the suitcase to 'em the evenin' before and they'll try to do the deed early the followin' mornin'. That's assumin' they're not on nights, but we'll know about that very soon. My men are confirmin' their identification and their work patterns this mornin'."

"According to Joe and George, the suitcase is very small. How much damage would the bombs do?"

"Usually, not a lot, but in the Woolwich Arsenal a huge amount. As soon as the device, or devices, go off, the ordnance will ignite and there'll be a buildin' full of explosions. A lot of people will be killed and our preparations for war will be set back by months."

"What about security? Surely they won't be allowed to walk in there carrying a suitcase?"

"Course not. They'll probably 'ide 'em in their lunch bags."

"When will I get to know about all this?"

"Ah hah! Ever the newspaper man, Mr Martin. I'll find out when we gonna make the arrests, in Woolwich that is, and you can be there with your photo boy. It'll most likely be early in the mornin', so you'll have to get up early."

"That's great. Thank you, Sergeant."

"Could be Inspector after this," Moss chuckled. "Anythin' else?"

"Just a couple of things. How will you cover up your tip-off?"

"Don't you worry 'bout that. 'Appens all the time. The other thing?"

"The German who supplied Donovan with the bomb is up to something else. Could you leave him for the time being? Should be another feather in your cap when you arrest him."

"And yours as well. Alright. Let's 'ope whatever 'appens, 'appens soon. If war starts he'll either be interned or kicked out."

"Right, I understand that. Thanks. I'll keep you posted. Bye, Sergeant."

"Thank you, Mr Martin."

◆   ◆   ◆

That had taken longer than he had expected, so he had to dash down the Strand, and was five minutes late for his meeting with Joe and George. They were waiting for him outside the refreshment room in Charing Cross station. Roger apologised and they went inside. After his early start, Roger was hungry, so he ordered himself a cup of tea and a bun. The boys seemed keen on this idea when Roger asked them what they wanted, and they found a table and settled down in silence to munch on their food. With three empty plates in front of them, they got down to business.

Roger started by giving them more money for their day-to-day expenses and reimbursing them for money already spent. Very efficiently, they gave him their receipts. All above board. They then told him how their switch of tails had gone. Roger congratulated them on showing initiative when their targets had left by car, by waiting for their return.

"If you hadn't done that, we wouldn't have a clue where the suitcase was. Brilliant."

"Thanks guv. We was a bit worried that we was lettin' you down," said Joe.

"There wasn't anything else you could have done. And it worked out well."

The boys smiled their appreciation and Roger continued.

"I've spoken to the police just now. Sergeant Moss wants you to know how grateful he is for all you've done. All being well, the Irish stuff should be wrapped up in the next couple of days."

"What do we need to do?" asked George.

"Nothing. Let the police do their job and arrest and lock up these people." Before the boys' faces had a chance to drop, Roger continued.

"I've got something for you to do that's far more important."

Their faces lit up.

"Remember that girl you spotted on Hampstead Heath with the German, George?"

"Yes guv. I don't fink she liked him much. She was cryin' a lot."

"Well, I'm not sure why she was crying. Maybe it was a lovers' tiff or he was giving her some bad news or he was threatening her in some way. No idea. I want you two to find out."

"What d'yer know about 'er?" asked Joe.

"She's German, probably a Jewish refugee, and she works for a bigwig in the Foreign Office and lives in his house."

"Blimey. D'yer reckon she might be a spy?" asked George.

"That's what I want you to find out."

"There's gonna be a lot of 'angin around 'Ampstead 'Eath. 'Ow we gonna do this, George?"

"When I saw 'er she was with the German. 'E's the danger. One of us 'as to watch 'im and the other the girl. Make sure we know where 'e is."

"I reckon I should watch the girl. she's Jewish and so am I. I could wear me kippah and speak a few words of 'Ebrew to 'er."

"I thought we was just goin' to watch 'er. Now yer thinkin' of talkin' to 'er."

"Well, guv needs to know what's goin' on. 'Ow else is 'e goin' to find out?"

"'E could talk to 'er 'imself," Joe suggested.

"If she's in trouble, she's more likely to talk to me than 'im coz I'm younger an' Jewish."

"Anyway, 'ow many words of 'Ebrew d'yer know?"

"Couple. That's enough. I'll catch 'er attention wiv 'em."

"OK. I'll watch the Nazi."

"Right, that's good," said Roger. "You might need to keep at her to get the truth. You'll have to make your mind up about that."

"Right, guv. What'll I do then, when I fink I might 'ave got the truth out of 'er?" George asked.

"Persuade her to meet with me. I hope she can get out from her house more or less whenever she wants. You said you saw her near the gallery, didn't you George?"

"S'right."

"Ask her when she could meet me there—if there's a cafe, we could have a cup of tea. As soon as you make the arrangement, phone me. I'll drop everything to make sure I can make the appointment."

"Do you want me to be there ?" asked Joe.

"No. You watch the German. I don't want to be disturbed while I'm talking to her. If he sets off in the direction of Hampstead Heath, you'll have to stop him somehow."

Joe chuckled. "Leave that wiv us."

◆   ◆   ◆

With Joe on his tail, Klein made his way to Carlton House Terrace to meet with Wolf. George had briefed Joe on the best vantage point so, as soon as the German had entered the embassy, he nipped over the fence by the statue and hid himself in the bushes just as his mate had done. George was on his way to Hampstead Heath.

Wolf was seated behind his desk, full of his own self-importance as usual. Klein, ever the cynic but always the professional, by Gestapo standards at least, waited patiently. He wasn't smoking. He figured that abstaining for the duration of this meeting was worth the sacrifice, since he'd be avoiding his superior's regular lecture about the evils of smoking and the Führer's intense dislike of it. "Perhaps it would be better," Klein mused to himself, "if the Führer did smoke. The smoke coming from his mouth would mask that disgustingly bad breath that everyone knows he has."

"So, Klein. Update, please."

"The girl's up and running. I've given her a camera, with instructions to photograph any documents she can lay her hands on, and she's worked out a way to eavesdrop on Blum's meetings with important visitors."

"Excellent. Himmler, and indeed the Führer himself, is most anxious to know what England will do in the event that we move against Poland. You can put as much pressure on the girl as you like. Müller assures me that they have her parents under close surveillance in Berlin. You can tell her that."

"Thank you. That's good to hear. Hopefully the girl can give us an indication of what England's intentions are."

"Good. Now what about the sabotage?"

"I collected the explosive from Harwich and delivered it to Donovan. He's an expert bomb maker."

"Not so clever when he blew those fingers off." Wolf laughed at his own joke.

"That was some time ago. He's much more careful now. He'll assemble two small bombs and deliver them to his men. There'll be nothing to do—just set the bombs and clear off."

"Will the damage be extensive?"

"If they put the bombs in the right place."

"Will they?"

"Donovan will see to that."

"And the timetables?"

"I think Donovan will wait until the second half of the month. Many men are on holiday at the moment. When they're all back and normal production resumes, there'll be more damage and more deaths."

"And the girl?"

"I'm seeing her in ten days' time. I should have some information then."

"Whatever you get must be brought here to me immediately. I'll see it's radioed to Berlin. Our cypher machines are impossible to crack, you know, my dear Klein."

"That's good to hear, sir."

Wolf stood up and gave the German greeting with his ramrod stiff right arm. "Heil Hitler," he shouted, and clicked his heels together so viciously that Klein thought he might do serious harm to his ankles. The Gestapo detective followed suit, slightly less enthusiastically, and left. He walked to Piccadilly and went into the Eros News Theatre on the corner of Shaftesbury Avenue and Coventry Street. Joe followed and kept an eye on him from about six rows behind. Cartoons were on as the two entered, and these were followed by an episode of *The Lone Ranger Rides Again.* Then came the Pathé News, in which the most important item appeared to be some sort of celebration in Paris in which lots of old soldiers from the Great War marched up the Champs Elysees. The narrator said that Britain was fighting hard to maintain peace and wouldn't want a repeat of 1914–1918. "They're just cowards," thought Klein to himself. "No chance," Joe mumbled. "We won't let them Nazi bastards walk all over us."

Klein left after the news and Joe followed him to Franks hairdressing salon nearby. Joe loitered at the entrance to the London Pavilion next door to Franks, smoking his Woodbines while the German had his hair cut. Freshly shorn, Klein made his way to the Regent Palace Hotel and stepped inside. Crowds milled around the foyer, and there were enough people about for Joe to conceal himself. The German stepped into one of several dining rooms. Joe watched and waited. He was getting hungry himself and bought a sandwich from one of many shops in the hotel foyer. Emerging forty minutes later, Klein made his way down the Underground station steps.

◆   ◆   ◆

"My dear Esther, you must pull yourself round," Sir John said to the young German Jewish girl. "There's nothing that anyone can do at the moment. It's a fine day. Why not go for a walk on the Heath? You may meet some interesting people on your travels and, in any case, the fresh air will do you good. I'm going to the office now and won't be back until the evening, so stay out as long as you like."

"Thank you, Sir John. I'll follow your advice. I'll leave as soon as you've gone."

Esther went to her room and slipped on a thin green cardigan. The walk would do her good, she thought. She might even come up with a solution to what she would do in ten days' time when she met the German. Hearing the front door slam, she waited for five minutes, and then left the house and set off towards Hampstead Heath.

CHAPTER 18

Concealed

London, Monday 7 August 1939

Donovan was in and out of the Uxbridge house all day on the first Monday in August. Shopping in Uxbridge, walking in Richmond Park, the cinema in Hillingdon, drinking in any number of West London pubs, he was followed every inch of the way by Special Branch officers. Sometimes he used the car, and at others the tube, but he was never out of their sight. The only time he managed to give them the slip was when he used the toilets in an Uxbridge pub. The police had a man posted outside the back door, so there was no way he could escape that way. What they didn't know was that there was a public telephone in the passageway leading to the toilets. He dared not use his home phone because he assumed, correctly as it happens, that it was being tapped. Donovan, an experienced and hardened IRA operative, didn't think he was being watched, but he wasn't taking any chances.

The brief call he'd made had been to alert his men in Woolwich that he needed to see them on the following day at seven o'clock near the fountain in Victoria Park. He figured that on a fine summer's evening, which was forecast, three men walking and chatting wouldn't arouse any suspicion. Moss and Watkins, a detective constable colleague, were on duty when the IRA man set off for his assignation. He went by car. The traffic would be light going into London at that time of the day, he figured. The police car, an unmarked light green Morris, had little difficulty in keeping the Austin Six in view, even though Donovan took precautions by making one or two detours, all to no avail.

Donovan left his vehicle on Cadogan Terrace, and Moss jumped out and followed him, while the DC parked up and raced after his sergeant. Donovan was meeting his two confederates by the fountain as arranged, and was not carrying a suitcase. The two Special Branch officers were watching from a concealed spot in the trees.

"What d'yer reckon, Sarge? Nick the three of 'em now?"

"Don't think so. We need all three of 'em and the explosives. That'll send 'em away for a long, long time. When they've finished their business, you take Donovan and I'll track the others, probably back to Woolwich. I'll check out their address to see if it confirms what the journalist told us. Then I'll phone the Yard and put a team on 'em straight away. You stay with the paddy in the car until he's tucked up for the night. Go 'ome when the relief arrives."

Donovan's meeting didn't last long, and soon Watkins was on the road back to Uxbridge and Moss was on foot towards the river. The sergeant thought that things were approaching a climax. His emotions were a mixture of excitement at making a big arrest and apprehension at the terrible consequences if he messed it up.

◆   ◆   ◆

Roger was on edge. He knew that both of his projects would soon come to fruition. Whilst, as any good journalist should, he was looking for a juicy story or two, he knew that there was so much more at stake. Lives were at risk at Woolwich if, as seemed likely, that really was the target of the IRA bombers, and who knew what was going on at Hampstead Heath. So much did he value the contribution of Joe and George, he had a strong suspicion that matters in that respect would soon come to a head. But, for the time being, all he could do was sit and wait. He busied himself with the latest IRA news, which included girls with Irish accents trying to burn down hotels in Southport and other seaside towns, and three women amongst the five deported at the beginning of the week under the terms of the new law. He was pleased to note that the numbers of Special Branch officers had been increased to keep a closer watch on the IRA.

At the *Globe*, the bosses were putting extra pressure on the editorial staff and reporters to come up with something big to boost circulation. Roger's two stories fitted that bill nicely. No wonder he was on edge. Jane had noticed it as well; he seemed distracted when they were chatting in his parents' lounge the previous evening. Jane had tried to reassure him, saying that he had done all he could have, and in less than five months had uncovered what was probably a major IRA conspiracy and a potential Nazi spy ring. He had smiled weakly and thanked her, but his mind still wandered.

The country was also under pressure. Fear of the IRA bombers had momentarily distracted it from the threat from Nazi Germany. The Irish hadn't done any great damage to date, although a bomb in the left luggage area of King's Cross station the previous month had killed a man, and injuries were mounting. Something terrible could happen soon, people feared. They were worried about another war, twenty-one years after the last big one had finished, although British troops had been involved in a few minor skirmishes. Danzig was on everyone's minds. Would Germany invade? Would Russia join us in a war against Hitler if he marched into Poland?

◆　　◆　　◆

Another person with a lot on his mind was Joe.

The lad was loitering around Sussex Gardens keeping a look-out for Klein. Now that the Irish business was coming to a head, he knew that his new assignment would most likely be fairly boring. He'd resigned himself to visits to Carlton House Terrace, news theatres, cinemas, shops, pubs and restaurants. Add to this endless hours of trying not to be observed in Paddington, and the prospect was pretty dull. Yet, he told himself, it was crucial that he didn't lose sight of the German for one second. If he did, and Klein went to meet the girl in Hampstead unobserved, he knew that George might be in danger. So he refused to allow himself to drift into listlessness and kept his wits about him.

In Hampstead, her upcoming meeting with Klein drove Esther into an ever deepening depression, which was turning day-by-day into panic as her day of reckoning approached. The only visitors that Sir John had received over the previous week were friends who had nothing to do with his work at the Foreign Office. He was out for long hours, often leaving after breakfast and not returning until well into the evening. On a couple of occasions he had left after lunch and not made it back to the house until the following evening, having spent the night in a Central London hotel at the end of a long session at the Foreign Office. He hadn't once brought his briefcase home with him. She had nothing to offer Klein.

Esther could see that Sir John was preoccupied with the current crisis over Danzig, which Esther knew all about from reading the English newspapers. He still treated her courteously and gently, but she could see that his mind was elsewhere. She had five days to come up with something which would satisfy Klein, and she knew that if she didn't, her parents would suffer horribly and she would probably never see them again. Sir John was in London and not expected to return until the evening. She had finished her morning and lunchtime chores, and told Cook she was going for a stroll on the Heath. It was a warm and sunny afternoon. Perhaps, she thought, being out in the nice weather would provide her with some inspiration.

◆   ◆   ◆

Klein had made his way to the German Embassy with Joe on his heels. Inside he was briefing Wolf on the plans for a "big incident".

"Expect something terrible to happen to the English within a week," he reported to his boss.

"Good," said Wolf, "and the other thing?"

"Well within the week."

"You know that the Führer needs all the intelligence he can about English intentions in the event that he attacks Poland. The rumours are that he may do this within the next two weeks. To delay beyond the beginning of September risks the Wehrmacht not being able to complete the job before the bad weather arrives."

"Is he banking on another Munich style conference that'll give him what he wants without a shot being fired?" asked Klein.

"That is what he expects. The English are weak and unprepared. The Führer expects Chamberlain not to honour England's commitment to Poland. But we must be certain. That's where you come in, Klein."

"Of course, sir. Are the girl's parents still under observation?"

"Yes, Müller has made this a priority. There's not a chance they'll disappear, unless of course it's into a concentration camp."

The odious man laughed heartily at his own joke. Klein didn't find it funny at all, but joined in the mirth half-heartedly.

"Klein, if that happens it means that you have failed. Don't."

Suitably chastised, Klein left the Embassy and walked towards Piccadilly. "Not another bloody newsreel," thought Joe, about fifty yards behind the German.

It was another bloody newsreel. Klein's cover was that of a journalist and he submitted reports of the British people's attitude to war, if there was to be one, to the press attaché at the Embassy. Luckily for Joe, the next episode of *The Lone Ranger Rides Again* was just starting as they took their seats. The plot wasn't too demanding, so he was able to watch it while keeping an eye on the German. The pair left after the newsreel and, after a short tube journey, Joe found himself back in Sussex Gardens. Joe took up his station and let his mind, but not his eyes, wander. "I wonder how George is getting on," he thought.

◆　◆　◆

George was hot. The sun was beating down on Hampstead Heath, although the trees in which he had concealed himself did give him some shade. He'd even climbed up one of the trees and was sitting on a strong-looking branch eating a sandwich and taking swigs from a bottle of lemonade. "Must take the bottle back," he reminded himself, so that he could collect a penny on the empty when he returned it. He had a banana in his pocket for later.

Not surprisingly, the Heath was busy with the usual assortment of prams and walking sticks. From his perch, he could see the girl's house, and he felt a surge of adrenaline when he saw her emerge and head his way. He slipped down from his vantage point and hid behind a tree until he could see which direction she was taking. To his frustration, he could see she was walking very slowly with her head down, as if she was completely immersed in thought. He cautiously set off after her, deep into the woods. Finding a bench in a quiet spot, Esther sat down and tried to collect her thoughts. Nothing came, and she felt tears begin to form in her eyes. Her head went forward and she went into a fit of uncontrolled sobbing.

George saw all this from his concealed spot behind a tree. What should he do? Somehow he felt a need for great urgency. "This is important," Roger had told him. He had to reveal himself and tell her everything now.

"Shalom miss, are you OK?"

Esther looked up and, through the tears, saw a young man looking anxiously at her.

"I'm alright. Just leave me alone."

She stopped crying and pulled a handkerchief from her brown leather handbag and wiped her eyes. He hadn't gone away.

"Please leave me alone."

"You look very un'appy to me, miss. You sure nuffin's wrong?"

Esther looked at him again, and realised with a slight shock that he wasn't a young man at all, but a boy, probably about fifteen or sixteen.

"No. Nothing's wrong. I'm just a bit upset, that's all."

"Boyfriend trouble?"

Esther immediately saw an opportunity to get rid of this troublesome youngster.

"Yes, yes. That's it. We've just split up."

She sounded far from convincing, and both George and she knew it. George decided he was going to get nowhere quizzing her like this, so he took a risk and changed tack.

"Was yer boyfriend that fair 'aired geezer 'oo was shoutin' at yer near the gallery a while back?"

Fear flowed through Esther's veins.

"What do you know about that? Have you been following me?"

"No miss. I was followin' 'im."

Stunned, Esther looked up and studied the boy's face. A kippah was perched on top of his black hair. His weather-beaten features only partly disguised his Jewish face. He was, she could see, growing tall, and had a strong muscular body, as far as she could judge. Brown eyes smiled sympathetically at her, but she recognised a strength of purpose that wouldn't easily be weakened. Could she trust him? She'd no idea, but felt that she could hardly be worse off than before he'd come onto the scene.

"You're Jewish?" she asked him.

"Yes miss, and you are too I fink. Nor British either, judgin' from the way yer speak."

"I'm German. I came over here to escape from the Nazis."

"That man you was arguin' wiv wasn't yer boyfriend, was 'e?"

"No, he was a German, a Nazi. Why were you following him?"

Now things were getting tricky for George. He reasoned that he wouldn't get much further if he didn't tell her the whole story. He decided to give her a short summary.

"You see, miss . . . "

"Please stop calling me miss. My name's Esther. And sit down."

George did as he was told, and looked at her.

"I'm George. My mate and I work for a newspaperman. My mate's called Joe, by the way. The guv'ner's name is Roger, Roger Martin. You might 'ave 'eard of 'im, 'e works for the *Globe*?"

"No, I haven't. I can't read English very well yet."

"You speak it pretty well."

"Thank you."

"The guv put us on a job followin' a geezer 'e thought was IRA. One day we spotted the paddy."

"What's a paddy?"

"Irishman. Anyway, we saw this paddy meetin' another bloke in Trafalgar Square. We 'ad no idea 'oo 'e was, so we split up. Joe carried on with the IRA guy and I followed the other bloke. 'Oo is 'e by the way?"

"I don't really know, but he is German."

"One day when I was trackin' 'im 'e came up 'ere to 'ampstead. That's when I saw 'im wiv you. 'E looked like 'e was being nasty to you and givin' out threats, so I told the guv."

"What did he say?"

"'E said 'e'd no idea what was goin' on, so 'e told me to keep an eye on you. Business is over with the IRA man, so Joe's keepin' watch on the jerry. If the Nazi sets off for 'ere while were talkin' 'e'll skip ahead of 'im and warn us before 'e gets 'ere. So don't worry."

"I'm not due to meet him again till Saturday, so he probably won't come up here before that."

"Why are yer meetin' 'im Sat'day?"

"He wants me to steal secrets from the man I work for, Sir John Blum."

"Tell 'im to bugger off."

"I can't. If I don't get something useful he'll send my parents in Berlin to a concentration camp, where they'll probably die."

"Blimey, y'are in a bit of a pickle. Roger was in Berlin when the Nazis smashed up them Jewish shops and synagogues last winter."

"Reichskristallnacht."

"That's it. Roger wrote a big piece in 'is paper when 'e got back sayin' what 'e'd seen and what a set of bastards the Nazis are. It 'elped to turn the British people against the Nazis."

"He sounds a good man, but what can he do for me?"

"Don't know. But if anyone can get you outta this, 'e can. 'E's got friends in 'igh places."

Esther relaxed for the first time in weeks.

"What happens next?"

"As soon as you've gone 'ome, I'll phone the guv and tell 'im what's gone on. 'E told me to tell yer that if you was OK with it, 'e'd come up 'ere and meet you tomorrer afternoon and you can go through the 'ole business wiv 'im. He says 'e'll see you in that caff near the art gallery. Know it?"

"Yes. What time?"

"Whenever yer say."

"Three o'clock."

"I'll tell 'im."

"What does he look like?"

"Big tall bloke wiv brown curly 'air. Yer can't miss 'im."

Esther leant towards George and kissed him on the cheek.

"Thank you, George. I feel so much better after talking to you."

George blushed scarlet, and for the first time was lost for words.

"That's OK miss, err, Esther. My mate Joe will keep an eye on the jerry, so 'e won't disturb you."

"Will you be there, George?"

"Oh yes, Esther, but you won't see me."

CHAPTER 19

$\mathcal{F}ear$

Berlin entered August 1939 nervously. Hitler's rantings about Danzig and Poland had put most people on edge. The population fell neatly into three categories. The majority of the population wanted peace, and relied on the Führer to reacquire Danzig using his renowned diplomatic skills. Then there was the vocal minority of fanatical Nazis, who wanted the Führer to put on some massive show of strength, to demonstrate that Germany was now the major European power and well on the way to becoming the world's most dominant country. Destroying Poland and restoring Danzig to the Reich fitted that bill nicely. The quiet minority, which included those Jews who had not managed to escape from Germany, loathed Hitler and the Nazis and all they stood for.

Simon and Deborah Abrahams were, of course, in the third group, but, like all their fellow Hitler haters, dared not whisper a word about their discontent. Just even talking quietly to one another about their unhappiness would lead to a visit from the Gestapo if their conversation had been overhead by one of the tens of thousands of informers who infested Berlin. So they spoke of such things only in the confines of their apartment. Never would they discuss their circumstances with anyone, even fellow Jews—there were also collaborators in their ranks. Each night they sat miserably in their small room listening to the gramophone which, for some unexplained reason, they'd been allowed to keep. They spoke quietly for fear of unfriendly eavesdroppers. Not that there was much to talk about. The Gestapo seemed determined to keep them in Berlin.

Their daily lives had fallen into a monotonous pattern. After breakfast, Simon would go to a converted apartment on the ground floor of a Jewish tenement off the Alexanderplatz—a Jew House. Queues of wretched people waited to see him, all Jewish of course, to ply him with their problems, big and small. Most of these were financial or domestic, but occasionally clients who had fallen foul of the Gestapo, by, for example, sitting on the wrong seat in the Tiergarten, sought advice. There was little he could do but listen and offer what comfort he could. Simon was good at that. Deborah spent her mornings cleaning. A dump compared with their previous residence it might have been, but she was determined to keep up some sort of decent living conditions. Sometimes she met Jewish friends for coffee and went shopping most afternoons, although, as a Jew, she often had to wait until the end of the day to be served. The Aryans had first pick of everything. Occasionally though, at the end of the day, the shops' shelves were empty when the turn of the Jews came. So they continued, day by day, with Simon setting off after breakfast with his briefcase and returning in time for his evening meal. On one of his trips, Simon noticed a man who appeared to be following him. It wasn't as if the man was acting particularly suspiciously, but Simon had seen him on several occasions. He told his wife about his concerns.

"Look darling, we haven't done anything wrong. If he wants to follow us, let him. At least we now know to look out for him."

"You're right," replied her husband. "When you're bringing my lunch, keep your eyes open for him, or anyone else who might be tailing us." From time to time Deborah took her husband a lunchtime snack to his office.

Simon came to expect being tailed everywhere as another part of the daily ritual. Three Gestapo men operated on eight-hour shifts, so he was under surveillance twenty-four hours a day. Any attempt to conceal themselves was completely unnecessary. All Simon needed to know was that he was going nowhere. They followed him to his office, loitered outside all day to make certain that he didn't go anywhere unexpectedly, tracked him back to his room at the end of work. and completed the cycle by keeping watch on his flat from the street. Simon was disturbed by this, but he had no idea why he was being singled out for this special attention.

Hartmann, a brute of a man with thinning brown hair, bushy eyebrows and a moustache, was glad to be relieved near Simon's office by his colleague Schultz. Ten years the younger, in his late twenties, Schultz was also smaller than Hartmann, but had blonde hair and blue eyes. So aware was he of his Germanness, he seldom wore the trilby hat favoured by many Gestapo agents.

"Don't go home," Schultz told Hartmann, "the boss wants to see you in the Alex office now."

"OK. It's not far. I shouldn't be too late for my supper."

The Alexanderplatz Gestapo office was much smaller that the Prinz-Albrecht-Strasse headquarters of the Gestapo, but regular shrieks, screams, moans and cries emanated from the basement. Schultz smiled when he heard some distant evidence of these noises as he entered the Alex. Müller was waiting for him.

"Come in here, Hartmann," he said indicating a small room usually used for "soft" interrogations.

Seating himself opposite Hartmann, Müller asked, "How is the surveillance on the Jew Abrahams going?"

"Very well, sir. He hasn't been out of our sight since this operation began, except, of course, when he's inside his apartment or his office."

"And what does he do each day?"

"Walks to the office and then returns to his apartment in the early evening. At weekends, he and his wife usually go for long walks."

"Do they meet anyone?"

"Only fellow Jews, and then only to chat and pass the time of day."

"Nothing suspicious?"

"No sir."

"Good. I've heard from Wolf in London that the project he's running there should be about to bear fruit. It's absolutely essential that we know where he is at all times. Understood?"

"Yes, sir. There was just one thing."

"Yes?"

"Well, sir, it's all very well watching the husband, but what about the wife?"

"What about the wife?"

"She could be planning something."

Müller burst out laughing. "You'll never reach high rank, Hartmann. You're like the Brownshirts, a bit dim, but good at what I order you to do."

Hartmann blushed and Müller continued.

"One thing all Jewish women have in common is that they spend their time giving birth, raising families and cooking and cleaning. Whoever heard of a dangerous Jewish woman?" More laughter. "Besides, we don't have the men to cover them both."

Müller stood up, signalling the end of the meeting. After an exchange of German greetings, Hartmann asked his boss one final question.

"Could you tell me what this is all about?"

"No."

◆　　◆　　◆

Roger was talking to George on the phone. The boy gave a full report on the day's events and told him that the girl was expecting to meet him at the gallery at three o'clock on the following afternoon.

"I fink she's in bad trouble, guv. I 'ope you can 'elp."

"I do too. Description?"

"She's quite small, 'bout five foot two I'd say. And thin, but not too thin. She's got black curly hair like me mum's. 'Er eyes are definitely brown. Oh, and she 'as nice lips."

Roger chuckled. "Good looking, was she?"

"Smashin', an you can keep yer eyes off 'er, yer engaged to Jane. In a year or two I might ask 'er out meself."

Roger laughed again. "I won't be standing in your way, George. Good luck."

"Thanks guv. Joe's gonna watch the Nazi and I'll be lookin' after you and Esther, that's 'er name by the way. You won't see me, but if you need me just shout out me name."

"Thanks George."

Another fine afternoon greeted Roger as he drove towards Hampstead. He gave himself plenty of time and motored past the end of road in which Esther was living. After he'd parked up, he made his way to the cafe, looking for signs of George. Not surprisingly, there were none. Having bought himself a cup of tea and a scone, he sat down and waited for Esther. A very pretty dark-haired girl who looked to be in her late teens came in and looked nervously around. She was wearing a blue blouse and grey skirt. Roger stood up and walked towards her.

"Esther?"

"Yes."

"I'm Roger. Can I get you a cup of tea and a scone?"

"Thank you. Just a cup of tea please."

With the food and drink in place, it was Esther who spoke first, in a timid voice.

"Is George here?"

"Yes, but don't ask me where. I've no idea."

"He's a very nice boy."

"He is, and tough and brave as well."

"And kind," Esther added.

"And kind," said Roger. "I'm very lucky to have him and his pal Joe on my side. George's told me your story. I understand you've a younger brother with a family in Cambridge, but he's not under any sort of threat."

Esther nodded.

"Let's be clear from the start, none of this goes in the papers until it's all been sorted out."

"Thank you," said Esther, growing in confidence ever so slightly.

"Tell me if I'm wrong, but the German has told you to get some secrets from Sir John Blum and photograph them."

"Yes. He's given me a camera to photograph documents and told me to listen in to visitors. But he hasn't brought his briefcase home from the office recently, and he hasn't had any visitors in the last few weeks. In any case, I wouldn't let down Sir John if I could help it."

"And you're due to meet the German here on Saturday?"

"Yes. But if I've nothing for him he'll have my parents sent to a concentration camp."

"I know. George told me."

"These Nazis are really horrible. George said you were in Berlin on Reichskristallnacht and wrote about it in your paper."

"I did, but it means I'm no longer welcome in Germany. They'd snatch me, give me a beating and then send me back as soon as I crossed the border."

"I can't see a way out of this. What can I do?" she said in a panicky voice.

Roger finished his scone, sipped his tea and looked at Esther.

"I know. There's a desperate race against time here with your Saturday deadline coming up. I think I know how we can keep the German sweet for the time being, but it does depend on a lot of things. For a start, Sir John has to know what's going on."

"Oh no, I couldn't. He's been so kind to me."

"You have to. You've done nothing so far to let him down."

"What would I say to him?"

"Nothing. I'll talk to him with you in the room."

"Do you think he'll see you? He's a very important man, and very busy."

"I'm not very important, but I do have contacts who are. I'll get in touch with them before the day's out and see if I can fix up to see Sir John at his house tomorrow."

Esther looked at Roger. She saw determination in his eyes. She'd no idea how he'd sort it out, but she knew he'd do everything he could. Roger got up to leave and Esther followed.

"There's no way I can let you know what time I'm coming, but it'll most likely be in the early evening, before dinner I hope."

"Thank you, Roger."

Roger called, "George," who immediately materialised as if from nowhere.

"Afternoon guv. Afternoon miss, err, Esther."

George had dispensed with his kippah and replaced it with a grey flat cap. He took this off and shook Esther's hand, and then Roger's.

"I'll take you home, George."

"Will Esther be OK getting to 'er 'ouse?"

"Of course I will." Esther laughed. "Thank you anyway."

She shook Roger's hand and then put her hands on George's shoulders and gave him a light kiss on the cheek. Then she set off home.

Roger was driving in silence with George in the passenger seat. He seemed to be full of thought. He let out a breath and then said, "She definitely likes you, George. You could be OK there in a year or two."

"Maybe, but will she be OK, guv?"

"I hope so. We've got to do everything we can to help her. But I have some ideas."

◆   ◆   ◆

The IRA bombing campaign continued throughout August. Despite the increase in Special Branch numbers and the new powers of arrest given to the police by Parliament, the Irish showed little sign of giving up. Young women set fires in more hotels, terrorists were arrested in Liverpool trying to enter England from the Isle of Man, and more clumsiness from the Irish saw their ammunition dump blow up in Coventry.

There was little sign either of Great Britain or France striking any treaty with the Soviet Union, and in fact things were getting worse; Germany was palling up with their would-be Russian enemies, with a trade agreement signed between the two. The warm, fine weather drove many families to the seaside resorts while, back in Westminster, politicians and civil servants were doing all they could to prevent the country being dragged into war. "Danzig," "Danzig," "Danzig," Hitler raged, as intelligence revealed that Germany was gearing up for war.

◆   ◆   ◆

Back in Belmont Road, Uxbridge, Donovan was carefully assembling the two bombs which he expected would wreak havoc at the Woolwich Arsenal sometime in the following week. Outside, Special Branch were monitoring the IRA man's every move, waiting for the moment that they could catch all of these dangerous people in a trap. George and Joe were watching Klein and Esther like hawks. Meanwhile the people of Great Britain sat and waited. Most accepted the inevitability of war. There was a small but vociferous peace movement, and a tiny number of potential traitors, but most of those who had admired Hitler in the early years of Nazi Germany now saw him for what he was; an anti-Semitic gangster who was using terror tactics to quell any opposition to his dictatorship in his own country, and was preparing to seize Poland and any other mainland European countries he could get his grubby hands on. Most British people were ready, but whether the armed forces were was quite another matter. Few expected Chamberlain to pull another rabbit out of the hat as he had done ten months before in Munich. Hitler was a liar and an aggressor. It was up to Britain, her Empire and France to stop him.

This was the gist of the conversation on that balmy evening in New Malden, where the Walkers, Roger and Jane were chewing the fat in Richard's garden. Not far away young and old cricketers were having their weekly net practice, trying, for the time being at least, to shut any thoughts of a possible conflict out of their minds. Against the distant sound of leather on willow, Roger only half-listened as the others discussed the situation.

"You seem distracted, Roger," Inge said. "Any trouble at the office?"

Roger hadn't really come up with a big story for months and was getting fed up with sitting in various courts watching IRA men and women be sent down.

"No not really. Just a bit bored. It's all rather predictable on the Irish front."

"You're right. That seems to be petering out. But you're not just bored. You're worried. Come on, tell us what's on your mind."

So Roger did, starting with Klein meeting Donovan, and then the appearance of Esther and his meeting with her earlier that day.

"Heavens," said Jane, "poor girl. What on earth can be done?"

"First of all, Sir John must be told. I would suggest you do that, Roger," said Richard.

"I said I would, but I can't just walk up and knock on his door and tell him he's got a potential spy in his house."

"Of course not. I'll get in touch with Harry tomorrow and ask him to get Van to speak to Sir John and let him know what's going on—well, roughly what it's all about. If there's not much going on at the FO, I'll try to arrange for you to see him at his house tomorrow night."

"What d'you mean—not much going on at the FO—they must be up to their ears in it."

"Yes, you're right. I could have put it differently. But this is important. A chance of capturing a major German spy ring. And, perhaps, some other opportunities."

"What are they?"

"Wait and see. We must keep this away from Cadogan and the other Foreign Office people, and definitely no politicians. None of those can be trusted, except maybe Churchill. As soon as they hear about it they'll have the girl arrested, banged up, and probably deported to Germany."

"Surely not," cried Inge. "She'll be taken to a concentration camp as soon as she sets foot on German soil, and her parents with her."

"Exactly. that's why we have to rely on Van getting you an introduction to Sir John."

"Can we trust Van?"

"Sure. He hates Germany, doesn't trust Chamberlain, and isn't too keen on MI5. He's got his own spy ring with his friend Churchill. He's ruthless and cunning as a fox. We can trust him."

Roger breathed a sigh of relief. He'd got exactly what he'd come for without saying it outright. Richard was crafty too. He recognised his friend's tactics because they were exactly those which he himself would have used in similar circumstances.

"One other thing, Roger. The girl will have to be present when you meet Sir John. She'll need the confidence to do what I'm guessing Sir John will suggest."

"What do you mean?" asked Roger.

"Wait and see," Richard said again.

Inge and Jane looked at Roger and raised their eyebrows.

"By the way, Roger, there's no chance that this German will spot you at Sir John's house, is there?"

"None at all. There's no reason for him to go to Hampstead before his scheduled meeting with Esther on Saturday. And if by any chance he does, George and Joe will warn us beforehand. I'll get Sir John's phone number and have them call with a warning if he's heading our way."

"Of course, the irregulars," Richard said with a smile. "Now let's have another beer."

☞eceit

London, Thursday 10 and Friday 11 August 1939

Roger was sitting in the press seats at the Old Bailey. He'd been in and out of the Central Criminal Court for the past few days, watching O'Shaughnessy on trial for possessing explosives. It was a cut and dried case. Mrs O'Shaughnessy's evidence that she'd found explosives in the garden shed of the family home, together with the police confirmation of this, had made a guilty verdict inevitable. His wife had appeared nervous in the witness box, but performed capably and handled the defence cross-examination without difficulty. The outcome was never in doubt and O'Shaughnessy had been sentenced to ten years in jail.

Roger flipped his notebook shut and left the court. He was surprised to see the convicted man's wife waiting for him outside. She smiled at him and said, "Thank you, Mr Martin. I'm so glad it's all over and he's been locked up. I can get on with life now."

"Are you working now, Mrs O'Shaughnessy?"

"Oh yes. Bit of a surprise really. I had a call from Bentall's offering me my old job back in haberdashery. I start next Monday."

Roger felt a sense of satisfaction flow through him.

"That's wonderful. I'm sure that everything will be alright for you now that this is out of the way," nodding towards the courtroom.

"I'm sure too. There is one thing though. Was the information I gave you of any use?"

"It most certainly was. I can't tell you anything about it now, but if you'll keep your eye on the *Globe* for the next couple of weeks, all will be revealed."

"That's good. I'll do that. It will be under your name I expect?"

"It will."

"Thank you, Mr Martin."

"No, thank you, Mrs O'Shaughnessy. It's a big story. Goodbye."

Roger walked back to the office and wrote up the conclusion to the O'Shaughnessy trial. He'd just finished when the phone rang. It was Richard, who told him that Sir John would see him that evening at seven o'clock. He'd already briefed Joe and George that this was likely to happen later that day. He'd given the boys Sir John's telephone number, with strict instructions that they were to call him there if Klein was to come anywhere near Hampstead. Joe would start the day at Sussex Gardens with George, and then late in the afternoon, the latter would set off for the Heath. Roger was very nervous. How would Sir John react to the news that he was harbouring a potential German spy? And what could be done to protect Esther? What would come next? So many unanswered questions.

Esther answered Roger's doorbell ring. She looked terrified.

"Good evening, Mr Martin. Sir John is expecting you. Please follow me."

As they walked towards the sitting room, she whispered, "What will happen if the German turns up and sees you here? Won't he be suspicious?"

"He won't. George is down the road, and his friend is keeping track of the German in London. If he comes within a mile of Hampstead he'll call and warn us. But he won't."

The mention of George made Esther relax a little, and she opened the door to let Roger into Sir John's presence.

"This is Mr Martin, Sir John."

Roger was surprised to see a man with a full head of thick curly hair walk towards him and offer his hand. Roger shook it, trying to match the firmness of his host's grip. Esther turned to leave.

"Sir John. The story I'm about to tell you involves Esther. I'd very much like her to stay while we talk."

"Curiouser and curiouser," Sir John replied. "I'll just ask Cook to make us three cups of coffee."

Esther stood, embarrassed, with her hands clasped in front of her. Sir John returned and asked Roger and Esther to sit down. He asked Roger about his background, noting with satisfaction that he was, like himself, a Cambridge man and a rugby player and athlete. Cook returned with the coffee and the rather strange discussion, for Sir John particularly, began.

"Mr Martin, may I call you Roger?"

"Of course."

"I have to say that this is highly unusual. I don't normally welcome journalists into my home. In fact, I do my best to avoid them altogether," Sir John said, with a hint of a smile.

"However, Sir Robert Vansittart insisted that I see you. Van doesn't know you, but knows of you, and regards you as some kind of ally."

Roger smiled.

"It seems that you have no love for our Prime Minister's approach to dealing with Hitler and his henchmen and that you have written in the newspapers of your dislike for his foreign policy."

"That's true, Sir John."

"Fortunately for you, I feel the same. Now, why is Esther here?"

"I think it best that she tells you that herself."

Esther sat in silence for a full thirty seconds, began slowly and quietly, and then it all flowed out. She recounted her abduction by the Germans at King's Cross, how it turned out that they'd been following her, had taken her to a quiet spot in a car, used physical violence on her and threatened her with her parents' lives if she didn't co-operate with them. She told him about the meeting with one of the Germans near the gallery, how he'd given her a miniature camera to photograph secret documents and listen in to his conversations when Sir John was receiving important visitors. If she didn't come up with something useful to the Nazis, her parents would be sent to a concentration camp and probably killed. By the end, she was in floods of tears.

Sir John stared at her ashen-faced, in silence. After a while he looked at her with pain in his eyes.

"My dear. How awful for you. These Nazis will stop at nothing to get what they want. They're the scum of the earth. But tell me Roger, how did you find out about this?"

Roger told him the full story. How he'd been on to the IRA man Donovan, how the boys working with the journalist had seen him meet the German, and how one of them had followed the Nazi back to his house in Sussex Gardens. Eventually, Roger said, one of the boys had seen the German threatening Esther.

"George, that's his name, befriended Esther when she was crying on the Heath the other afternoon and got the whole story from her. He reported back to me and I met Esther yesterday and promised to help."

Esther looked up, red-eyed, and with a weak smile said, "George is a lovely boy."

"And most resourceful and determined. He sounds remarkable."

"He is," Roger continued, "and so is his friend Joe. In fact, I owe Joe my liberty, if not my life. But that's another story."

"You must tell it to me one day, Roger. But what on earth are we going to do about this mess?"

He'd put that question to himself, and sat in silence for a moment.

"When do you have to meet this German, Esther?"

"On Saturday, Sir John, after my return from Cambridge."

"Heavens, that's only three days, we're going to have to move quickly. There aren't too many people I trust at the FO. You've met Mr Williams, haven't you Esther?"

"Yes, Sir John."

"I'll talk to him at the office tomorrow. Meanwhile I suggest the three of us reconvene here at seven o'clock tomorrow evening. Is that alright for you, Roger?"

"Yes sir."

"Not one of your cinema nights, is it, Esther?"

"No, Sir John. And, Sir John . . . "

Sir John interrupted.

"You were about to say that you wouldn't have spied on me or done anything you shouldn't. There's no need. I trust you completely."

At last Esther gave a full smile, with a little bit of optimism in it.

"Thank you, Sir John."

The meeting broke up. Handshakes were exchanged.

"Thank you, Sir John," Roger said.

"It is I who should thank you and your lieutenants, Roger. Esther will see you out. Good night."

As she opened the door to let him out, the girl turned to Roger and asked, "Is George with you, Mr Martin?"

"Roger, please. I'm sure he's somewhere around here. I'm just going to find him and take him home."

"Please give him my . . . um . . . best wishes."

"I will. See you tomorrow."

Roger drove to the end of the road near the Heath. George stepped from the trees.

"Everythin' alright, guv?"

"Better than it was, George."

"'Ow's Esther?"

"OK. She sends her, err . . . best wishes."

George was glad it was getting dark so that Roger wouldn't see him blush.

They drove off. Roger sat in silence, thinking about how this could all work out. He couldn't come up with anything. He gave up. He was tired. Perhaps a good night's sleep would provide some answers.

George sensed Roger's mood.

"It's alright. There's three of us plus Esther and 'er guv. The Nazis ain't a match for us lot."

◆   ◆   ◆

Less than twenty-four hours later Roger was back in Hampstead. George was keeping his eye on things outside, while Joe was back in London keeping eye on Klein. It was easy to watch the German, who was on the lookout for Special Branch and MI5 agents rather than adolescent boys. So for Joe it was another round of visits to the German Embassy, the Eros News Theatre, pubs and restaurants. One new thing that caught the young lad's attention was that, for the first time, he realised that Klein wasn't alone in the Sussex Gardens house. While he was waiting for his mark, he spotted three others emerging from the premises, all of them shifty looking, wearing belted raincoats and trilby hats. Rain seemed far away, and Joe felt that they were dressed in some kind of uniform. The three men jumped into a car and drove away while the boy waited patiently for Klein.

◆   ◆   ◆

"Hello Esther," Roger said to the pretty young girl at the door of Sir John's house.

"Good evening sir, err, Roger. Sir John is waiting for us."

They walked together to the lounge where Sir John was sitting on a large settee. He got to his feet as Roger stepped into the room. As handshakes were exchanged the journalist noticed signs of strain, and Roger thought to himself that this wasn't surprising, what with Sir John having Nazi spies targeting his house, as well as playing his part in coping with the threat of Hitler. Sir John was still in his pinstriped suit and black shoes and looked as if he had bolted down his dinner after a late return from the office.

Settling down, Sir John began the meeting.

"I've spoken to my colleague Nigel Williams and he, like me, is horrified. By the way, he's very much on our side and will not breathe a word about this dreadful affair to anyone. One exception to this is his secretary, Miss Danvers, who has prepared some papers for tonight's meeting. She doesn't, of course, know the details, but is sworn to secrecy about what she believes is a matter of national security. Which it is. Her role in all this will become evident later. I forgot to ask you, Esther, to bring the camera. Please would you collect it now and fetch it here?"

"Certainly sir."

As Esther left the room, Roger began to wonder what all this was about. As she returned the penny dropped and he smiled to himself.

"I think we're all agreed that Esther has to have something to give this Nazi on Saturday. If she doesn't, her parents are in extreme danger."

Roger and Esther nodded.

"What I propose is that we give her a mixture of information to give to him, some false, some meaningless, and one or two important documents which will be of great use to us if they fall into German hands."

He reached down to the side of the settee and lifted his briefcase onto his lap. A number of documents were pulled out and Sir John spent a moment or two sorting them out.

"There are two objectives to this exercise. One is to prevent Esther's parents from being imprisoned and the other is to ward off another world war. Astonishing as it may seem, we may be able to achieve both. This paper," Sir John said holding it up, "is a memorandum from senior Foreign Office staff to the Prime Minister, stating that we believe that His Majesty's Government should stand by its commitment to Poland and give them all the support we can in the event that the country is attacked by Germany."

He put the paper on the floor and lifted another.

"Here is the Prime Minister's reply to that memorandum. Equivocally, he states that we will honour the Polish guarantee, but, in best Chamberlain fashion, he adds a footnote in which he states that he hopes that the disagreements between Germany and Poland can be settled through diplomacy. Another Munich, in other words. I can assure you both that if Germany does attack Poland, Great Britain will declare war on the Nazis."

Sir John paused while he put down that paper and picked up three others.

"Each of these is based on a fictional series of memos from the War Office. It details the state of preparedness of our armed forces in the event of war. Two of these are barefaced lies, while the third is completely accurate and will confirm to the Germans what they know already, and that is that our navy will outgun the Germans, sink their ships, and blockade their coastlines to stop food, oil, ammunition, iron, steel and all other commodities from reaching them."

"So, Sir John, you think that, having read this intelligence, Hitler might think twice about invading Poland?"

"Precisely."

"Obviously I can't let you read these documents. I'm taking a great risk in bringing them here, but I feel that it is a risk worth taking on all fronts. Now, we must not inform either MI5 or Special Branch, because if this man is arrested Esther's parents will be seized and the Germans probably won't be dissuaded from going to war. Esther, please come over here and photograph the documents."

Esther took the miniature camera and quickly snapped the five documents.

"That was remarkably efficient, my dear. Anyone would think you'd done this before," he laughed.

Esther blushed, then replied, "This is a brilliantly simple camera, Sir John. It's easy to operate and simple to conceal. Probably invented by a Jew," she concluded.

"More than likely," replied Sir John, and the three of them laughed.

"Presumably the German will wind on the film, take it out, load another and return it to you," Roger said.

Before Esther could answer, Sir John interrupted.

"Let's hope there's not a next time. Which brings me to the second part of our deception. I intend to invite a number of friends for drinks and snacks here, followed by dinner on Monday night. Only Nigel Williams will have a clue what's going on. We will not be discussing anything secret, but no doubt the conversation will turn towards the possibility of war. Please tell the German that this is happening and that you hope to learn something from the gathering that may be of interest to the Third Reich. Arrange to meet him on the following Saturday. I'll give you a prepared script."

"That's excellent, Sir John. Thank you very much."

"Esther's too precious to me to be left to the disgusting plots of these vile hooligans. Besides, I made a promise to her parents."

"They know they owe you everything, Sir John. Thank you."

"Two things remain. I don't know what kind of an actress you are, Esther, but you're going to have to convince the German that you're not giving false information. Pretend to feel dirty in betraying me and the country that adopted you, yet demonstrate your acceptance that this is the only way of saving your parents."

"I think I can do that. Will George be there, Roger?"

"Yes. Unseen as ever. What was the second thing, Sir John?"

"The truth is that while this deception is helping us it's only buying time for Esther's parents. They may be free to walk the streets of Berlin, but sooner or later this game will run out and they'll be arrested. What then?"

Sir John and Esther turned to Roger, who shrugged his shoulders.

"We'll just have to get them out. And soon."

CHAPTER 21

Young Love

London, Tuesday 15 to Friday 18 August 1939

"'Ere guv", Joe began, "there's three more of 'em in that 'ouse in Sussex Gardens. I let the other three go coz I was down to follow the usual Nazi, but d'yer think them others might be bad guys too?"

"I'm sure they are," Roger replied.

"Wot yer gonna do about 'em?"

"I'll pass this on to my police contacts. You stick with target number one."

The three of them were sitting in their usual spot at Charing Cross station having what Roger called a "catch up" meeting. All of them sensed that things were coming to a head, both in their own operations and in the approach to possible war. The newspapers were reporting that German troops were heading east towards the Polish border, and Britain and France's efforts at forging an alliance with the Soviet Union seemed to be floundering. The boys read the *Globe* every day and kept abreast of events.

"Do you have descriptions of the other three men, Joe?" Roger asked.

"Course."

Joe then gave Roger comprehensive details of the other three. The journalist jotted it all down.

"Brilliant. Thanks, Joe."

George joined the conversation.

"Is Esther gonna be alright, guv?"

Joe gave a wide-eyed glance towards his friend. Roger pretended not to notice.

"I hope so George, I really do. We're going to have to be on our toes now if we're going to get her out of the trouble she's in."

"Count on us."

"You needn't say that," said Roger. "I know you're both one hundred per cent behind this. Now, on Saturday, do your usual jobs. Esther's going to meet the German up in Hampstead at their normal spot in the evening. Joe, you follow him there, and George, you keep an eye on Esther until Joe and the German arrive."

"Wiv pleasure," said George with great enthusiasm. Joe glanced at his friend again with a smirk on his face.

"Don't bother getting too close. Esther will tell us later what went on. Just keep an eye on her, and if she gets into trouble, create some sort of diversion so she can get away. I'm sure that's not going to happen but, just in case, think about it."

"No problem," said Joe. "I'll saunter up to 'im and ask 'im for a light. I'll drop me fag and while he's distracted the girl can scarper."

"Sounds good. But we're desperate that this shouldn't happen, and there's no reason why it should. The last thing we want now is for one or both of your faces to be known to the German."

"Guv," asked George, "if 'e turns really nasty can we lay into 'im?"

"No," Roger replied firmly. "I could never live with myself if either of you got hurt."

"Just askin'. 'E deserves a right kickin' for what 'e's doin' to Esther."

Joe looked at his friend for the third time, a big broad smile on his face.

"Right, that's it lads. Good luck and keep in touch. Thank you."

◆   ◆   ◆

Roger walked back up the Strand to his office. Once again he thanked his lucky stars that he had Joe and George on his side. Despite the optimism he'd shown to the boys, he was becoming increasingly worried about the Hampstead end of things. Happy as he was with the Irish business, safe in the hands of Special Branch, tangling with Gestapo agents was quite another matter. He had no doubt at all that the boys would set about the German, but he was a big, tough man and, although George looked strong for his age, he wouldn't stand a chance. Joe, much slighter, would be blown away like a paper bag.

Roger rang Moss at Scotland Yard, but he was busy elsewhere. He left a message asking if the Sergeant would call him back and then got on with his work. After answering the phone several times with disappointment, Roger was relieved to hear Moss's voice just before lunch.

"Good afternoon Sergeant. Thanks for ringing."

"'Ello, Mr Martin. what's the latest?"

Roger recounted to the policeman everything that Joe had told him, including full descriptions of the four Germans, or rather the men he was sure were German.

"Right. I'll get on to this right away. Now we've got plenty of extra men I can cover this lot and the Irish. We might even crack open a Nazi cell. That'll be a feather in the Branch's cap and put MI5's noses well out of joint."

"Just one thing. Could you just follow them, keep them under watch, and leave the person whose description I gave you first to us. There's two people in Germany whose lives are at stake here, and if we arrest any of the Germans, those two people are going to die."

"Sounds complicated to me, but I'll do it coz it's you. I 'ope yer know what yer doin'."

"So do I, Sergeant. So do I."

◆　　◆　　◆

Richard Walker and Roger were enjoying a pint of bitter at the Anglers at the end of Kingston High Street. Roger had dashed there straight from work and Richard had enjoyed a slow stroll from the store after his day was finished. Of the day's three meetings, this was the one that Roger thought was the most important. After exchanging some small talk, Roger began.

"We're well on the way to sorting out that business at Sir John Blum's house. The old boy has allowed her to photograph some documents, either useless or fake, and she'll pass them on to the German."

"Leading them up the garden path, eh? Sounds good."

"And Sir John's having a meeting of so-called 'important colleagues' on Monday evening at his house. They'll probably talk about cricket or something. After it's over Sir John will feed Esther some more misleading titbits and she'll give them to the German when they next meet."

"Sounds better and better, but . . ."

Richard could read Roger like a book and knew full well that his young friend hadn't asked to meet him just to give an update.

"All this helps Esther, but it does nothing for her parents except keep them alive. As soon as the information dries up, Berlin will be informed, and her parents will be whisked off to a camp. That'll probably be the last she or her brother see of them."

"So, what do you suggest?"

"We get them out."

Richard was visibly taken aback, and spluttered the beer that had just entered his mouth. He wiped his chin with a handkerchief, cleared his throat and looked up at his friend.

"You must be barking mad. It would be easier to climb Mount Everest. There's every sign that war's on the way, and the Nazis will have their borders locked tight. It'll be impossible to get anyone out, especially a couple of Jews. Anyhow, who's going to bring them out?"

"No idea," said a crestfallen Roger. "I thought that perhaps you might have some suggestions."

"Well I'll tell you who isn't going to be doing it. You! As soon as you step over the border you'll be arrested. You wrote all those nasty things about them after Kristallnacht. They won't have forgotten that. After they've roughed you up a bit you'll be deported. Anyway, what contacts do you have in Germany? This can't be a one-man show."

"Of course, I know that, but . . . "

"Before you ask, I'm a lame duck as well. Last time I was there was to help the Gerbers get out. Before they escaped and after I'd left, Benjamin

Gerber was arrested by the Gestapo and interrogated about his relationship with the 'English spy' Walker. Apart from that, any past association with the Gerbers is likely to lead to more than just deportation for me. On that abortive voyage of the *St Louis* Jonathan Gerber beat a couple of Nazis to a pulp."

"I heard that. He sounds like a good lad."

"He is, but he only got away with it because the ship's captain was anti-Nazi. The Germans have memories like elephants and files on everyone. As soon as I arrived I'd be taken to some basement, beaten up, then shipped off to Sachsenhausen. I'd probably meet up with Esther's parents there."

Roger's beer was untouched. He sat with head bowed, hands clasped between his knees. A moment or two passed before he sat up straight and looked at Richard.

"What about Harry?"

"Ah! I wondered when we would get round to him."

"Any chance there?"

"Not a cat in hell's of him going into Germany. He wouldn't survive minutes. He's even more unpopular than you or me. Not that they know anything about his, err, activities. But a former German, now British citizen . . . Well, you can see what I mean."

"Of course, I understand that, but what about his contacts?"

"Obviously our man in The Hague would be the best bet. He absolutely loathes the Nazis, as you know, and might relish the opportunity to put another one over the Hitler mob. He did a good job for you tracking that Irishman in Brussels, or rather his man Willi did."

"You can say that again, and that's really what's led us to the present Nazi agent who's bothering Esther."

"Our agent in the German Embassy in The Hague is very well known, so he wouldn't be able to undertake any of the legwork himself. But, and this is what Harry tells me, he knows plenty of people in the anti-Nazi underground. That could be very useful. But it won't be easy."

"OK, that's a given, but where do we go from here?"

"I'll get in touch with Harry and see what he thinks. There may not be a lot of time given the present situation over Danzig, so we'll have to move fast. First job is for you to get a full description of the Abrahams from Esther, as well as their address. She mustn't breathe a word about this to anyone."

"What about Sir John Blum?"

"Excepting him. She might need him later on if the parents reach our shores, His influence could stop the police deporting them as soon as they arrive."

"Surely they wouldn't?"

"Indeed. A couple of Germans arriving at Dover or wherever with war possibly about to break out? I wouldn't fancy their chances. Of course, they might be interned. That could be sorted out later. We're a long way from that. Let's just take one step at a time. One more thing. When you see Esther, ask her if she has any photographs of her parents. Could be useful for fake passports."

"No use in Germany, I would imagine, but some form of disguise might be important."

"Definitely not, but once they're over whichever border they cross, they'll need them. Germany doesn't have any allies in western Europe—well, perhaps Italy—but all the countries that border them are anxious not to create any diplomatic incidents that might upset their warlike neighbours. Hang on. you mentioning disguises has given me an idea."

"What's that?"

"I'll tell you when I've thought it through. By the way, be careful not to let this German see you with Esther. The Nazis might be dreadful, but some of them aren't that stupid. They'll soon smell a rat."

"Don't worry about that. My lads will watch my back."

"Of course."

"Thank you very much, Richard. Another pint?"

"Why not?"

◆　　◆　　◆

Joe and George were kicking a football about in the park near to their East London home while Richard and Roger were sinking pints in Kingston.

Temperatures were still high, but it was cloudy and humid. They were sweating profusely and after a quarter of an hour decided to take a break. Sitting on their jumpers, which had been serving as goalposts, they were silent for a while, and then Joe spoke up.

"Wot's wiv you and this Esther?"

"Wot d'yer mean, wot's wiv me and Esther?"

"When we was wiv the guv this mornin', you kept mentionin' 'er."

"So wot? I'm worried about 'er. That German's treatin' 'er like shit."

"Are yer sweet on 'er?"

George was in full blush, and he looked away from Joe, who asked, "Is she pretty?"

"I suppose so."

"C'mon George, own up, yer've got a crush on 'er."

"Wot if I 'ave?" George replied, his voice rising. "Any 'ow, she's older than me. Not much can come of it."

"Rubbish. Me mum's four years older than me dad and they get on OK."

"Well per'aps. We'll see."

"Is she pretty?"

At last George relaxed. "Not 'arf. You'll see her yerself on Sat'day, all bein' well."

"Yer know," continued Joe, "what we're doin', we're doin' for England and the guv, in that order. Now this bloody jerry's bein' 'orrible to my best friend's girl. 'E'd better watch out."

The pair of them burst into laughter.

"C'mon. Fifteen more minutes of three and in, then we'll go 'ome."

◆　　◆　　◆

Klein was sitting opposite his boss Wolf in the Carlton House Gate office. Joe was behind the bushes opposite keeping watch.

"You've done very well, Klein. Berlin is pleased with you."

"Thank you, sir."

"We may be reaching the end of our mission here. The Führer's patience is running out with Poland. We desperately need to know what the British will do if we attack Poland."

"I hope to find that out tomorrow. I'm meeting the Jewish girl in Hampstead. I'm sure she'll have some information for us."

"What makes you so certain?"

"Her parents. She knows what will happen to them if she doesn't come up with the goods. She won't like what she's doing, but she'll do it. Blood, as the English say, is thicker than water."

"Excellent. On that front, my colleagues in Berlin assure me that they continue to have the mother and father under surveillance twenty-four hours a day. They can't possibly slip through our net."

"Thank you, sir. That's good news."

"And the Irish business?"

"All set for next week."

"I look forward to reading about it in the English newspapers. It should be a front page story."

"It will be, sir."

"Now Klein, on another matter. We have to prepare for the worst, like their boy scouts. If we attack Poland and Chamberlain keeps his promise and tries to go to the rescue of the Poles, we'll have to leave England, obviously. You must be ready to leave, and don't leave any loose ends. If necessary, kill the girl. That will be one less Jew to worry about."

"Is that really necessary, sir?"

"Of course. You'll be serving the Führer."

Klein sighed inwardly to himself. He was a policeman, not a murderer. The thought of killing an innocent person, Jewish or not, was total anathema to him. Slapping the odd person about in order to get them to do as he asked was something he was prepared to do. But murder—no. He was enjoying outwitting the English in his role of a spy in the country of a potential enemy. He was a patriot and he did what he did for Germany, not for the tinpot Führer, whom he despised. As much as he hated Hitler, he detested Wolf and his ilk almost as much—black-uniformed, heel-clicking self-servers. When Hitler came to power, Klein had been a young policeman, relishing his job. Then the slimy Himmler had swept all of Berlin's detectives into the SS and he found himself working for the Gestapo. Well, he thought, I'll complete my duties here to the best of my ability and that would not include killing the girl.

"Right, sir. Will there be anything else?"

"Yes. I myself will be returning to Berlin early next week. I'm wanted at the centre of things, of course. These are momentous times for the Reich and my superiors insist that I'm present to play my part."

Klein had to swallow hard to prevent himself from being sick. If Germany goes to war and we have to rely on slimy toadies like Wolf, we'll lose, he thought to himself.

"We shan't meet here again and I'm leaving you to wind down our operations before we leave. I have here the names and addresses of the other agents working for me in London. I want you to use the other three in your team to inform these on the list to be ready to leave at a moment's notice. They've done a fine job and, thanks to them, we have all of the necessary information; locations of airfields, docks, factories, roads, bridges and so on, necessary for the Wehrmacht when they launch their no doubt successful invasion of England. They also have details of English people sympathetic to our cause, and this includes Members of Parliament, members of their ridiculous aristocracy, civil servants, even a bishop. Those lists and the contact details of those on them must be taken back to Germany. We may need those people in the years to come. Do you understand?"

"Yes sir. I'll brief my men as soon as I can."

These must be a revolting lot, thought, Klein, to be ready to betray their country for Hitler. On the other hand, he reminded himself, my country comes first. I'll do my duty.

"Right, Klein, you may go. I'm glad that you have been able to flourish here under my leadership. I look forward to meeting you again in Berlin."

Klein stood up, awaiting a special rendition of the German greeting from Wolf, and it wasn't long in coming.

"Heil Hitler," roared Wolf, with his right arm stretched so tight that Klein believed that his superior officer might damage a muscle in his shoulder. Heels clicked smartly.

"Heil Hitler," responded Klein with as much enthusiasm as he could muster.

Klein stood on the top of the steps outside the embassy and lit a cigarette. God, I need a drink after that, he thought to himself as he drew the smoke into his lungs. Less than fifty yards away the watching Joe heaved a sigh of relief. "Thank 'eavens 'e's on the move. I'm dyin' for a smoke," he thought. Joe hadn't dared light up in his place of concealment. Smoke rising from the bushes would have betrayed his presence. He set off in pursuit of Klein, whom he hoped would visit the Eros News Theatre so that he could see the latest episode of *Flash Gordon*.

CHAPTER 22

Conspiracy

London, Saturday 19 and Sunday 20 August 1939

It was a sunny Saturday in Uxbridge as Donovan put the final touches to his plans for the following week. Unaware that he was under close surveillance but, as always, suspecting the worst, he'd spent the last few days using pub and shop phones to issue orders for the plot. Despite the arms dump in Coventry being accidentally detonated, he still felt that next Friday's "exercise" there would go ahead as planned. The Woolwich bomb, ready but not primed, would have to be delivered on Tuesday evening, with the action scheduled for early on the following morning. A quick telephone message, and the arrangements were made for the suitcase to be handed over at the busy Holborn station during the rush hour. That business being concluded, Donovan decided to take advantage of the fine weather, and spent the afternoon sitting, strolling, smoking and reading in Richmond Park.

Not many miles to the north of Richmond, Esther was becoming increasingly anxious about meeting with Klein later in the day. She tried without success to focus on her duties, and by the time Sir John's coffee was due to be served she was a bag of nerves.

"Esther, my dear, you are understandably very upset about this evening's meeting with this German."

"I am, Sir John. I'm not sure that I can carry it off, you know, telling him a pack of lies without him becoming suspicious."

"Yes, that may well be difficult. But what I suggest is this. You are upset about your parents, about seemingly letting me down, and that's how you must appear. After you've handed over the film, appear aggressive, demanding news of your parents and asking if he would keep his promise. Tell him if he sticks to his part of the deal, you will get him more useful information. Then tell him about next Tuesday's meeting here and ask for fresh film for the camera. That should convince him."

"Thank you, Sir John. I'll do my best."

"Oh, and another thing. Mr Martin has telephoned. He'll be calling in to talk to you after he's seen the German safely on his way back to London. He's bringing his fiancée with him, I believe."

"Do you think he's been able to do something about my parents?"

"I've no idea, but he does seem a remarkably resourceful young man. After all, he uncovered your business with the German, didn't he?"

"I suppose so. I hope he can do something."

"The reason that he was able to get permission to visit us here was because a very senior colleague of mine vouched for him. He described him as a most courageous young man who wasn't afraid to say what he thought and back it up with action. I'm certain that if anyone can sort this mess out, he can."

"Thank you, Sir John."

Esther left the room and resumed her duties, aware that time would pass agonisingly slowly and that a long afternoon lay ahead.

◆   ◆   ◆

Sussex Gardens was also bathed in sunshine. Outside, Joe watched the house like a hawk, while taking regular drags on his Woodbine. Inside, Klein and his team were also smoking. They sat in a back room surrounded by dirty dishes and empty coffee cups.

"Right, gentlemen," Klein began. "We have some very important tasks to undertake. Wolf," he said with a look of distaste on his face, "is on his way back to Berlin. We shall soon follow. He expects that the Reich will invade Poland very soon, possibly as soon as next weekend. If that happens then the British and French may well honour their pledges to the Poles and declare war on us. Then, of course, we'll be interned and of no use whatsoever, locked up in a cell for the duration of any war."

"That won't be much fun," one of the men added. "How long do you think the war will last?"

"No idea. What I do know is that we must prepare to leave soon. That doesn't mean packing your suitcases and not forgetting your toothbrushes, it means tying up all loose ends. I've got a big job on tonight and there may be more of it to follow. I hope to be bringing a film back with me. I'll give it to you straight away. Please get it to the darkroom immediately," Klein said, nodding at one of his subordinates.

Köhler nodded and Klein continued.

"When the film's developed, please take it to Harwich, Meier. It'll need to be rushed to Berlin as soon as possible. Meet the contact in the usual place. He'll take it to the MS *Elbe*."

Meier indicated his assent and Klein continued.

"Each of you will make contact with one of our other cells and tell them to tie up loose ends and be ready to leave."

"But isn't that a bit dangerous?" asked Werner. "The whole point of our operation here is that very few people know who our colleagues are and what they're doing. If one of us gets arrested by the English police we won't be able to tell them anything because we don't know anything."

"Of course," Klein replied, "but we'll have to take that risk. Wolf has left me in charge."

"If Wolf got arrested the English torturers would only have to pull one hair out of his head and he'd be singing like a bird," Schwarz said.

Klein joined in the general laughter. "Good job he's already safe back in Berlin. So, see your agents and get all final information from them—notes, photographs, drawings, timetables, maps, plans, whatever they've got, and get everything down to Harwich. The *Elbe* and the *Ganter* are the two ships we'll be using, with rendezvous in the usual place."

"How do we pass this information to the other cells?" asked Werner.

"I'm just coming to that. Werner, you will contact Schmidt, Schwarz, get in touch with Fischer, and I'll deal with Weber."

Klein handed around sheets of paper.

"Here are their contact details. When you've passed on the messages, destroy these. I wouldn't like them to fall into the wrong hands. And Werner, bring the car to Hampstead this evening and collect me after my meeting is concluded at, say, six thirty. I'm tired of the trolleybus and Underground."

Outside, Joe was waiting patiently. So, he noted, were others. Roger had told him that the police were likely to turn up, but wouldn't be interfering with his job. "Funny," he thought, "I can spot them, but it doesn't look like they can see me." The front door of the Sussex Gardens house opened about an hour later and three men trooped out, climbed in the car and drove off. Klein wasn't amongst them, Joe noted. After the Germans' car had departed, followed by an unmarked police Wolsey at a respectable distance, Joe settled back and ate a sandwich and watched. If he'd got this right, it looked like a tube trip followed by a trolleybus ride later in the day.

◆   ◆   ◆

George was already on Hampstead Heath, also enjoying the fine weather. He didn't expect to see Esther before the evening but, he thought to himself, better safe than sorry. Sometimes during these long hours of surveillance he'd wished he smoked. Anything to pass the time. But today that wasn't a problem. He could daydream about Esther all day long.

Roger was at home talking to Jane. He was like a cat on hot bricks and couldn't sit still.

"For heaven's sake," said Jane. "Calm down. You've done all you can."

"Yes, I know that, but will this deception work? There are lives at stake, you know."

"I know, but worrying about it won't guarantee its success."

Further conversation was curtailed by the ringing of the telephone and Roger went into the hall to answer it. It was Richard.

"Got some good news, Roger. Harry's on board."

"That's brilliant, Richard. Thank you."

"There's a heck of a lot to be done and not much time to do it. Do you want to come round or shall I tell you over the phone?"

"No, I'll walk round. I need the exercise. Jane's with me."

"Good. Bring her too."

Half an hour later the three of them were sitting in short-sleeved shirts or blouses in Richard's garden, sipping tea and munching on scones.

Richard started the ball rolling.

"Harry was delighted to be asked. He spoke to Willi by telephone in The Hague, and said he would be coming across on Monday with all the details for an important operation. How far are you with collecting all the information needed for this job?"

"I should have everything tonight. We're both going up to Hampstead."

"Great. Bring it all round first thing tomorrow and I'll see that Harry gets it straight away. It's going to be incredibly tight, you know. Harry reckons that Hitler's all ready to invade Poland. It could be as soon as next weekend. If we can't get the Abrahams out before any war, they've had it."

"I know. We'll just have to hope that Hitler gets cold feet and either postpones the invasion or even cancels it," Roger replied.

"How on earth can this be organised at such short notice?" asked Jane.

"No idea," Richard replied. "That's up to Harry's man in the German Embassy at The Hague. I presume that the photographs are needed both for recognition and to prepare documents."

"Documents? You mean identification cards, passports and so on?"

"Yes, but I'm not sure exactly what."

"How will they get out, Richard?"

"No idea. One thing's for certain, it won't be by train. You can hardly move without having your papers checked. And with the Gestapo paying particularly close attention to these two it will be impossible. My guess is they'll have to be hidden and smuggled out by car."

"To where?" persisted Jane.

"Again, no idea. They won't go east, that leads to Poland. North to the Baltic would mean a longish sea trip to Sweden, and there's no knowing how they might react to two German refugees. South is Switzerland, who would send them straight back—they don't want to upset the Germans—

and south-west is France. That would be the most heavily protected border of all. There's been a big build-up of troops there. The Nazis are worried that if they attack Poland, France will retaliate. No. My best guess would be west to Belgium or the Netherlands, and then to England by steamer."

"And then what?" continued Jane. "Will they be welcomed here?"

"Now that's the big question," answered Richard. "The police could put them on the next ferry back across the Channel."

"Surely not?" Jane said with her voice rising.

Roger joined the conversation.

"Didn't you read about those two Jewish teenage boys who fled from Berlin, rode on lorries to the Swiss border, crossed it, got arrested and thrown into a cell? The Swiss took them to the French border, where they were again arrested, this time jailed, and taken to one of the Channel ports—I can't remember which. They crossed the Channel and landed at Folkestone, where they were again handcuffed, spent a night in the police cells, and were brought up in front of the magistrates the following morning."

"Then what happened?" asked Jane.

"The magistrates recommended they be deported, but the court solicitor who was defending them got in touch with the Home Office, and they've been allowed to stay."

"That's a blessing," said Richard. "I thought your story was going to have an unhappy ending, Roger. Having said that, there are plenty of anti-Semites in this country, nothing like Germany of course, who'd like to see the back of the Jews. Folk like Moseley, William Joyce, that awful MP Maule Ramsay, Lord Londonderry, even the recent King, the Duke of Windsor."

"I bet they'll all be locked up if war breaks out?" Jane said.

"Let's hope so," the other two said in unison.

◆   ◆   ◆

Klein and Joe were on the trolleybus en route to Hampstead. Roger and Jane were in the Morris heading for the same location. George was already there, relishing another chance to see Esther and perhaps even speak to her. It must have been one of the hottest weekends of the year and he was glad of the shade afforded by the trees on Hampstead Heath.

◆   ◆   ◆

In Berlin Hartmann was sweating profusely, despite the fact that he'd hardly lifted a finger or moved a muscle since morning. He was watching the Abrahams' flat and had not had a sight of them all day. He knew they were in there, however, because figures had been seen through their windows. Why didn't they go out? Then again, perhaps he was glad they hadn't. It was far too clammy to go chasing people around the city. Schultz was due to replace him in an hour. Stick it out till then, he told himself.

Nothing happened until his partner's arrival.

"Nothing to report," Hartmann told Schultz. "They haven't moved a centimetre outside the building since I took over from you. Good luck with the night shift."

"Thanks. I hope it'll cool down when it gets darker."

"Bound to," replied Hartmann. "Do you ever wonder if this isn't all a waste of our time?"

"I reckon you're right. Every day the same thing. Man goes to his office. Woman goes shopping mid-morning, then goes to his office, presumably to take him his lunch. They're there for about an hour or so, and then she goes home and waits for him to return. I can't imagine they're up to much."

"Nor me. See you tomorrow."

◆   ◆   ◆

Roger parked in view of the trolleybus, but further down the road from the route he knew the German would take. He didn't want Klein walking past the car and seeing him and Jane sitting together in the front seats. Three more passengers got off, then a teenage boy with a flat cap set at an angle on his head. Joe headed straight into the woods, while Klein didn't enter the trees until about fifty yards further up the road. Esther crossed the road from Sir John's house and followed the same path as Klein.

Joe made his way into the woods and was wondering where George was when his friend emerged from behind a tree.

"All set?" asked George.

"Course. Let's find a spot where we can keep an eye on 'em. Remember the drill if fings go wrong."

Esther was sitting on a bench at the agreed spot when Klein appeared. Her head was looking down at her feet and she seemed totally miserable.

"Got anything for me?" asked Klein.

She looked up at him.

"Yes. Here's your wretched film," passing the small cylinder to Klein.

"What's on it?"

"How should I know? It means nothing to me."

"Heard anything?"

"No. He's not been coming back from London until late most nights. I just give him his supper and he goes to bed. He sets off early most mornings. What about my parents?"

"If there's anything on this film, I'll see they won't be arrested, for the time being at least."

Angrily, she stared at her German tormentor.

"You said you'd leave them alone if I co-operated."

"And I'll keep my promise, for another week or so at least."

"A week, is that all?" Esther shouted.

"Look at it this way. Every little job you do for me buys your parents a short spell of freedom. As soon as you dry up as a source, I'll have them arrested."

"You're a horrible man."

"I'll take that as a compliment. We'll review the situation next Saturday. Same time, same place. Here's another film. You know how to load it into the camera?"

Esther mumbled a yes and then took a deep breath.

"There is one thing. Sir John has told me he's expecting some important visitors next Tuesday at seven. I have to prepare drinks and snacks for them."

"Ah, you see. You may be able to keep your parents out of a concentration camp after all. Will you be able to listen in?"

"Of course. I'll be in and out of the room all evening."

"Excellent. Good night, Esther. I'll see you next Saturday. Don't disappoint me."

Klein strode off, thinking to himself that he might put in an appearance on Tuesday night to see what kind of guests would be at Blum's party. The girl was clever and could be making up the event just to keep him satisfied. She might even feed him a load of nonsense just to keep her parents safe. Unlikely, he thought, and if she led him into a trap her parents would be behind bars in Sachsenhausen within twenty-four hours. He turned right out of the woods and walked fifty yards to a car, waiting with its engine idling. The German climbed in and the car drove off.

As soon as the vehicle disappeared around a corner, Joe appeared, accompanied by George, who'd found a place of concealment, and Esther. She's gorgeous, he thought to himself. George is a lucky boy. Roger's Morris drove up and he wound the window down.

"I'll find a place to park. You three head to the house. I'll meet you there."

"Wot, all of us, guv?" George asked with surprise.

"Yes. All of you. If we get Esther out of this mess, it'll be mostly down to you two."

Sir John opened his door and welcomed the three. He showed no surprise at the presence of George and Joe. Roger and Jane hurried to the door. Introductions were made and the plotters were ushered into the lounge.

"Esther, my dear. Just for a moment would you be kind enough to resume your normal duties. Cook's prepared sandwiches and cakes and the kettle will be warmed. Bring it all in on a tray and, oh, two large glasses of lemonade."

George and Joe, both of whom were very nervous, were clutching their caps in front of them, but relaxed and smiled with the mention of lemonade. The boys sat forward on the edge of a settee smarter than anything else they'd seen in their lives. They began to relax further when Sir John congratulated them on the work they were doing which, he promised them, was of vital importance to their country.

Esther came in with the tray and everyone settled down to what was, to Joe and George, a feast. Jane and Sir John were chatting about the world of finance, and Roger was getting a report from Esther and the boys on the meeting with Klein.

"Well," began Sir John, "it all seems to have gone rather well. Let's hope we'll have similar success on Tuesday. What's next?"

"To get Esther's parents out of Berlin," Roger replied.

"And how are the arrangements for that progressing?"

"OK so far, but we need some help from Esther—names and addresses of her parents, and as many photographs of them as you have."

"I'll go and get it all straight away."

Esther reappeared five minutes later with a sheet of paper and several photographs. Roger seemed happy. He pocketed them and stood up to leave, thanking Sir John for his hospitality. The boys thanked him too, but Esther seemed strangely withdrawn. Jane took her hand.

"Tell me what's the matter, Esther?"

"You're all wonderful people, but what chance have they got of pulling this off? The Nazis have so many policemen and informers and they're terribly cruel."

"Roger knows that. He was in Berlin on Kristallnacht. He knows what they're like. He's got some very capable friends. If anyone can arrange for them to escape, he can."

CHAPTER 23

Success And Failure

London, Monday 21 to Thursday 24 August 1939

Roger went to see Richard on the Monday following, after the usual Sunday lunch with his family and Jane. He told Richard that all had gone well in Hampstead, but that this deception had only a limited life and that, sooner or later, the Germans would smell a rat.

"And what's more, war could be just a week away if intelligence reports from Berlin are reliable," Richard began. "If Hitler's going to attack Poland, he must do it in the next two weeks or he risks the army being held up by the late autumn rains. It's not like the old days, you know, when campaigning couldn't begin until the harvest was in."

"In other words, another good reason to get the Abrahams out of Berlin before it's too late," added Roger, who then handed over the photographs and address that Esther had given him on the previous evening.

"Thanks. I'll take these to Harry first thing in the morning. Please tell your father I won't be in until after lunch."

"I will. I'm sure he'll understand."

◆　　◆　　◆

The following day, Roger was busy chasing up a story of spying in Perth, Scotland, where he'd been for the notorious by-election during the previous winter. Throughout the summer, there had been a number of cases in which seemingly perfectly respectable people had been caught trying to sell secrets to a "foreign power", as Germany was described in the press. Rather oddly, three of the most recent had taken place in Scotland. "Rumblings of Scottish independence", Roger thought to himself.

His thoughts were interrupted by a call from Moss, the Special Branch detective.

"All quiet at our end, Mr Martin. We're watchin' all of the Irish suspects very closely. One thing you should know is that, as soon as we know they're about to act, we'll grab 'em first thing the followin' mornin'. You'll need to be up early to catch your story."

"Thanks. I'm planning to stay in a hotel at the top of the Strand. Our photographer will be there too. Any idea when?"

"No, but we're assumin' that it'll be the day after the bomb's been delivered by Donovan. Some of our men'll be in place to arrest 'im as soon as we've tied up the Woolwich end of things. I'm guessin' that Donovan will get the bomb to 'em soon after the two at the Woolwich end have finished work. I'll phone you in your office as soon as we know it's on. The whole thing's bound to 'appen in the next day or so. They can't risk the explosive becoming unstable and the thing goin' off, where the only damage'll be to 'emselves."

"OK. I'll go out and buy myself a toothbrush and book us in tonight. We'll stay there until it's over. As soon as I've found a hotel, I'll let you have the number."

"Right you are, Mr Martin."

◆   ◆   ◆

Charlie, Roger's photographer, was out on a job, so he had a quick word with Ben, his boss, and excused himself while he walked down to the Strand Palace Hotel and booked two rooms for that night and the following one. The hotel had been refurbished in art deco style about eight years ago, and the handsome building on the opposite side of the street from the Savoy now enjoyed splendid art deco interiors. Roger thought that expenses would run to his hotel, but not to the more famous establishment opposite. He walked back to the office, telephoned Moss to leave the hotel's telephone number, told Ben what was afoot and settled down to wait.

Charlie returned about teatime and Roger told the photographer to buy himself a toothbrush on his way to the hotel. Charlie pulled a face, then gave an ironic smile before leaving to telephone his wife to tell her that he wouldn't be home that night, and perhaps the following one as well. Roger had also phoned to both home and Jane to tell them where he was. The two of them walked to the hotel, checked in and went to their rooms, arranging to meet in the hotel restaurant an hour later.

Fifty minutes elapsed before Roger remembered that he should telephone Sir John to update him on the situation. Roger was told by Esther, who answered the call, that Sir John was still at the Foreign Office, so he told her that all of the information she'd given him had been passed to the people who were helping her. He asked her to convey this message to Sir John and said he might not be there the following night for the fake meeting, but she wasn't to worry because George wouldn't be far away. That seemed to reassure her.

Roger and Charlie had an excellent meal. They talked mostly about their jobs at the paper. Charlie called Roger "Prof", but, despite the difference in age and background, they got on well. The journalist briefed the photographer on their current mission. The meal ended, and the two of them drifted into the bar where they drank and chatted, waiting for the call that wouldn't come that night. At eleven o'clock they went to bed.

◆   ◆   ◆

George watched from his concealed spot as large cars containing important people pulled up at Sir John's house. One or two had chauffeurs, but most visitors drove themselves. All were dressed in dark suits, and their ages ranged from the mid-thirties to the over-sixties. At first it was light enough to leave the curtains open, and from time to time he caught sight of Esther and his heart beat faster. But George wasn't going to let Esther or anyone else distract him from his observation, and a short time afterwards he caught the sound of a car coming up the road. Klein left the car about one hundred yards from the house and walked casually past it, glancing at the gathering discussing what he thought were state secrets. To his satisfaction he noted that Esther was there serving drinks and snacks. He looked forward to hearing what had been discussed when he met her later in the week. Pleased, he walked back to his car and drove off. In the house the curtains had been drawn as darkness began to fall. Inside the discussion ranged from the final weeks of the cricket season through to the latest films, the health of everyone's families and the West End theatre. The international situation was never mentioned. George reluctantly set off home. His job was done for the night.

◆   ◆   ◆

Donovan awoke early. He had a busy day ahead of him. Assuming as ever that he was being followed, he concocted an elaborate plan to shake any pursuers. He studied the map of the London Underground and plotted a route. After that he left to do some shopping, before returning to prepare the bombs. His men would enter the armaments factory at eight. Donovan allowed them fifteen minutes to find suitable places to conceal the devices for maximum impact, and then a further quarter of an hour to somehow slip out of the factory to safety. The timers were set for eight thirty the following morning.

◆   ◆   ◆

Roger was sitting in the refreshment room at Charing Cross station sipping coffee. He and Charlie had enjoyed an excellent breakfast before the photographer had left for another job. Assuming the call to action didn't come during the day, they agreed to meet in the hotel restaurant at six. George and Joe arrived at Charing Cross a couple of minutes after Roger.

"Sorry we're late, guv. Trouble wiv the buses, lotsa traffic," said Joe.

"You're not late. I'm early."

"I couldn't foller the jerry last night. 'E set off by car. I reckon I'll 'ave to take lessons if I'm to do this job prop'ly."

Roger laughed and George began to speak.

"The jerry turned up at 'Ampstead. 'E wasn't there long. Parked up, took a walk up the road past the 'ouse, 'ad a look in, walked back to 'is car and drove off."

"Good. He was obviously checking up to see Esther was telling him the truth. How did the gathering inside the house look, George?"

"It was all toffs in suits. There was about ten of 'em. If I was watchin' the 'ouse like the jerry was I'd guess that summat important was goin' on."

"That's what we wanted him to think. Just keep doing what you're doing. I might not be about for a day or two, but it's important to keep a close watch on Klein and Esther. We're hoping to polish off the Irish business in the next couple of days. There might be something in the paper if all goes well, but it won't mention you. We can't have all the crooks and spies thinking that the British use teenage boys to keep an eye on them. Klein might read it, and instead of just looking for grown men following him he might be looking for the likes of you. Then you two could be in real danger and I'm not having that. But you'll get your just deserts, I promise you."

"Anyfin' else?" asked Joe.

"No. We'll meet here on Friday at the same time."

"Right. We'll get on wiv it."

◆   ◆   ◆

Just after four, Donovan left his house in Uxbridge. He was on foot and carrying a small suitcase. The Special Branch men followed him to Uxbridge Underground and on to a Piccadilly Line train. The Irishman was, as usual, reading a paper. At Piccadilly Circus he changed trains and caught a southbound Bakerloo Line service. He got out at Waterloo and, at the last minute, jumped onto a bus bound for Russell Square. Two Special Branch men managed to get on the same bus, but they were now seriously exposed. It was easier to follow on a tube train with its several carriages. Still, they persisted, and followed Donovan into the tube station. One went in the lift and the other raced down the narrow steep steps, arriving just in time to see the Irishman climb onto a westbound Piccadilly Line train. The policeman hoped his colleague was still about and was relieved to see him standing in an adjacent carriage.

From Piccadilly Circus the Irishman went south again on the Bakerloo Line, changing trains at Waterloo, boarding a northbound Northern Line train. Getting off at Tottenham Court Road, he walked briskly to the Central Line platform. Somehow the Special Branch men kept up and were still on Donovan's tail when he got off at Holborn, but the crowds in the station concourse area made it almost impossible to keep a close watch on him, so they didn't see the suitcase change hands and lost sight of their quarry completely. Panicking, they raced back to Uxbridge. The Irishman hadn't made it back. Perhaps he didn't intend to. One detective watched the house while the other phoned Moss at the Yard, who was annoyed that they'd lost Donovan, but not as angry as he might have been, as the watchers in Woolwich had spotted the suitcase being carried into the house in Wellington Street. The Uxbridge end of the operation was to continue and they were to wait for the IRA man's return. They'd be relieved at midnight.

◆   ◆   ◆

Roger and Charlie were enjoying another splendid dinner at the Strand Palace. Roger was on edge. He'd staked his reputation on this big scoop, and besides he had felt that he would, hopefully, put a spoke in the IRA's wheels and undermine their bombing campaign in England. For Charlie, on the other hand, this was just another job, although he realised, from what Roger had told him, that this was a big one. They were just enjoying their apple crumble and custard sweet when a voice at the entrance to the dining room announced, "Telephone call for Mr Roger Martin." He put down his spoon and fork and walked quickly towards the man who'd summoned him. He was directed to the reception desk and was pointed towards a telephone at the end of the counter.

"Hello. Roger Martin here."

"Sergeant Moss here, Mr Martin. We're goin' in first thing in the mornin' . . . We're not goin' to let 'em anywhere near the factory. We're gonna pick 'em up with the bombs in Wellington Street. Know where that is?"

"Yes. I've got my A to Z in case I get lost."

"Good. We'll make the arrest between seven and eight. We'll 'ave the 'ouse watched back and front so there's no chance the micks'll escape. Come on foot. We'll spot you before you see us. Don't forget your photographer."

"I won't. He's with me now at the Strand Palace."

"The Strand Palace eh? Alright for some."

"You'll soon be able to afford it, on an inspector's pay."

Moss laughed. "Another thing. We've lost Donovan fer the time bein'. A couple of me lads lost 'im at 'Olborn tube. Should've left it to your boys."

Now it was Roger's turn to chuckle. Moss was probably right, but he didn't want Joe and George in any more danger. Let the police deal with it, he thought to himself.

Moss continued.

"'E'll probably make 'is way back to Uxbridge. We'll snatch 'im there. See you tomorrow."

Roger thanked him, hung up, and made his way back to the dining room to rejoin Charlie.

"Right, we're on for tomorrow morning. We need to be in Woolwich by seven."

"Blimey, that'll mean a six o'clock start. I'll miss my beauty sleep."

"I'll go and order an early call and try to persuade them to give us some breakfast to take with us. Then I'm off to bed."

Roger went to the reception desk, asked for an early alarm, and enquired whether some packed food might be available. It would be, sandwiches and a couple of flasks. Setting off for his room, he wondered if the excitement would prevent him from sleeping. Probably, he concluded.

◆　　◆　　◆

Donovan knew his cover was blown. He was an old hand at avoiding surveillance, which was why he'd taken such precautions earlier in the day.

It was the two men jumping onto the bus at Waterloo that had confirmed that he'd been rumbled. Still, he'd lost them at Holborn and the case was in safe hands. Nothing could stop tomorrow's explosion. That he'd be in the Germans' good books pleased him, but he was much more satisfied when he thought of the delight of the IRA officers back in Dublin. The planned death and destruction of tomorrow might at last persuade the Brits that the IRA meant business. Perhaps that would convince them to get themselves out of the north of Ireland.

Reaching Uxbridge by a roundabout route, the Irish terrorist thought he'd got back unseen. He was wrong. The two Special Branch reliefs saw him sneak into his house just after midnight. One went to phone Moss, who was working a twenty-hour shift, or perhaps more, to ask for orders.

"Leave 'im for an hour, then break the door down and arrest 'im. 'Opefully 'e'll be asleep. I'll call the local nick and get some uniforms round to give you an 'and. I'll ask for firearms support just in case."

Inside the house Donovan was preparing his escape. Papers containing lists of codes and contacts were burned. He packed a small case, shoved his revolver into his coat pocket. He had several passports in different names and multiple tickets for various sea crossings. What came next he'd planned for a long time. Taking his shoes off, he left via the back window. The ground was baked dry, so his feet didn't get wet. Climbing carefully over the garden fence, he walked along the lane at the back of the house before setting off, cross-country towards Hillingdon. Here, in a garage, he'd secreted a Ford car, which was full of petrol and ready to go. He climbed in and pointed the car northwards, towards the Midlands.

Less than half an hour later there was a commotion in the street. A burly sergeant broke down the front door of the Uxbridge house. Two other uniformed officers did the same at the back. A local plain-clothed policeman led the others into the house, pistol at the ready. One by one he searched the rooms, each time finding nothing but emptiness. No sign of Donovan anywhere. He'd gone.

Moss was getting the bad news as Donovan was heading north. His destination was Coventry, where he had a bit of business to conduct before trying to leave the country. Just how he would do this was anybody's guess.

All the ports were bound to be watched, especially after the bombs went off at Woolwich. Still, he concluded, the Coventry business was more important. Escape would come later.

◆   ◆   ◆

Roger was woken up at quarter to six. As he predicted, he'd slept badly, but the thought of what lay ahead pumped adrenaline through him. A bleary-eyed Charlie joined him in the lobby and, after collecting their packed food and flasks, they walked out of the hotel into the London dawn. As Roger drove over Waterloo Bridge, the photographer chewed on his sandwiches and sipped from his flask. Heading east, traffic was light, and most of the few vehicles on the road were travelling toward the city rather than away from it. They reached the Woolwich Ferry in good time, but were alarmed to see a long queue of cars and other vehicles waiting to cross to the other side of the river. Probably early workers, most likely managers at the Arsenal, thought Roger. They parked up and joined the line of foot passengers waiting to board.

By twenty to seven Charlie was finishing his breakfast and Roger was just starting his. The sun was up and it looked like a hot day. As they approached Wellington Street a hand reached out from a doorway and pulled the pair towards him inside.

"You the boys from the *Globe*?"

"Yes."

"You're to wait 'ere. Sergeant Moss says you can take as many pictures as you like of the arrests but none of the bomb disposal boys or the armed officers. Understood?"

The clop of horses' hooves announced the arrival of the milkman.

"Get a move on," the policeman whispered in a nervous voice.

The milkman left bottles on some, but not all, doorsteps. The horse trudged slowly behind him. Roger glanced at his watch. Half past seven. Suddenly he spotted Moss appear from another doorway and flash his warrant card at the milkman, who picked up speed and disappeared around the corner. As soon as he had disappeared, the front door of the target house opened and two men stepped out, each carrying a satchel-type bag slung around his shoulders and looking nervously up and down the street. Suddenly, two policemen in plain clothes appeared and grabbed both men. The policemen carried knives, and quickly cut a strap on each bag, lowered it gently to the ground, grabbed the men by the scruffs of their necks and dragged them a hundred yards up the street. Two more policemen raced towards the bags and carefully opened them.

There was no bang. The two bomb boys fiddled away inside the bags and then looked up the street, where Moss and several uniforms were waiting for some sort of signal. One of the bomb disposal men gave the thumbs up and called out that the bombs were on a timer, which they had now disconnected. They were harmless. Moss blew his whistle and a small jeep appeared, followed by a black police van. The jeep paused beside the bomb disposal officers, who lifted the devices into the jeep, climbed in and were driven off.

"Right lads. It's all yours," the officer said to Roger and Charlie, who reached the prisoners just as Moss was reading them their rights. Charlie was snapping away furiously as handcuffs were produced and the two Irishmen were frogmarched into the waiting police vehicle, which then sped off, presumably to the nearest police station. The whole thing had lasted no more than five minutes, and those curtains not already opened were now pulled back, with at least one face staring anxiously out of each and every window.

"Right, let's get out of 'ere," said Moss. "'Appy, Mr Martin?"

"Very. Thank you, Sergeant."

"I am too. Thanks to you and yer lads. The only disappointment is that Donovan got away. 'E won't get far. We've got all the ports covered. Let's go and 'ave some breakfast. One of the local plod 'as told me there's a great caff just round the corner."

CHAPTER 24

Murder

Birmingham, London, Coventry and Berlin,
Thursday 24 and Friday 25 August 1939

Donovan was staring at himself in the mirror of a modest safe house in Birmingham's Small Heath district. The car was safely hidden in a garage a short distance away. He examined his dark beard and moustache, which he had been growing since the previous weekend. The failed Woolwich bomb plot would cause an enormous hue and cry, and the beard was part of the disguise which he knew he'd need to get safely out of England. He looked at his false passport in the name of Lewis, and noted with satisfaction that the photograph bore some resemblance to the face in the mirror. Hair cut short and with a pair of horn-rimmed spectacles perched on the end of his nose, Donovan reckoned that he would look like Lewis within two or three days. In the meantime, he had some preparation to do for the next day's action but, apart from that, he would stay in the house smoking, drinking, daydreaming and contemplating his escape from England.

But Donovan wasn't a happy man. Having pinned his hopes on blowing up the Woolwich Arsenal, he accepted that the whole thing had been a disaster. His men were in custody and probably singing like birds, the bombs had never reached the Arsenal, and he was almost certainly a hunted man. How had this come about, he asked himself. He'd been so careful and positive he hadn't been followed, until the very end. He knew

Special Branch were clever but he prided himself in spotting a copper a mile away. Certain that they hadn't been tracking him, it crossed his mind that someone else had been on his tail. But who? He soon realised that he would probably never find out. Then there were the Germans. He'd let them down. Their days as allies were probably over. Still, they would soon be at war with Britain, and there was every chance that they would win that war and that a united Ireland would be one of the outcomes of their victory. That, at least, would help to make up for the Woolwich disaster. The papers were full of it, and there were photographs of his men being led away in handcuffs. There was mention of a Roger Martin, a journalist on the *London Evening Globe,* whom it was said had tipped off the police, which had resulted in the abject failure of the bomb plot. Where had this Martin bloke got his information from? Donovan wondered. What else did he know? Definitely time to get out, he decided.

Turning his attention to his escape, Donovan decided that he would have to reach the south of Ireland. Fetching up in Belfast via Heysham, Liverpool or Stranraer was not an option. There'd be a large police presence when he docked. It would have to be Wales, either from Holyhead to Dublin or Fishguard to Rosslare. Once at sea he would be safe. He made a mental note to get hold of another car. By now he assumed the police would know all about the vehicle he'd had in London. Slipping his raincoat and hat on, he left the house to find a telephone box. He had one last important job to do.

◆　　◆　　◆

Richard Walker was drinking coffee in a small establishment opposite the British Museum. Sharing his table was a very small man with receding black hair and dark eyes who smiled at his companion and said, "Well Richard, how can I help you this time? Arrange to assassinate Hitler?"

"That would certainly be a good idea, Harry, but not practicable I'd guess."

"Oh, I don't know. You'd be surprised how many Germans would like to see him dead. Since he came to power there have been nine attempts to get rid of him. None have really come close, but it shows you just how many people have been prepared to risk their lives to get rid of that monster. One day, somebody might succeed."

"We live in hope," Richard said. "No, it's not that. It's helping the two Jews I told you about to escape."

"I thought so. Have you got the information and photographs?"

Richard handed Harry a thick envelope.

"Good. I'm going to The Hague this afternoon. I'll pass them over to our friendly anti-Nazis."

"Will they help?"

"Certainly. They'd do anything to put one over the black-suited boys. And this is especially important. It's not just helping a couple of decent Jewish people to escape. It's closing down their source of information here. That could be vital as war approaches."

"What's the latest on that?"

"Extremely likely. You'll find out later today that Ribbentrop and Molotov have signed a non-aggression pact on behalf of their countries, leaving Hitler free to invade Poland without fear of retribution from Russia."

"Good God! What on earth do you make of that?"

"I'm only guessing, but I don't think that Stalin is ready for war. He wants to buy himself a bit of time. He probably thinks that Germany will turn to Russia as soon as Hitler's mopped up Poland and then polished off Britain and France."

"Do you really think that'll happen?"

"Chamberlain may dither a bit and contemplate some kind of Munich style diplomacy, but, yes, he'll honour his pledge to Poland. How the British forces will fare is anybody's guess."

"How soon do you think all this'll happen?"

"The latest intelligence we have is have is that German troops are massing on the Polish border. German newspapers are reporting daily about crimes committed against German citizens by Poles, as well as border infringements by them. It could be as soon as this weekend."

"Heavens," replied a startled Richard. "If that's the case, it'll be impossible to get the Abrahams out."

"Exactly," Harry replied. "That's why the information that the Jewish girl in Hampstead gave to the Germans is so important. If Hitler thinks that Britain and France might declare war on Germany if he attacks Poland, he may cancel the invasion, or at least postpone it. That will buy us some time. So I'm off to Holland this afternoon with the material you've given me. I'll meet with Willi and see what can be done. He'll have a word with his boss, who's called Putlitz by the way, and plan something. These two Germans have plenty of contacts in the anti-Hitler underground in Berlin. They won't be short of help. My only other worry is that Putlitz thinks he may be under suspicion from the Gestapo. I hope he remains at liberty until this job can be finished. By the way, I've one or two ideas that should help."

Harry tapped his nose and Richard smiled.

"Thank you, Harry."

◆   ◆   ◆

Donovan's man, Joby O'Sullivan, woke up early in his small bedsit not far from the centre of Coventry. He had hardly slept, which was not surprising considering that in a short time he might be committing mass murder, although that was not his intention. He'd dismissed this from his mind. They were the enemy after all. And the IRA was at war. More worrying was the bomb. There'd been plenty of accidental detonations, including one just recently in this very town. If his bomb went off before its time he might end up like Donovan, with three fingers missing or perhaps a limb or, even worse, dead.

The bomb had been delivered by a reliable IRA man on the previous day. He hadn't liked it being in the house overnight. In a shed in the tiny back yard there was a brand new bicycle, brought from Halford's a few days before by another terrorist. A basket was attached to the handlebars. Donovan had told him that the bomb was likely to make a very big explosion and that he had to leave it in the street with time to spare so that he could escape and follow his orders to return to Cork.

No specific instructions had been given to him about where to actually place the bomb. O'Sullivan, like all of his comrades, hated the British, but had no desire to kill innocent people. He would find a place where it would cause the maximum amount of damage without risking civilian lives. He could place it near a barracks or another place where soldiers might gather. Their lives didn't matter to him. In the end, he decided that outside the police station was best. It would make a big mess of the building and if a passing policeman bought it, so much the better. O'Sullivan didn't count the police as innocent either. Carefully, as he had been instructed, he prepared the bomb. Setting the alarm clock for two thirty that afternoon, he calculated that he would leave it in place about five minutes before it was due to detonate, time enough he was sure to get away in the confusion, and catch a train to London before making his way back to Ireland.

The Irishman, the bicycle and the bomb set off from the small house just before two. At first everything went smoothly but, as he approached the city centre, it all went wrong. Not being a very experienced cyclist, the wheels of the bike kept getting caught in the tramlines, forcing him to stop, dismount and lift it clear of the rails. Coventry's main shopping area, Broadgate, was packed with shoppers, more than usual because Friday was market day. Panicking, he saw that it was already two twenty-five. He wouldn't reach the police station in time. Apart from perhaps a number of innocent people, the only person killed when the bomb went off would be himself.

A young girl was returning to the store where she worked as a shop assistant just before half past two, having enjoyed a late lunch. Her head was full of her wedding, which was due to take place in two weeks' time. She paid no attention to the bicycle propped against a lamppost nearby. Instead she gazed dreamily in a jeweller's shop window. She was still there two minutes later when the bomb went off, blowing her to pieces as she took the full force of the blast. Police investigators could only identify her by her engagement ring. Nearby four others were dead; a young boy of fifteen, two men aged eighty-two and fifty, and a thirty-year-old man who had also expected to be married in the near future, according to the following day's *Coventry Evening Telegraph*. Glass from nearby shops was strewn over the pavements. Other shoppers lay dazed, moaning and bloodstained. Seventy people were injured, some of them seriously.

Broadgate was a scene of abject terror and confusion, filled with the screams of the shocked, injured and dying. There was a brief lull in the hysteria as a stunned silence filled the air for a full five minutes before the arrival of the fire brigade, police cars and ambulances began the process of dealing with the scene of total confusion.

O'Sullivan had made it to the station and was anxiously awaiting the London train, which soon arrived on time, and he stepped aboard, bound for safety back home in Ireland. Only when he reached the capital did he learn of the Coventry horror, which he knew would haunt him for the rest of his life.

The police were quick to begin their investigation and had soon arrested the two men who had provided the bomb and the bicycle. They were brutally interrogated, charged, and told they would shortly appear before the city's magistrates. Despite claiming that they had not intended to kill anyone, they knew that their days would end in the hangman's noose.

Donovan smiled in satisfaction back in Small Heath. He was surprised and elated that there had been five deaths in Coventry. Not planned perhaps, but maybe this would persuade the Nazis that the IRA was still both active and effective. He looked again in the mirror. Not long now, he thought. Soon he would be ready to return to his beloved Ireland, possibly even a hero, at least amongst his IRA colleagues. Failure at Woolwich would soon be forgotten. Little did he know that those plans had been foiled by a pair of brave and resourceful teenage boys.

◆   ◆   ◆

George and Joe were watching, unseen, the latest meeting between Klein and Esther. The girl was putting on another convincing performance, telling the German of the previous Tuesday's meeting, which appeared to confirm much of the information he'd obtained from the film the previous week. This needed to go to Berlin immediately, he thought. Esther had explained that she'd hardly seen Sir John since the Tuesday meeting. He had spent long hours at the Foreign Office, returning only to snatch a few hours of sleep before making his way back to Whitehall after breakfast.

He'd never brought his briefcase with him, she explained. Klein seemed happy, and assured her that her parents would be unharmed. Same time, same place next week, he told her, and then left to wait for his lift back to Sussex Gardens.

After he'd gone, George and Joe emerged from their place of concealment and congratulated her on her performance.

"You should be an actress," Joe said. "Yer better than Katherine Hepburn."—the pair had recently seen her in the very funny *Bringing up Baby.*

"An' I could be yer Cary Grant," George added with a chuckle.

"You two are wonderful," Esther said and leaned forward and kissed them both on the cheek, lingering slightly longer on George's face than his friend's. "All this is very well, but what's going to happen to my parents?"

"Don't worry. Roger'll sort that out," George said.

"'E definitely will," added Joe.

"I hope so," Esther said. "Good night."

Joe and George caught the trolley bus back to King's Cross.

"Can't wait fer the guv to sort this out," George said. "Then she'll smile a lot more."

"She really likes you yer know. I could see she gave you a longer kiss than me."

"Are you jealous?" asked George.

"Not a bit," replied Joe. "There is one fing though."

"Wot's that?"

"Promise me I can be best man at yer weddin'."

◆　　◆　　◆

Harry and Willi were having a drink in an MI5 safe house in The Hague. The little spy had told the German everything.

"This is going to be very tough," Willi said. "I'll talk to Gans as soon as I get back to our residence."

The familiarity with which Willi referred to his boss suggested that the two were more than just master and servant.

"Tell him I'm hoping to use one of Korda's people, that might help."

"I know what you're thinking. It's a good idea. I'll get on with it straight away. When are you coming back?"

"Can you get the ball rolling over the next couple of days?"

"I'll have to and yes, I think I can."

"In that case, I'll meet you here on Tuesday. Is the Dutch border the best way out?"

"Probably. I'll ask Gans."

"OK. I'll get in touch with Korda's organisation and tell them that."

"We'll sort out the passports. Dutch I think."

"Thank you, and thank Gans for me."

"I will. From what he's been saying we may not be far behind you. He reckons that the Gestapo are on to us."

"I've heard that from him as well. It's all arranged for you at our end."

"Good. We'd better be getting on with this. There's not much time."

◆   ◆   ◆

At the Reich Chancellery in the heart of the government district of Berlin, Hitler looked like a man with much on his mind. Himmler and Ribbentrop were with him. Both remained silent while he sat motionless with his head in his hands. Himmler had already told the Führer of the intelligence that had come from the British Foreign Office, which suggested that Britain, and probably France, would fight if Germany invaded Poland.

Ribbentrop disagreed. The English, he argued, were weak and cowardly, and their Prime Minister Chamberlain was the worst of the lot. As soon as the Polish border was crossed, he'd come running with offers of talks. Then Poland could be overrun while the English congratulated themselves again on avoiding war.

Hitler remained silent. He looked at each man in turn with his dark piercing eyes. He still kept quiet. After what seemed an eternity, he looked at his two acolytes and told them that he was postponing the invasion until the following weekend. If the English didn't show any signs of aggressive diplomacy by then, he'd give the order for the destruction of Poland to begin.

$\mathcal{P}$uzzles

Berlin, Saturday 26 August 1939

Deborah Abrahams glanced anxiously at her husband.

"Looks like war, doesn't it? What will happen to us?"

"Funnily enough, nothing. If Germany attacks Poland, or anywhere else for that matter, the Nazis will be far too busy to bother about a middle-aged Jewish couple. The problem will come if they win. Then they'll have time to deal with the Jews."

"Let's hope they lose, then."

"That depends entirely on the British and French. If they keep their word to Poland, Hitler and his gang might have to scuttle back to Germany with their tails between their legs. And that might bring about the downfall of the Nazis."

"Let's pray to God that's how it works out."

The late summer weather was holding out brilliantly, and Berliners continued to enjoy themselves, although deep down they were growing ever more fearful of the war they'd been expecting since the beginning of the year. Two-inch high newspaper headlines screamed at them.

POLAND LOOK OUT
COMPLETE CHAOS IN POLAND—GERMAN FAMILIES FLEE
WARSAW THREATENS BOMBARDMENT OF DANZIG

There was a popular fear of war, but the SA were relishing the prospect, drunkenly marching along the streets in their brown uniforms shouting insults at Poland and the Polish people. In Wedding and other working class districts of the city there was total confusion. Despite years of Nazi purges, a strong Communist presence still existed. Their uncertainty was caused by the Nazi-Soviet non-aggression pact two days previously. The British ambassador, Sir Neville Henderson, was flying between London and Berlin almost daily trying to persuade Hitler not to attack Poland. The Nazis didn't think much of British Premier Neville Chamberlain, and he was frequently portrayed in the Nazi newspapers as a figure of fun. Nobody in the Nazi hierarchy took his threats seriously, except perhaps Hitler, who considered the intelligence that the Gestapo had collected from London thoughtfully. He wasn't sure, but nevertheless set full mobilisation of the German armed forces in motion on that last Saturday in August, the 26th.

Berliners now felt that war was certain and the city was plunged into desperation and fear. As part of the preparation for war the Gestapo began rounding up Social Democrats and Communists, many of whom had already undergone a period of "re-education" in a camp.

"They're starting to arrest all of the old comrades and members of the SD. I wonder when they'll get round to me," Simon said as he prepared to go to work.

"Never, I hope," his wife replied. "By the way, why are you going to the office? Surely you won't have any clients today on the Sabbath?"

Simon who, like his wife, was very much an "arm's length" Jew, smiled at her.

"No. It'll be very quiet, but there's a bit of paperwork I need to deal with."

"Shall I bring your lunch as usual?"

"No. I'll be home by lunchtime. We can eat here."

Over the past weeks, Deborah had taken to shopping in the morning and then calling in at her husband's office, where they ate snack lunches together.

"Tomorrow, though, is likely to be busy," Simon began. "While Christian Berlin is on its knees, Jewish Berlin is on its feet trying to earn a crust."

"OK. I'll see you back here at lunchtime." They kissed briefly and Simon left.

◆　　◆　　◆

With Schultz in tow, Simon made his way to the office. He knew the Gestapo man was on his tail but there wasn't a great deal he could do about it, so he decided to ignore him. At least on that fine morning he had nothing on his conscience—yet.

Back in their room Deborah did some rudimentary cleaning. Most of their possessions and property had been seized in the aftermath of Kristallnacht. Albert Speer's Rental Law had allowed Jews to be booted out of their properties, which were then demolished to make way for Speer's ridiculously over-ambitious design for the new Reich capital, Germania. So this task took up very little of her time, and it wasn't long before she set off to do the shopping. She always enjoyed this. It got her out of their poky little room and she often met people she knew with whom she could exchange gossip, usually about nothing at all.

This Saturday was no different from any other. Most of the chat was about rationing, which was expected to be announced on the next day, a sure indication that war wasn't far away. Deborah was unsettled by this because she guessed that the number of coupons earmarked for Jews would be considerably smaller than that given to the rest of the population. Still, she smiled to herself, a black market was bound to flourish, and she knew plenty of Jewish comrades who would make up the shortfall in weekly provisions.

Shopping was soon complete, including bread and cheese for their lunch. It was almost noon and her bag was nearly full. The crowds were growing by the minute as she threaded her way through them towards home, bumping against and apologising to her fellow shoppers. Suddenly she felt a gentle squeeze on her arm.

"Don't look at me, Mrs Abrahams," a man's voice urged her, "just carry on walking."

Deborah was more than a little bit frightened, and her first inclination was to look at the man. But she did as she was told.

"You'll be taken out of Germany on Monday. Read every single word of the newspaper I've put in your bag, I repeat, every word. All your instructions are there. Don't look at me after I'm gone. Good luck, Mrs Abrahams."

Deborah was totally shocked. Her legs felt like jelly and her heart was racing. She struggled home, put her bag down, flopped into a chair and pulled out the newspaper.

◆   ◆   ◆

"What on earth is that filthy rag doing in our home?" Simon exclaimed noisily as he returned home at lunchtime.

Deborah re-told the story of her strange encounter with the man who had shoved a copy of the Nazi newspaper *Völkischer Beobachter* in her shopping bag and told her to read every word when she got home.

"Why pick that paper?" Simon asked loudly. "It's a testament of lies from cover to cover."

"Perhaps not to arouse suspicion. A Jew would hardly read the *Völkischer Beobachter*."

"Hmm. I suppose so."

"And another thing. He said we would be taken out of Germany on Monday."

"Now you tell me," Simon said, staring incredulously at his wife "How's that going to happen?"

"All the instructions are in the newspaper."

Deborah stood up and went to the tiny kitchen to make lunch. When she returned Simon was still sitting staring into space, as he had been when she'd left.

"Do you think it's some kind of trick?" she asked.

Simon thought for a moment.

"I don't think so, no. The Nazis don't need to play tricks to get their hands on us. We're Jews, after all."

"In that case, as soon as you've eaten your lunch and drunk your coffee we'll start looking at the paper."

"We'll have to go out for a walk some time, otherwise our tail might become suspicious. After all, we always take a stroll on weekend afternoons. He might think we're up to something if we broke that pattern."

"Right," Deborah said, "drink up. We'd better get on with it."

Simon recognised that his wife was responding to these odd circumstances much better than he was, but then he silently excused himself by mulling over the fact that she'd known about this strange situation a little bit longer than he had.

Staring at the front the page of the paper, they began to read every word, as Deborah had been instructed. Painstakingly they closely examined every column. Simon sank back in his chair.

"I've read every word on that page and—nothing. What do we do now?"

"Read it again."

So they did. Suddenly Deborah let out an exclamation.

"*I see it.*"

"See what?"

"The letter *o* in that column," she said, pointing to the middle of the page. "It's got a finely pencilled dot beneath it. See if you can find some more letters with dots beneath them."

Simon started again at the top of the page and soon found a *y*, and Deborah came across a *u* towards the bottom. Simon took a blank sheet of paper from his briefcase and wrote in pencil: *you*. Then they started on page 2 and repeated the process. After about forty-five minutes they'd got three or four sentences. A walk beckoned, and they temporarily abandoned their challenging task. They were back an hour later, having innocently strolled to Unter den Linden and back with the faithful Schultz not far behind. They drank some tea and resumed their labour.

The sun was going down as Simon and Deborah read the message.

You will be taken out of Berlin on Monday. A car will collect you from Simon's office not long after noon. Deborah must have delivered the lunch just before that time. You will leave immediately to get a head start on the

Gestapo, who will become suspicious after an hour or so when Deborah doesn't leave the office for home.

You must not bring any large items of luggage. Simon should bring his briefcase and it must be empty, but Deborah must bring nothing. Wear ordinary clothes suitable for the time of the year. Any valuables you bring must be concealed in your clothing or in Simon's briefcase. Leave everything else behind, including your passports and identity cards.

Your journey will be long, uncomfortable and possibly dangerous. You must eat and drink and use the toilet before you set off. Now destroy the newspaper and read the copy you've probably made of this message one more time and then destroy it.

Good luck.

The Abrahams were seized with a combination of excitement and fear. They thought out loud a host of questions, not necessarily to one another:

"Who will collect us?"

"Where are we going?"

"Who is organising this for us and why?"

"What if we're caught?"

Simon it was who got things going this time. He tore both the newspaper and the message into hundreds of tiny pieces. They daren't risk a fire on a warm August day. Then he turned to his wife.

"We'll have to take things out that are both valuable and easy to hide."

"In other words, my jewellery."

"And my store of banknotes."

"I'll wear that light jacket and skirt with a blouse underneath. I'm often seen in that at this time of the year. You take your lightweight grey suit, raincoat and hat. I'm going to collect them now and bring my sewing gear in. We'll start tonight and finish the job tomorrow."

For more than an hour and a half the two of them were unpicking seams. Even Simon was entrusted with this work, knowing full well that when it came to restitching everything into their hiding places he wouldn't be allowed near this delicate aspect of their activity. The family carving knife made short work of Simon's old briefcase and cut strips of leather to create false compartments in his current one.

By ten o'clock they were exhausted and had a final hot drink before setting off to bed. The excitement had long worn off. They knew that tomorrow and Monday they would have to be at their cool and courageous best. They were soon asleep. Outside, Hartmann smoked his fifteenth cigarette of the shift, reflecting on what an easy, if dull, job this was. That's not to say he didn't recognise its importance. But these Jews would never escape the clutches of the Gestapo, not on his watch, anyway.

CHAPTER 26

*P*ursuit

Germany and the Netherlands, Sunday
27 to Wednesday 30 August 1939

That Sunday, the last in August 1939, was, Simon and Deborah hoped, the last they would spend in Berlin for perhaps some time. They expected to return some day; they assumed the Nazis would be toppled from power eventually. This was, after all, their home town, where they had been born, educated, married, had raised a family and ran a profitable business. They loved it, or rather were used to it. For the time being, though, they recognised that it was wise to get out of Germany.

Deborah's expertise with needle and cotton was proving priceless as she secreted valuables all over her and her husband's clothing and in Simon's briefcase. By the time she'd finished, they'd squirrelled away a small fortune, mostly in jewellery, either Deborah's own or pieces inherited from both sets of parents. Wherever they ended up, they'd be able to survive for a long time if they could get out of Germany with their stash intact.

They worked hard all day, pausing only for their traditional Sunday afternoon walk, accompanied on this occasion by Schultz. Simon was smiling to himself, thinking that, if all went well tomorrow, it would be the other man, Hartmann, who would carry the can for letting them slip away. The walk completed, Deborah finished off the sewing while Simon prepared a meal. Sparse though it was, neither of them could eat much at all. Staring into space after their dinner, their nervousness shone like a beacon.

"We can't afford to look like this in the morning," Deborah said. "We'll look suspicious, and the Gestapo might guess we're up to something."

"You're quite right. Let's go to bed. We need a good night's sleep."

Which was exactly what they didn't get. They lay in each other's arms wide awake for the best part of the night, dozing intermittently, before fully waking up at dawn. They'd hardly spoken in the night, but when Simon returned from the bathroom while his wife was dressing he seemed full of optimism.

"This isn't a trap. It's an opportunity. Heaven knows where we'll be in twenty-four hours' time, but it'll be far from here. I know it."

"You're right, Simon. Wherever we end up, I'm sure it won't be in Germany and we'll be able to see the children again."

After a pause, Deborah continued, "OK. Breakfast and off. I'll do my usual shopping, and come to the office just before noon to give us time to eat our food and so on."

Hartmann was waiting for Simon to emerge from the apartment. Smugly he thought to himself how easy it was to track this Jew. the Führer was right. They were inferior to Aryan Germans intellectually and physically. Having safely seen the Jew to his office, the Gestapo man settled down to a morning of reading the paper, smoking and sipping coffee from his flask. Inside the office, Simon was dealing with his first client, who was seeking an exit visa without any success. Miserable faces trotted in one by one with tales of unhappiness, until, fifteen minutes before noon, the lawyer stuck a notice on the outside of his office door:

Gone for lunch. Back at 1400.

Hardly had he finished doing this than his wife arrived with her shopping bag. They ate bread and fruit and drank water, then used the rather scruffy toilet in the passageway just outside the work space. Simon had just re-entered the office when the back door swung open and a tall blonde-haired man wearing a black suit came in. In his lapel was a swastika badge.

"Oh my God," Simon exclaimed, and a look of terror passed across his wife's face.

"Don't panic," the man said. "I'm a friend. I'm taking you on the first part of your journey. Take your coats and briefcase and climb into the boot of the large black Mercedes outside. It's going to be uncomfortable but short."

Moving quickly though the back door into the lane outside, the Abrahams immediately spotted the car with the boot already open. Swastikas fluttered on either side of the windscreen. They squeezed their way in and the young man slammed the boot down. He climbed into the driver's seat and the car began to move. All this was witnessed by a small gang of youths and men who were loitering at the end of the lane.

Inside the boot it was stuffy and hot and the two were incredibly cramped. They whispered to one another and came to the conclusion that, if they were going to be snatched by the Gestapo, this was hardly the way it would be carried out. The boot of a government Mercedes was not the normal way the Gestapo made arrests.

The powerful Mercedes cruised onto Unter den Linden, through the Brandenburg Gate, past the burnt out Reichstag on the right and the Tiergarten on the left, rather sparsely populated considering the fine weather. The Abrahams couldn't see, but the driver was now approaching the Siegessäulle and going on to Charlottenburg. Turning left towards Grunewald, the car entered the forest and pulled up alongside a parked cream-coloured Maybach saloon. The Mercedes' driver let the Abrahams out of the boot. He smiled at them.

"That wasn't too bad, was it? This is Eddie. He's going to take you out of Germany."

"Hi folks," a craggy-faced short man with thinning blonde hair said to them in his obvious American accent. "The Maybach's got a bigger boot than the Merc and I've drilled some small holes in the lid to help you breathe. I'll try and stop every hour, and once we're out of Hanover you can sit up front. Now let's be off—go behind the trees for a minute if you need to, but be quick."

Neither did. The German turned to them. "I must be off now and return this car to the Wilhelmstrasse before it's missed. Good luck."

"Thank you."

"My pleasure."

With that he was into his car and gone.

"He never told us his name," Simon said.

"He probably didn't want you to know it," said Eddie. "Now into the boot and let's get away. I'll try to stop between here and Magdeburg."

By the time the Maybach rejoined the road more than forty minutes had elapsed since they'd left the street behind the Alexanderplatz. In half an hour or so the Gestapo would become alarmed. Eddie understood this and put his foot down as he headed west. He knew that, long before they reached Magdeburg, the alarm would be raised.

Shortly after one o'clock, Hartmann realised that the Jewish woman had not emerged from her husband's office. This didn't unduly alarm him, since she often stayed longer, so he decided that if he didn't see her by half past he'd go into the building and investigate. Twenty-five minutes passed and the Gestapo man's patience finally ran out. He walked briskly into the block and immediately spotted the *gone for lunch* note on a door, which he quickly opened. Empty. He tried several other doors, and even had to break one down. Finally, he found someone in, an elderly Jewish lady whose face was covered in fear.

"The lawyer. Which is his office?"

The old woman got to her feet with some difficulty and shuffled into the corridor, nervously pointing at the door displaying the *gone for lunch* sign. Hartmann rushed back into the office. Still no sign of anybody. Glaring feverishly around the room, he spotted another door. He wrenched it open and stared down the empty lane. Horrified, he sprinted across the Alexanderplatz to the Gestapo office.

"Get me headquarters," he screamed at the receptionist, "and when you've done that run around the building and bring every agent you can find to me."

The girl handed the phone to Hartmann who shouted down the line.

"Get me the chief—NOW!"

As three men joined him after the receptionist's quick round-up, he explained to Müller what had happened. The Gestapo chief was furious, but saw little point in hurling abuse at Hartmann.

"How many men have you got?" asked Müller.

"Three plus me, sir."

"Get straight back to the Jew's office and question everyone in the building. Hurt them if necessary. I'm sending a truck full of men to question everyone in the surrounding area."

More than two hours had elapsed since the Abrahams had fled from Berlin, and Eddie was now past Magdeburg and on the way to Wolfsburg. They had a stretch and toilet break and another was planned in an hour. Eddie seemed to know the road like the back of his hand. He'd also worked out that the alarm would have been raised by now, and he needed to get his passengers to the safe house in Hanover before the road blocks were set up. He knew that it would be sensible to start using smaller roads where he could avoid the Gestapo and the police. In the boot the passengers were cramped and hot, though less so than in the Mercedes, and the holes were making their breathing easier, if not exactly easy.

In the area around Simon's office, the team of four were soon joined by six more from headquarters. They banged on every door, and rushed in without being invited.

"Do you know the Jew Abrahams?" they bawled.

None of the petrified folk did.

"Pick up people from the streets. Stick them up against a wall and use your knuckledusters if necessary," Hartmann ordered.

Eventually, after many blows and threats, they came across the group that had been loitering in the lane when Simon and Deborah had fled. Most denied knowing anything about it, but one rather scruffy young man piped up.

"I saw two people get into a car driven by an old bald-headed man."

"What make of car was it?"

"A Horch, dark red."

"What time was this?"

"I'm not sure. Nearly one o'clock, I think."

"How did you see it and not the others?"

"They were walking away. I just turned around when I heard the engine start up."

"OK. You may go."

Around the corner and out of earshot and sight, the young man smiled at his mates.

The Gestapo men either walked back to the Alexanderplatz or returned to headquarters in their transport. Hartmann rang Müller.

"They've gone, sir. Seen being driven away in a red Horch. The witness thinks at about one o'clock."

"Do you think he's telling the truth?"

"He's no reason to lie, sir."

"Hmm. I'm a suspicious person. Find him and bring him here. We'll question him together."

"Right, sir."

"By the way, how did they escape your notice?"

"Back door, sir."

Müller realised that the shortage of agents had come back to haunt him. Had he put two men on surveillance of Abrahams, this wouldn't have happened. No point in taking it out on Hartmann.

"Thank you, Hartmann."

He replaced the phone in the cradle and had his secretary call senior colleagues for an emergency meeting.

◆   ◆   ◆

It was early evening, and several more stops, before Eddie cautiously approached the safe house in Hanover. It was a large car, so he decided to find a place of concealment, let the Abrahams out, and walk back with them to the house. Luck was on his side as he came across a building site where several industrial vehicles had been left for the night. He squeezed the Maybach in and opened the boot, where the Abrahams sighed with great relief. They climbed out, grabbed their coats and Simon's briefcase, and walked back to the safe house. Eddie was sure the car was OK. They'd be gone long before the workmen appeared in the morning.

◆   ◆   ◆

"They must not escape," Müller said with great emphasis. "Get in touch with every office in the Reich and circulate descriptions. I want every train and bus passenger checked. Road blocks set up on every main road. Double-check all passengers on flights and ferries. Double the number of officers checking at the borders. Each of our offices must order the local police to co-operate. Track down every red Horch in the country."

One of Müller's colleagues spoke up.

"What about our agents in the ports outside the Reich, sir?"

"Good idea. Get in touch with our people in Belgium, the Netherlands and France and warn them to be on the lookout for these Jews. They must not escape."

◆   ◆   ◆

Eddie's gentle tap on the rear door of the safe house was answered by a short pretty brunette with blue smiling eyes. Her hair was cut in a bob.

"You must be Eddie. I'm June. You must be Mr and Mrs Bakker, or at least that's how you will be known from now on."

The four of them sat around a kitchen table and tucked into the food that June had prepared. Then she took over.

"I work for London Films in their Rotterdam office. The four of us have been in Hanover scouting locations for a forthcoming film about a romance between a Nazi army officer and an aristocratic English girl. We're on our way back to Rotterdam. If we're questioned, that's our story."

June dropped a couple of Dutch passports on the table. "Here are your passports. They were delivered to me by a man on a motorbike this morning. Please open them and look at the photographs."

"They look nothing like us," exclaimed Deborah.

"I should hope not. From what I know, every law enforcement officer and every snitch in the country is on the lookout for you."

"But why?" asked Simon.

"No idea. I neither know nor care. I've got a job to do and I intend to see it through."

Eddie was chuckling away through all this. He guessed what was coming and was looking forward to seeing the outcome.

"Eddie, please go and get some sleep. You've got a lot of driving ahead of you tomorrow."

Eddie left the room with a sheepish grin on his face.

"You've probably worked out that Eddie and I work for British Intelligence. I also still work for my previous employer, London Films. I'm a make-up artist. I've got until dawn to turn you two into your passport photographs. One at a time. Mrs Bakker first. Mr Bakker, get some sleep. Your wife will call you when I'm ready for you."

Simon was dog-tired and, despite all the excitement, soon fell asleep. It seemed only a few minutes later when his wife's hand was nudging him awake. He sat up, remembered where he was, reached over and switched on the light.

"Good God."

The face smiling at him bore no resemblance to the Deborah he knew and loved. Instead it was the image of the face in her passport; short curly brown hair, high cheekbones and a smaller mouth.

"I prefer the original, but this is brilliant," Simon said.

"And what's more, June says I can be back as I was in a matter of minutes."

"She's brilliant. My turn I suppose."

Two hours later the four were eating a very early breakfast. Simon's hair was lighter too, and his sideburns extended down the side of his face, under his chin and up to form a very distinguished looking beard and moustache.

"You look like Orson Welles," Eddie said, grinning at Simon.

"Who is Orson Welles?" asked Simon.

"Theatre and radio guy. Last year he broadcast H. G. Wells' *War of the Worlds* on the radio. It was so realistic people started fleeing their homes."

"He sounds an interesting man."

"He is. The theatre world was blown away by his stage production of *Julius Caesar*. The players wore modern dress."

"We need to be off soon. Mr and Mrs Bakker, please go and dress in the clothes I've put out for you in the front bedroom. There's a large suitcase there as well. Put all you other clothes and the briefcase in there. Lock it and we'll put it in the boot of the car. There'll be plenty of room in there, I believe," June said with a grin.

Eddie fetched the car. It was still dark when the Maybach pulled out of Hanover with its four passengers. He told them of the day's itinerary.

"We're crossing the German/Dutch border near Ahaus. We should be there in about an hour and a half. Once inside the Netherlands we'll travel via Arnhem to Rotterdam, where we'll leave June and proceed to the Hook of Holland for the overnight ferry to England."

This news threw the Abrahams into a frenzy of joy and excitement.

"England! How wonderful. Will our children be there to meet us?"

"I expect so, well, probably not at Harwich, but not long after. They won't be told until you're safely at sea. When you board the ferry go straight to your cabins and stay there until you dock in Harwich. Here are your tickets. We'll pick up food and drink for your crossing in the Netherlands. Now let's rehearse your roles if we're questioned by the Gestapo at the border."

"Let's hope we're not questioned," said Deborah.

"Well we might be, so let's be prepared. I'm an American putting some money into this movie. Mr Bakker is the location scout for the movie—looking for various places for outdoor scenes. Emphasise that we don't want this to be a studio-based movie—gives it more realism. By the way, do you smoke?"

"No."

"Here, stick this in your mouth," Eddie said handing over his pipe. He laughed.

"Now you look even more like Orson Welles."

June told him that she'd filled his briefcase with old film scripts.

"June works for London Films and can prove it. She's just keeping an eye on things for Korda."

"Who's Korda?" Deborah asked.

"Alexander Korda, the owner of London Films."

"Seems simple enough," Simon said.

However big the search for the Abrahams was, it didn't yet extend to the approach to the Dutch border, but, as they drew closer to the frontier, there was a long queue of vehicles waiting in line at the checkpoint. Just short of Ahaus the passengers rearranged the seating so that the two men were seated side by side in the front. As the car crept forward, the tension mounted. Uniformed customs officials were carefully scrutinising passports, with leather-coated Gestapo men, one either side of the line of traffic, picking out some cars for extra attention—questioning and searches.

They reached the custom officials, one of whom took their passports and asked, "Where are you going?"

"Rotterdam," Eddie replied.

The official looked at each passport in turn, stamped them and returned them to their owners.

"Just a minute," interjected a tough-looking Gestapo man with angular features beneath a type of small grey fedora, "Where have you been in Germany?"

"Hanover," Simon replied. "We're hoping to shoot a film there."

"What sort of film?"

"It's a love story about an affair between a German soldier and the daughter of an English aristocrat."

"And who are these people?"

"The young lady in the back is a colleague of mine in Rotterdam at our film company's office there, and the other lady is my wife. This gentleman," gesturing at Eddie, "is an American businessman who is providing the money for the film."

Turning towards Eddie, the Gestapo man asked, "And what is your business?"

"I own several factories that make shoes."

"Why would a man who makes shoes give money to a film?"

"I love the movies, and besides it helps with my tax returns."

Floored by this answer, the Gestapo man looked at his colleague, who was giving the boot the once over, rummaging through suitcases and Simon's briefcase. He shook his head and started to replace the luggage in the boot.

"You're free to go," he growled.

Cruising off after just a show and stamp of passports on the other side of the border, the passengers let out a collective sigh of relief and then, for no apparent reason, burst out laughing.

"You were terrific," Eddie said to Simon. "We should use you on more jobs like this," he chuckled.

"Thanks, but no thanks. I may have looked calm on the surface but, just like a swan, I was paddling like mad unseen underneath just to keep afloat. I've had enough excitement to last a lifetime."

Provisions were taken on board at Arnhem and then an incident-free ride to Rotterdam ensued. There June left them after kisses, thanks, and expressions of good luck. Arriving in the Hook of Holland in plenty of time for the night crossing, there were more hugs and handshakes.

"Straight to your cabin and stay there till you're ready to disembark in Harwich."

Much to Müller's intense frustration, it had taken more than a day to track down the witness to the escape from Berlin in the fictitious dark red Horch. As the Abrahams boarded the ferry at the Hook of Holland, he and Hartmann were sitting opposite the witness at Gestapo headquarters.

"How do you know it was a Horch?"

"I'm keen on cars, even though I can't drive. I know all about them."

"In which direction did the car go?"

"Towards Unter den Linden."

"What did the driver look like?"

"I told this man," gesturing at Hartmann, " the driver was bald. I only saw the back of his head."

"Describe the passengers," rapped Hartmann.

The man gave an accurate description of the Abrahams.

"Wait outside," ordered Müller.

The head of the Gestapo looked at Hartmann.

"I think he's telling the truth. As you said, what has he got to gain by lying? I reckon they're long gone, and I haven't got time to follow this up. I've got to send an advance party into Poland with the Abwehr to prepare for this weekend's events. Let him go."

Deborah and Simon boarded the ferry, not noticing a man wearing a motorcycle helmet and goggles sitting astride his machine on the quayside. The man was watching another obvious Gestapo agent, who had a sheet of paper in his hand and was checking the faces of each passenger who boarded the ferry. Had he taken his goggles and helmet off, and had they looked, they would have seen a smile of deep satisfaction.

CHAPTER 27

Together

London and Harwich, Wednesday 30
August to Friday 1 September 1939

"They're out, Roger. On the night ferry from the Hook. Docks at eight tomorrow morning."

Worrying as he had been since first uncovering the conspiracy, Roger now let go of his concern, as initially relief and then excitement flooded through him.

"That's great Richard. Thank you very much. And please thank Harry and ask him to pass on my gratitude to all those who made this happen."

"I will. Don't forget you need to tell your Special Branch man that somebody needs to be at Harwich when they arrive to stop them becoming embroiled with the immigration people. They could get arrested. They're travelling on Dutch passports with the name Bakker."

"I know. I'll ring Moss now. He'll sort it out. I need to ring Sir John and warn him that they're on their way."

"More success then, Roger. Well done."

"Thanks Richard. Not quite done yet."

Less than a minute later he was speaking to Moss.

"Good evening, Sergeant. I'm sorry to be calling so late."

"It's only ten, Mr Martin. Early yet. What's the latest?"

"Our fugitives from Hitler are at the Hook of Holland on board the night ferry to Harwich. I need to ask you to meet them when they disembark. They're travelling on false passports under the name of Bakker."

Roger gave Moss Sir John's address and asked the policeman if he would deliver them to Hampstead.

"Certainly, Mr Martin, and as soon as the parents are safely tucked up we'll move against the Nazis. Get your cameraman ready."

"Thanks. He's on standby."

Next Roger telephoned Sir John, who answered himself. Roger explained what had happened.

"That's wonderful, Mr Martin. Congratulations."

"Thank you, Sir John. I'd like the reunion to take place at your house, if that's possible?"

"Good heavens, man. Of course it is, and Esther's parents can stay here as long as they like. How will they be getting here?"

"My Special Branch contact will meet them at Harwich and drive them to you. One more favour, please. Would you give Esther the news and ask her to phone her brother in Cambridge and get him to come to your house in the morning to meet his parents?"

"Certainly, my dear fellow. I'll do it straight away. Will you be here?"

"No sir. Sergeant Moss, the man who's bringing Esther's parents to Hampstead, is expecting to round up all the Nazis who've caused this trouble. I'd like to be there."

"Of course you would. Good luck from me. I'll rouse Esther with the good news. Good night, Mr Martin."

Roger called Jane with an update, while Sir John went up to call Esther. He tapped gently on her door. She answered promptly, full clothed.

"Oh! Sir John. I was just going to bed. What can I do for you?"

"My dear, I've got some wonderful news. Your parents have escaped from Germany and are currently on the overnight ferry from Holland to Harwich. Mr Martin's police contact will bring them directly here from the boat in the morning."

Esther burst into tears. She was almost speechless. "That's marvellous, Sir John. Thank you." She threw her arms around him and cried into his jacket. Sir John was so pleased for her, but he needed to gently push her away.

"You need to phone the people in Cambridge where your brother lives and ask them to give him the good news, and see if he could be brought here for noon tomorrow."

"Yes sir. I'll do it right away and give them your address."

They walked downstairs together.

"Sir. Will Roger and the boys be here tomorrow?"

"No. I expect they'll be helping to see that that awful Nazi gets his dues, but I intend to hold a party here on Saturday evening for all those who've helped your parents, including Roger and, of course, the boys. It'll be like the old days before my wife died. I'll speak to Cook in the morning."

Esther called Cambridge. Her brother was in bed, most likely fast asleep. The Richardsons were thrilled and said they would tell him in the morning and then drive him to Hampstead.

As their good news was being spread around England, Simon and Deborah were sitting in their cabin eating their food. They were still too excited to sleep, and still on edge. One final hurdle remained—the British immigration authorities. When the ferry docked at Harwich they left their cabin carrying the suitcase and Simon's briefcase, and made their way off the boat towards the customs shed. Both were showing signs of being very nervous. Their next stop could easily be a night in a cell at a British police station, followed by a return trip across the North Sea. There were several queues at customs, but they moved fairly quickly and soon were showing their passports to a pleasant fair-haired young man. He quickly glanced at the documents and then said, "Excuse me for one minute."

Concern was etched on the Abrahams' faces. To come through so much and be foiled as soon as they stepped on English soil filled them with fear and frustration. But it didn't last long, as the customs officer returned less than a minute later with a shortish, tubby man with ruddy cheeks and thinning black hair. He'd ditched the moustache and the tired old raincoat some weeks ago in an effort to spruce up his image in anticipation of the hoped-for promotion.

"Mr and Mrs Bakker? I'm Detective Sergeant Bert Moss of the Special Branch of the Metropolitan Police. I've come to take you to your son and daughter."

Relief flooded through the Abrahams, who had been struck speechless. This was not what they'd been expecting, even in their wildest dreams.

"Here, let me take your bags," Moss said, leading them towards a smart black car. They set off towards London.

"I expect this has all come as a bit of a shock for you, 'specially after suffering as Jews in Nazi Germany."

"Yes, we can hardly believe it," Deborah said. "We must find out who has done all this for us and thank them in person."

"Lots of people, I expect, but the main bloke is a journalist called Roger Martin."

"We must thank him in person. Will he be where we're going now?" asked Simon.

"No. He'll have a lot on with war on the horizon. But I'm sure you'll meet him soon."

"Where are we going now, Sergeant?"

"'Ampstead in North London. To the 'ouse where your daughter lives."

Could we stop somewhere on the way so that my wife and I can remove our disguises, please? Our children won't be able to recognise us."

Moss laughed with good nature.

"Blimey, I 'adn't thought of that. Course we can."

They stopped half an hour later at a roadside cafe, and while Simon and Deborah were removing their disguises, Moss treated himself to a cup of tea and a bacon sandwich. Emerging a few minutes later two totally different people, apart from their clothes and the length of their hair, the "new" Abrahams drew a gasp from Moss.

"Good gawd. 'Oo ever did you up made a fantastic job of it. 'Ere's a couple of cups of coffee. I wasn't certain if you drank tea, but everybody drinks coffee. Anything to eat?"

"No thank you. We had plenty on the boat. By the way, Germans do drink tea, but more often with lemon rather than milk, but," Deborah continued, "now we're in England we'll have to get used to taking it with milk."

The light traffic and the fast car meant that it was before noon when they reached Hampstead. After a couple of wrong turns, they found Sir John's house, and hardly had they got out of the car than a pair of wildly excited children rushed to greet their mother and father. Behind the children, Sir John strode towards the family with a huge smile on his face. Shaking Moss's hand, he thanked the policeman for delivering them safely. Moss smiled his appreciation and said, "I 'ave to go now, Sir John. Now that Mr and Mrs Abrahams have been safely delivered we can pick up the Germans responsible for all this."

Sir John shook his hand and he said his farewells to the deliriously happy parents and their children before setting off to Scotland Yard.

"Please come in, everyone."

He ushered them into the lounge, where Esther took orders for hot and soft drinks. The visitors actually numbered six, because the Richardsons had stayed inside the house while the initial reunion was taking place outside. Peter's guardians were introduced to his parents, and the tears stopped flowing and were replaced by laughter and excited chatter.

"I am so delighted to welcome you here. You are all very brave people. You will know of the uncertainty of the international situation, and I must go to the Foreign Office immediately. I hope everyone will join me here on Saturday evening when we can celebrate your extraordinary escape."

"Will Mr Martin be here?" asked Deborah.

"I'm sure he will be, with his fiancée Jane, and—I'm sure no one will begrudge me saying this—the real heroes, George and Joe. I'm sorry, but I've been unable to contact them with the news, but I'm sure we'll be able to pass it on very soon."

Esther returned from the kitchen just in time to hear this and her face lit up.

◆   ◆   ◆

Unaware of the fabulous news from Hampstead, George and Joe were keeping an eye on Klein's house in Sussex Gardens. They'd had a few dull days of waiting for him outside of cafes and pubs. One consolation had

been a visit to the cinema to see *The Four Feathers*, which the boys had
thoroughly enjoyed.

Klein appeared on his own at mid-morning. He was strolling towards
the Underground station as if he didn't have a care in the world. A raincoat
slung over his arm with slacks, sports jacket and a smile on his face, his
mood matched the fine weather.

"'E looks in a good mood today," Joe said.

"I 'ope that don't mean another day of news theatres and pubs," Joe
replied.

It quickly became obvious that Klein's destination was the German
Embassy and, as he went in, George and Joe set themselves up in their
usual spot.

"Urgent telegram for you, sir," one of the female staff said, thrusting
the message into Klein's hand. It was from Wolf.

*Girl's parents escaped. Get out now. Brown launch David V 200m from
Harwich ferry terminal. MS Auslang to bring you home.*

It was a much-changed Klein who emerged from the Carlton House
Gate building less than five minutes after he'd gone in. His face was creased
in worry and urgency, and his stride brisk and purposeful. The police, he
reasoned, would be waiting for him in Sussex Gardens and he knew he
must head straight for Harwich.

"'E's on the move, Joe, and quick. Let's go."

Joe and George were over the fence and in pursuit, although Klein
already had a hundred yards' lead on them. They increased to jogging
speed and just caught sight of him on his way down the steps to the tube
at the end of Piccadilly. Breathless, the two boys just made it onto an
eastbound Piccadilly Line train with Klein in view in the next carriage. A
change at King's Cross, then the three of them, the fugitive and the two
pursuers, reached Liverpool Street twenty minutes later. Joe closed right
up on him as he queued at the ticket office and bought a single to Harwich
Parkeston Quay. The next train would leave in thirty minutes, he was told.
Joe bought a couple of tickets and rejoined George.

"Keep an eye on 'im, George. I'm gonna phone Roger. "

Roger was at his desk and had just briefed Charlie to be on standby with his camera. His phone rang.

"Moss 'ere, Mr Martin. We've arrested fifteen Nazi spies and they were carryin' loads of stuff, but the main man wasn't amongst them. Looks like 'e's done a runner. Any ideas?"

Roger was about to reply when a bothered-looking boy thrust a piece of paper under his nose.

Joe on the line urgent.

"I might have in two minutes. I'll call you back."

Joe was put through.

"Guv, 'e's at Liverpool Street. Gettin' a train to 'Arwich Quay. Train leaves in 'arf an hour. We got tickets."

"Brilliant, Joe. Listen, Esther's parents are safe. They're at Hampstead. Keep on the German. We'll get to Harwich somehow. For God's sake, be careful. He's desperate and will try anything to escape back to Germany."

Roger called Moss back and gave him the news.

"I'm on my way. Wait outside your office for me."

Roger called Charlie the photographer and the two made their way to the street. Five minutes later a large black Austin pulled up with Moss in the passenger seat.

"Get in."

They were hardly seated and were in the process of closing the door, when the police car pulled away with the screeching of tyres. Fortunately, they were on the east side of London, and were soon heading for Chelmsford on the A12.

"This is gonna be tight. we've eighty miles to go. It'll be a one and three-quarter hour trip compared with an 'our and an 'arf on the train. Use the bell, Bourne, if we get 'eld up."

"Yes Sarge," replied the driver.

"The local boys will meet us near the customs shed. This is the second time I've been to 'Arwich today. By the way, the lads tell me that the 'ouse in Sussex Gardens was a right treasure trove. Names, addresses, codes maps, targets, the lot. And most of the names are ours, not coppers, I mean British. Traitors. Bastards."

As the time approached for the train's departure, George said to Joe, "We're gonna 'ave to sit close to 'im. Remember, I've been to this station before when 'e went to pick up the suitcase. It's 'uge, with a long platform. It we're not near 'im, we'll lose 'im."

A flustered-looking Klein got into the third carriage, so the boys settled into the second. The train pulled out on time. The police car was racing towards Chelmsford.

"Why not have the train stopped?" asked Roger.

"Can't," replied Moss. "Some people might miss their crossin', then there'd be 'ell to pay."

"Well, why not radio through and have him picked up at Harwich?"

"None of the 'Arwich boys know wot 'e looks like. And wot's more," continued Moss, "I doubt 'e'll be usin' the ferry. More likely a small boat to take 'im to a merchant ship anchored outside territorial waters where we can't get our paws on 'im."

The train was on time as the police car passed through Chelmsford and careered along the road to Colchester. Moss was beating his fist on the window as they were held up for three or four minutes behind a tractor, which eventually pulled off into a field. By the time they were through Colchester and onto the final lap, they knew they wouldn't beat the train.

At Parkeston Quay, Klein leapt onto the platform almost before the train had come to a halt. The lads, showing their agility, were soon after him. Not wishing to attract attention, Klein presented his ticket at the barrier and walked unhurriedly towards the customs shed. Just before the entrance he increased his speed, walking quickly around the outside of the building. He had a clear view of the harbour and the area where the *David V* would be waiting. There were two large buildings between the German and safety. He started running around the outside of the one furthest from the water.

"Keep on 'im, George. I'm gonna intercept 'im."

Joe sprinted flat out along the gap between the buildings and arrived at the end just after Klein had turned left and was heading towards the quay. Repeating the trick that had once saved Roger from falling into the hands of the bad guys, Joe stuck out his left foot, and Klein went flat onto the floor. He rolled onto his back and stared into Joe's eyes, the German's face a mask of shock and hatred.

The police Austin sped into the car park by the railway station. They could see the train stationary and empty. Three uniformed bobbies joined them as they got out. Roger was scanning the quayside when he spotted George dashing along the outside of one of the large buildings.

"That's George," he shouted. He ran off, joined quickly by the others.

Klein had his hands by his side and had murder in his eyes as he tried to get up to hurt Joe, who was standing defiantly beside him. In the distance, they could both hear the faint sound of police whistles. Klein was scrambling to his feet when George appeared, ran in full tilt and delivered a mighty boot between the German's legs. The whistles grew louder. Klein screamed and let out a stream of foul-mouthed oaths as he tried to get to his feet, before Joe kicked him in the face, breaking his nose and dislodging several teeth.

"There, yer Nazi bastard. That's fer puttin' the frighteners on my best friend's girl."

But Klein wasn't finished. He leapt to his feet and drove a hefty punch into George's midriff. George staggered backwards. All the air had been knocked out of him and he was briefly out of action. the German turned his attention to Joe and grabbed hold of the smaller boy and hurled him against the wall of the building. There was a loud crack as Joe's forearm splintered on impact. "Christ," Joe cried out, as he fell into a sitting position against the wall.

As he tried to get back on his feet, Joe spotted Klein advancing on George with an evil-looking knife in his hand. George had regained his upright position and just managed to sway out of the knife thrust. The German had a wild look on his face and was screaming. Bravely, George moved towards the armed man.

Forgetting his agony, Joe rushed towards Klein and aimed a vicious kick at the back of his knee, throwing him momentarily off balance. Seeing his chance, George ducked beneath the German's knife and drove a shoulder into his midriff. Startled, Klein found himself flat on his back for the second time in less than a minute.

The whistles were deafening now, but Klein still wasn't done. Lying on his back and still clutching his knife, he was about to resume his attack when Roger appeared with the five policemen. Sensing the danger, the young journalist went straight for the knife and stamped violently on the German's wrist. A loud scream followed by more foul language showed that, for the third time in the skirmish, a bone had been broken.

Three burly uniformed policemen jumped on Klein, pulled him to his feet and handcuffed him. There were more obscenities from the German.

"What's 'e saying, guv?" Joe asked, clutching his injured arm.

"Dirty words in German. You OK, Joe?"

"I think my arm's broken," Joe laughed.

Moss read Klein his rights, and arrested him on suspicion of being an enemy agent and of attempted murder.

"No pictures," ordered Moss. "Clean 'im up first. We don't want any accusations of police brutality."

One of the bobbies produced a handkerchief and wiped the blood off the face of a cursing and struggling Klein. Charlie's camera flashed. Klein looked at Joe and George.

"Who are you? I've never seen you before."

The boys said nothing, just smiled with the deep sense of satisfaction that came with knowing that they'd done their jobs well.

"Told you, Mr Martin. These two 'eroes would make great coppers. Right, back to the local nick. I'll arrange for a secure van to transfer 'im to the Yard, then we'll take the lads to hospital."

"What'll 'appen to 'im?" George asked.

"Dunno until after we've questioned 'im. Dependin' on the evidence we'll either lock 'im up, 'ang 'im or turn 'im."

"By the way boys," Roger began. "We're all invited to Hampstead on Saturday evening. Esther's parents want to thank you. I'll collect you just after lunch and buy you some new clothes for the occasion."

"Will Esther be there guv?"

"I should think so."

The three of them laughed.

CHAPTER 28

Joy And Then War

London and Berlin, Saturday 2 and
Sunday 3 September 1939

The British Ambassador in Berlin, Sir Neville Henderson, was in and out of various offices in the German capital trying to persuade the Germans to withdraw from Poland, which had been invaded the previous day. Roger, George and Joe were still fast asleep after their exertions of the previous forty-eight hours. Klein had been charged with espionage and attempted murder, and was lying in a cell waiting to be tried. Simon, Deborah and their children, Esther and Peter, were still in bed in Hampstead. Thrilled as they were by being a united family again, there was still the matter of who was going to live where and with whom to be resolved.

The hospital had confirmed that Joe had broken his arm and he had left Harwich with it encased in plaster of Paris, with the assurance that it would heal perfectly. Apart from a sore stomach, George was unscathed.

Roger had written another smash hit, the Klein arrest being the main front page story on the day following the excitement at Harwich.

DANGEROUS NAZI SPY SEIZED AT HARWICH
***GLOBE* AGAIN ON THE SPOT WHEN IT MATTERS**
from Roger Martin in Harwich

Roger shared the details of the story with Claud Cockburn, as he had with the Woolwich bomb story. There was no threat to exclusivity, since Cockburn's news sheet, *The Week*, only appeared every seven days, but Roger had made the promise in return for acquiring the services of George and Joe and he felt that he'd had the better of the deal by some distance. At the *Globe*, Ben was ecstatic.

"You've done it again, Prof. The editor's over the moon. Those pictures of Charlie's were bloody great. Talk about bein' on the spot. Anythin' else to report?"

Roger was at home preparing to collect Jane and the two lads.

"Thanks, Ben," Roger spoke into the phone. "We could be at war by Monday, so I thought a nice little anti-Nazi piece later in the week. I need to interview three of the rescued passengers who came off the *St Louis*. They've got quite a story to tell."

"Blimey, that sounds good. Whenever you're ready. Enjoy the rest of the weekend."

Roger put down the phone and then immediately picked it up again and made a second call.

"Sergeant Moss, please," Roger requested.

"There's no Sergeant Moss 'ere," a man replied with a chuckle.

"Must have the wrong number. Sorry."

"'Ang on sir, perhaps it's Detective Inspector Moss you want."

Roger smiled to himself.

"Yes please."

Moss came on the line.

"Good mornin', Mr Martin. Congratulations on your front page scoop."

"And the same to you, Inspector, on your promotion."

"Thanks. It's worked out well for both of us. Old wounds healed, d'you think?"

"Totally," Roger replied. "What's the latest on the other fifteen?"

"We're still quizzin' 'em. Got an extension from the magistrates. Now that war seems likely we might as well 'ang on to 'em. If we can't get anythin' to charge 'em wiv, they'll be interned."

"Please keep me posted."

"I will, and thanks, and thank them lads. Sorry I can't be there today, but more duty calls. Give them all my best."

"Certainly will, and thanks to you, Inspector."

"Good luck, Mr Martin."

Roger ended the call knowing that almost certainly this period of his life was about to close, maybe temporarily. Just as infancy gave way to school, school became university, and university the world of work, Roger knew that a spell of duty would follow. If war came, he would volunteer for the army.

George was at Joe's house when Roger arrived with Jane early on Saturday afternoon. Both boys were wearing white shirts and blue or grey working trousers. Joe's arm was in a sling. They, their clothes and their shoes were immaculately clean. George had a light blue kippah perched on his head. The grown-ups greeted them warmly and they set off westwards, none of them noticing a Bentalls van drawing up outside Joe's front door.

"What d'yer fink about the Nazis, Jane?" Joe asked.

"What, going into Poland? I think we'll be at war after the weekend."

"Me dad don't like them Germans and Russians on the same side," George said, "but he reckons it won't last long."

"Mine says the same," Joe added.

Roger let the three of them chat while he concentrated on the driving. Jane absolutely loved the boys and he reflected that if he and she were blessed with children he hoped that they'd grow up to be like George and Joe.

It wasn't long before they were parking in Kingston. They made their way to Bentalls restaurant and had a tasty afternoon tea, before heading to the menswear department. The boys emerged wearing flannel trousers, ties and jackets—Joe's a black and white check, George's a cream and brown check. Joe had his good arm in a sleeve and the jacket slung over the shoulder of his broken arm. Jane inspected them and gave her seal of approval.

In Hampstead, Esther and Cook, assisted by Peter, were busy preparing the buffet for the evening celebration. Sir John was with Simon and Deborah and the Richardsons discussing the future. Esther was anxious to stay with Sir John and the diplomat was keen that she should stay. Peter had told his parents that he'd like to live in Cambridge so he could continue his friendship with the Richardsons' son Michael. The Richardsons were very pleased to hear this. Mr Richardson, with his university connections, was sure he could find Simon work. All was organised. Deborah would convert her jewellery into cash and they'd buy a small two-bedroomed house in Cambridge. Esther would sleep on the settee when she came to stay.

All were safely gathered in by early evening. Roger, Jane and the boys were introduced as heroes, and Roger was quick to deflect this praise to George and Joe, and also to Richard, whom he described as the brains behind the operation. The boys were, of course, the centre of attention, especially Joe, who had to endure everyone signing his pot.

Roger gave Bert Moss's apologies, sang his praises, mentioned his promotion to Inspector and passed on the Special Branch officer's best wishes to all.

Richard, who was there with his wife Inge, said a number of others, whose names couldn't be mentioned, had played a very big part in the operation.

Esther had changed into a pink blouse and light grey skirt after serving the food. To George she looked stunning. Little did he know that her heart had melted when her two young friends had made their appearance, with George her preferred escort. This, she knew, created a problem, because she recognised George and Joe were inseparable. She wrestled with this for a while, but soon came up with a solution.

"Let's go into the garden away from these stuffy adults who are mostly talking about the war."

Neither boy needed a second invitation.

It was warm in the beautiful half-light.

"Look," began Esther, "now all this is over, thanks to everyone, I don't want us never to see each other again."

George's heart was hammering.

"We'd like to go on bein' with you, Esther," Joe said.

"Well," Esther began, "I usually go into London on Saturday evenings. We could meet then. I have a friend Mary who works in a big house in Clapham. She's very nice and pretty. She could make up a four—Joe and Mary and George and me."

George thought he was going to explode with happiness, but Joe spoke next.

"That's a brilliant idea. Count us both in fer next Sat'day. Meet at King's Cross at six. We could see a film or go to Lyons or maybe even both."

"Wonderful. It's a date." She kissed Joe on the cheek and George on the edge of his lips.

"Better rejoin the adults now," George suggested. "They'll be wonderin' wot we're doin' out 'ere."

"Let 'em wonder," Joe said, and the three of them laughed.

◆   ◆   ◆

At 11:15 on the following morning, the British Prime Minister Neville Chamberlain declared war on Germany. He spoke gravely from the cabinet room of 10 Downing Street, and was apologetic that all of his efforts to maintain peace had failed. There were attempts, right up until the last moment, to persuade Germany to withdraw its troops from Poland, but all to no avail. Soon after he had finished, the air raid sirens went off, but it was a false alarm.

In New Malden the Martin family, together with Jane and Jonathan Gerber, listened to the broadcast with heavy hearts, but no one was surprised. Roger declared that he would immediately volunteer for the army and Jane said she was certain that there would be something for her to do. Reg was already a member of Bentalls' anti-aircraft gun team. Jonathan sat in silence.

A short distance away, the Walker family and their guests, Jonathan Gerber's parents, stared glumly at the radio. Richard would be working with his boss Reg on the anti-aircraft team. The Gerbers, Benjamin and Ruth, were due to move to their new North London home on the following day.

In Berlin's Reich Chancellery, Hitler leaned forward on his desk, and with his arms straight, drove his knuckles into the surface. He looked up, and one by one studied the faces of his acolytes, most of whom had predicted that Britain wouldn't fight. Knowing that some time later that day France would join Britain in a declaration of war against the Reich, he paused for a moment and then said, "Now what?"

George and Joe were kicking a football in the street outside Joe's home at eleven o'clock on that beautiful Sunday morning. Two new bikes, one dark green and the other dark blue, had been delivered by a Bentalls van on the previous day. There was a label tied around the handlebars of the bikes. Each said simply:

SORT THE COLOURS OUT YOURSELVES

THANK YOU

THE GUV

"Be a week or two before I can ride mine," Joe said.

Joe's father called from his house just before 11:15.

"In you come boys. Mr Chamberlain's on the radio."

Four of them, including Joe's mum, listened to the grim words of the PM without comment. The siren sounded and they sat in silence. Shortly the all clear went off and the boys went back out to the street.

"Will we be able to fight?" asked George.

"Not yet. We're too young," his friend replied.

"When we're old enough, I'm gonna join up with Roger.'"

"Me too."

"Let's forget about it for now. We've got Saturday to look forward to. I 'ope yours is alright."

"Bound to be," replied Joe.

"Why d'yer say that?"

"Stands to reason. Esther's very pretty, so 'er friend is certain to be the same. See, if a girl ain't all that pretty she usually 'as a friend less pretty than 'erself to show up 'er own prettiness. They'll both be gorgeous. You see."

"Great, I can't wait."

"Fancy a game of three and in, special rules. I'll keep goal," suggested George.

"Why not?"

AUTHOR'S NOTES

The Summer of '39 is a work of fiction based on fact.

Many of the characters in this book appear in my two previous novels *The Blue Pencil* and *Two Families at War*, both published by Sacristy Press.

The IRA bombing campaign of 1939 began on 16 January, following the IRA's declaration of war four days earlier. After the Coventry outrage of 25 August 1939, the number of incidents petered out. The last explosion was on 18 March 1940.

The plan to bomb Britain, known as the *S Plan*, was the brainchild of Seamus James O'Donovan (Donovan in the novel). He was a very senior man within the IRA and was their link with the Abwehr. He died in 1979 at the age of 83.

One of the IRA bombers was exposed by his wife, but she lived in Slough, not North Sheen.

The attempt to bomb the Woolwich Arsenal is a figment of my imagination, but there was a Communist spy ring there in 1937 and there were several fatal accidents in 1939.

Maurice Childs did receive the MBE for his part in foiling the Hammersmith Bridge bombing in March 1939.

The Coventry bombing did happen in August 1939, and five people were killed. Two of the three bombers were quickly arrested. Found guilty, they were hanged at Birmingham Prison on 7 February 1940.

Admiral Wilhelm Canaris was Head of the German Foreign Intelligence Service. He approved the link with the IRA. The Abwehr was a singularly unsuccessful intelligence-gathering organisation, especially in its attempts to smuggle agents into Britain and Eire. Many of these were turned and radioed false and misleading information back to Germany.

Heinrich Müller, known as Gestapo Müller to distinguish him from a general of the same name, was last seen in Berlin in early May 1945. No trace of him has ever been found.

Canaris hated the Nazis and especially their treatment of the Jews. On more than one occasion he made possible the escape of Jews from Germany. By the middle of the war he was in secret contact with MI6, although there is no evidence of treason within these contacts. The Abwehr was abolished by Hitler in February 1944. Canaris was arrested shortly after the failed July plot against Hitler and kept in custody until 9 April 1945, when he was garrotted naked with a violin string at Flossenbürg concentration camp.

The German diplomat who spied for the British in the Nazi embassies in both London and The Hague was Wolfgang Gans zu Putlitz. His manservant was Willi Schneider. After Britain and France declared war on Germany in September 1939, suspicion grew amongst the German intelligence services that Putlitz was working for the British. He and Willi fled the Netherlands a month after the outbreak of war. They made their way to the USA via Jamaica. Putlitz returned to Britain in 1944 without Willi. In 1946, he gave evidence at the Nuremberg War Crimes trials and became a UK citizen in 1948. Putlitz returned to Germany in 1952 and settled in the German Democratic Republic. He died aged 76 in 1975 and is buried in Potsdam.

Putlitz's contact throughout his periods of spying for Britain was Klop Ustinov, known in all three of my novels as Harry. Ustinov worked for the Weimar Republic as a press attaché in the German Embassy at Carlton House Gate. He was sacked with the coming of the Nazis, became a British citizen, and later became an operative for MI5. He died in 1962, aged 70. His son, Peter, became a double Oscar-winning actor, playwright, Chancellor of Durham University and legendary raconteur.

Sir Alexander Korda was a great figure in the pre-war British film industry. A Hungarian, he became wildly enthusiastic about Britain after coming to live there. He ardently encouraged MI6 agents, masquerading as film people, to be placed in London Films offices all over Europe.

SOME INTERESTING BOOKS

Barnes, James J. and Barnes, Patience P., *Nazis in Pre-War London, 1930–1939* (Sussex Academic Press, 2005).

Bielenberg, Christabel, *The Past is Myself* (Ward River Press, 1982): account of an Englishwoman living in Nazi Germany.

Day, Peter, *Klop* (Biteback Publishing, 2014).

Evans, Richard J., *The Third Reich in Power* (Penguin, 2005).

Gans zu Putlitz, Wolfgang, *The Putlitz Dossier* (Allen Wingate, 1957).

Gardiner, Juliet, *The Thirties* (Harper Press, 2010).

Lowther, David, *The Blue Pencil* (Sacristy Press, 2012).

Lowther, David, *Two Families at War* (Sacristy Press, 2015).

O'Donoghue, David, *The Devil's Deal* (New Island, 2010): covers the IRA and the Abwehr.

ACKNOWLEDGEMENTS

I am most indebted to Sacristy Press for their continued support of my writing. Special thanks are due to Richard Hilton and Thomas Ball, who grabbed hold of my ramblings and produced a good story.

Brian Cooper has patiently scoured the pages of my drafts and turned often illiterate nonsense into coherent prose. Thank you Brian, proof reader extraordinaire.

Nick Wiltsher did an outstanding job in preparing the final manuscript. My grammar and sentence construction have greatly improved thanks to his guidance.

The British Library's Newspaper Library has now been moved to St Pancras. The staff there were most helpful as I ploughed my way through every 1939 edition of the (sadly) now defunct *Star*, a London evening newspaper.

Recovering from the horrors of war and the Great Depression, Britain clings to dreams of peace as Europe slides towards Fascist dictatorship. Amidst a web of half-hidden alliances where rumour and reality interweave, Roger Martin begins his career in Fleet Street journalism. As he is drawn deeper into the murky world of international politics, he quickly realises that discovering the truth is only half of the challenge . . .

Two families . . .

One, escaping the horrors of Nazi Germany, reaches England after a perilous journey just before the outbreak of World War II.

But another family awaits the illicit opportunities that the blackout and blitz will bring.

As the bombs begin to fall on London, the paths of the two families cross with tragic consequences as their lives race towards a dangerous and thrilling climax.

*Available from **www.sacristy.co.uk**/books/fiction*

Lightning Source UK Ltd.
Milton Keynes UK
UKOW01f2345260917
309928UK00007B/351/P